FAMILY CHARMS

A NOVEL

MALENA LOTT

buzz books

ISBN-10: 1938493125
ISBN-13: 978-1-938493-12-6

For more information on the book or to schedule a speaking engagement, discuss a media opportunity or sales, please contact Buzz Books at buzzbooksusa@me.com.

PRAISE FOR MALENA LOTT' S NOVELS:

"An extremely well written story that captivated me from the very beginning. "   — Book Binge

"Delightful … compelling, heartfelt novel."
— Curled Up with a Good Book

"She delivers a novel of remarkable wit and insight. This book is a treasure."—Ellen Meister, author of *The Other Life*

"A romance-laced, emotional roller-coaster ride…."   — *Library Journal*

"A remarkable tour de force. This story will make you laugh, cry, and fall in love all over again. —SingleTitles.com

"Delightfully affirming romance." —*Booklist*

"A quick-witted page turner."— *The Oklahoman*

A Note from the Author

Though this is a work of fiction, the idea for the novel came from my own experience being estranged from my mother for twenty years. I am the eldest of three girls, each a year apart. When I was four, my mother took us across country to start a new life without my father, without his knowledge. In less than a year, all three of us were back in Oklahoma and my paternal grandparents became our legal guardians. Contact with my mother was infrequent, sometimes spanning years, and was primarily through short letters.

When I was twenty-five, the same age as Marlo in this book, I found my mother for my youngest sister. We did not get a trip around the world, though a reunion of any kind provides its own drama.

Advice to writers is to "open your veins and bleed on the page" and that's exactly what I did here. It was extremely emotional for me to write and I hope I did the story justice.

Relationships are difficult, even under normal circumstances, but it's the search for love that intrigues me and the story idea for this book was one I had asked myself over and over as I grew up:

"Where in the world is my mother?"

1
MARLO, THE OLDEST SISTER

I preferred to believe my mother was dead.

I imagined she'd died both tragically and quietly. Over the years, her deaths became my richest memories of her, fictional and yet far more real than the fuzzy truth. There was the fire, the first of many heroic deaths I gave her, in which she clawed through the smoky two bedroom house to rescue her three sleeping girls, a baby, a toddler, and me, a preschooler. After she'd handed my baby sister Amelia over to the fireman, the roof collapsed, and she screamed her final breath. There would be a big write-up in the paper and all my life I would hear how lucky I was to be alive. That I had a mother who would risk her life to save mine.

As I grew older, her death scenes became more vivid, darker, even comical. Like the time she ran off to join the circus and fell off the high wire dressed in her sparkling tutu, splatting next to the grinning clown on the floor below.

In history class, I imagined she perished alongside the nurses who blew up when bombs hit their medical tents in World War I, from the Black Plague in Europe or even in the concentration camps of Nazi Germany, her blue eyes the last bit of color on her bone-thin face. Even in her historical deaths, she typically played the victim and the savior. As the Titanic began to sink, she placed my sisters and I on a lifeboat with strangers because there was only room for us. As we drifted off into the cold night air, I watched her fall to her death in the icy sea.

So what was I to make of this, a letter from beyond the grave, received on my twenty-fifth birthday? I stare at the return address and realize for all the ways I'd killed her in my mind, my mother is still very much among the living. No address, only her name. *Elizabeth Barnes.* Her married name, unchanged after all these years. Could she not bother with the paperwork?

My fingers begin to burn so I drop the envelope onto the painted entry table. She did not deserve my father's name, a good man who had died a real death, years before his time.

The letter is silent, yet its presence blares through my small historic home like nonsensical rock music. I catch my reflection in the mirror and am ashamed I've let a single tear fall. I swore I would never cry another drop for her.

My husband would be finishing rounds at his medical internship, and besides, I knew what he would say. "Just open it." I'd married a practical man, a caring but logical guy who wanted to fix people for a living. I'm certain this is why he was drawn to me.

I contemplate opening the other mail instead, the bills even look pretty good right about now, or the two letters for Shane, bait from hospitals trying to lure him away. He wants us to relocate, but I've lived in Kansas all my life. I can't imagine home being anywhere but here. Anxiety crawls up my spine.

I could call my sisters, but they aren't like me, rational and self-controlled. My middle sister Taryn would blow up, curse until her face turned red and might even tear up the letter before it could be read. Amelia, the fragile one, the baby still, would either cling or run. I'm never sure which. I have to protect them from this letter, from my mother's hawkish caw from beyond.

They'd never have to know. I'd open it alone.

First I put the water on to boil and wait patiently for the whistle to bring me back. How long I'd waited, thirsted for some communication from her over the years, to hear that she was safe, that she hadn't fallen prey to any of my fatal daydreams, but I eventually gave up the longing. Or had I?

When I turned five, I believed in the magic of wishes on a candle and wished for her return. The next morning, dressed in my new pink pajamas, I had been so certain the sound and smells coming from the kitchen was my mother making me breakfast, my wish fulfilled.

"There's my pumpernickel," my father had said, holding his arms open wide for our usual morning hug. I had not run to him, as he deserved. Instead I looked feverishly in every room, behind every door, searching for her.

I had the kind of father, who despite knowing the truth, got down on his hands and knees and looked under the bed with me. When I finally gave up, he let me eat mint chocolate chip ice cream at eight in the morning.

Even with my black thumb, the back yard is beautiful this time of year, spring fully in bloom, the flowerbeds bursting with color. We could only afford the two lawn chairs I'd picked up at a garage sale the summer before, and I used an old fruit crate as a side table. I know how I want to die. I'll sit in my backyard, gazing into a flower garden, and simply drift off.

The letter, with its banging cymbal and booming drum, destroys the tranquility I normally feel here. I sip my tea, trying to clear my head, making room for whatever the letter would put there. I had grown so tired of imagining where she might be, with whom, if she'd had more children, gotten remarried. So tired of subconsciously searching the female faces in the crowds, the ones that would be my mother's age, just in case she was here, right under my nose.

And now, it seems, she is. For all I know, my mother is no more or no less than this letter. Ivory, linen, black smooth ink. The call I'd waited for. The letter is heavy, containing something small and round. Through the envelope, it feels like metal. I turn the letter up and down, listening to the small object slide from side to side, until it becomes two objects: one round, the other the shape of a small key.

With my index finger, I tear open the flap of the envelope and remove the letter.

I unfold it carefully, the objects falling into my lap. The key is shiny and silver, like one for a post office box or lock box. The other item is a charm, a tarnished locket with a scripted B engraved on the front. I use my thumbnail to pry it open and find two photos I have never seen before. I recognize the subjects. On the left is a picture of me holding my sister Taryn. She must've been about two. On the right is a baby picture of Amelia from her first birthday, taken just weeks before my mother left.

I close the locket and set it on the wooden crate, my heart booming in my chest. I no longer hear the birds in the trees. Even the wind has died down. I wonder if these are the only pictures Elizabeth took with her, if she has just given back her last reminder of us. Through my tears, I begin to read.

Dear Marlo, Taryn and Amelia,

I know it must be a shock to receive this letter, but the time has come. Marlo, you just turned twenty-five, the age I was when I left. It has been almost twenty years since I saw your face, held you in my lap, read you bedtime stories.

In my mind, you are all still my babies. I have no right to want this so much, but I need you to know why I could not be the mother you needed. I have written a dozen letters trying to explain my life before, during, and after you girls, and nothing comes out right. How to explain a life in one letter? Twenty years with just a few words?

The more I thought about it, the more the answer became so clear I could think of nothing else: I want you girls to see where I have been. To see who I was, who I have become, how my journey has culminated in this readiness to reunite. They say you can only truly understand someone by walking in their shoes, so what I am offering is not so much the shoes, but the footprints of my life since I left.

Tomorrow I will be sending you three tickets to the first destination. If you agree to this, then the tickets to the next destination will be waiting for you with one of my Keepers. The Keeper will have the journals I wrote while I lived there.

I am offering you a trip around the world. A trip back into the past, to understand who you came from. If you feel you don't need or want this journey, I will, of course, understand. I expect nothing, deserve nothing, but hope you will say yes, all the same. My hope is that the three of you can take four weeks off to see the world-- and if you so choose, to see me at the end of the journey.

Writing this letter is the hardest thing I have ever done, next to leaving you. I suppose your reading it has not been easy, either. Thank you for not throwing it, and this chance, away.

Your mother,

Elizabeth

P.S. Do you remember the charm bracelet your father gave me? Every year for Christmas, Mother's Day and my birthday he gave me a new charm to add to it. You and your sisters loved to play with it on my arm. I have not taken it off in twenty years. I have added a new charm for every stop in my journey. Though you never knew it, I bought the three of you identical charms, hoping one day I could give them to you. It has been my only constant in a life of chaos. The charms have such special meaning to me, and if you accept the journey, they could mean something to you, too. It is all I have to give.

I re-read the letter four times, each time disbelieving my own eyes. She included the charm to prove she is who she says she is. Otherwise, I would think it's a trick. Someone playing a very, very cruel joke.

A trip around the world? Before I check my own feelings, I think of my sisters. This is how it has been since I was four – thinking of their welfare first. I won't do this without them, and I wonder if this is in our best interest. Will it hurt them more than they've already been hurt?

My sisters and I could not be described as "close," though when we need each other, we we're there. We're a rubber band, stretching, but never snapping. Lately our communication has mostly been via text message. I'm usually the one that tries to get us together, but our schedules make it increasingly difficult. I try not to think it's because they just don't like me very much.

Amelia, who has no memories of our mother, has wanted to reunite with her since she was a child. She is the optimistic one, the glass half full one.

Taryn, on the other hand, rails against the world, giving it an "eff you" at every turn. She is everyone and no one at the same time. She's been a dancer, a model, a hairdresser, and, as far as I know, is currently employed as a tattoo artist. A damned good one at that, if you're into that sort of thing. Amelia tells me Taryn's gotten really "tatted up" since I last saw her six months ago so I imagine her skin to be a kaleidoscope of dragons and warriors and Betty Boops.

It's no surprise that I haven't met her newest beau. I'd long ago learned to reserve judgment until asked, and then word my reply with eggshell care.

I doubt any man has the power to dull the blade of her angst, but there goes my doubt again. From what Amelia tells me, Paul is too head over heels for Taryn, and in the past, she's only liked the ones who treat her like shit. Ones with names like Cash and Briston and Finlan. Ones you might expect to be covered in serpent tattoos. What Paul the Banker doesn't know yet is how good she is at leaving. One day he may wake up and find she's vanished from his life without a trace.

I close my eyes and think of Shane, and of the packed suitcase in the closet. This is what I know: when the going gets tough, you leave.

The bag contains the bare necessities for what I'd need to start a new life without Shane. Until today I hadn't thought that my mother had done the same thing: a single bag, a one-way ticket out of her life.

Yet I'm still here. As I saw Shane pull into the driveway, my heart went on blender mode and I snatched the suitcase from its spot next to the front door and ran it back into the closet where it still sits a week later, packed, and waiting.

I'm not sure why I didn't leave. Things aren't working out. I'm not sure what marital bliss is, but I'm sure I don't have it. So, therapy. Well, therapy sucks. It brings all the things I've pushed down for so many years to the surface. I'm covered in emotional boils, though no one can see them.

Trip therapy. I roll around the idea in my mind, to see if the heart will grow fonder or drift farther apart. I wonder if I've made the term up. I make a mental note to jot it down for a future article. Had my mother thought the same thing when she left us? What if I did the same thing? Left to find my mother but never returned to my husband? Is running away a genetic marker?

I hear Shane's low voice, from just the night before, creeping into my ear like a thousand sharp blades. "Why are you so unhappy?"

If only I could keep him in a box. If only I could predict the future. If only, if only.

Shane believes he can fix whatever is going on between us, but I'm not so sure. Perhaps screwed up DNA combined with a crappy early childhood has made us incapable of any semblance of normal. I don't like to sit on someone's couch and connect the dots from my mother leaving to my troubled marriage and my decision not to have children of my own.

It seems the universe is doing it for me. The letter.

I watch a bee buzz around a sunflower, wondering what I should do with the letter, the key, the charm. It somehow feels like stolen property, something I should turn over to a higher authority to deal with. It feels like anything other than a gift, an invitation for a trip around the world.

The world is a big place, full of dark alleys you'd never want to visit—let alone the people in the shadows. Let alone the mother you loved and hated in the same breath. What if the trip to paradise took you to hell instead?

As much as a part of me wants to protect my sisters by not showing them this mysterious invitation, I can't make that call. I stuff it in my messenger bag and head out to find my sisters.

2

The kindergarten classroom smells like crayons, dry erase markers and Windex. I hadn't *forgotten* that my sister Amelia had quit her nursing internship for a teaching internship; she simply hadn't told me. She knew the announcement might provoke a "making traction" speech about forward career momentum.

Amelia looks good in this setting. I prefer it to seeing her behind a bar mixing drinks and chatting up old men.

I've been squeamish around children all of my life-- even when I was one. Shane believes having children of my own would help move some psychological boulder, but I think my fear of children is incurable and having one of my own would only make things worse. It's a gamble I'm not willing to take.

I haven't been in a kindergarten classroom since I'd last held Amelia's five-year-old hand, one of my many duties as the eldest and retriever of my sisters.

Amelia's cheeks wet instantly as she reads the letter in silence. I can't bear to look. All my life I've tried to dry Amelia's tears while wishing Taryn would spill some. I have no idea what normal crying is when you're a child, but I'm fairly sure that whatever it is, it's all screwed up in my family. At least I only cry at night in the dark when I think no one can hear me.

I hear my sister sniffle and feel my own eyes begin to give out, but I blink hard and concentrate on the classroom.

The board blares a message in orange neon marker: *have a great summer*!!! In the distance, I hear the faint scream and laughter of little people on the playground. A couple of bright sunshine cupcakes remain on a platter on the side table along with leftover juice boxes. I'm certain the cupcakes were Amelia's idea. Though she didn't tell me, I guess Amelia's distance from me meant she was on a down cycle, which could last anywhere from four weeks to four months. I gave her space.

The cupcakes indicate, perhaps, things are looking up again. She probably even made them from scratch.

My gaze falls on a pink Strawberry Shortcake backpack slung over a tiny chair and my throat tightens. I resist the urge to go to it and see if my mother's last note still sits inside the front pocket.

Have a nice day at pre-school. Be a good girl. Love, Mom

I'd gotten on and off the bus myself. While other kids were greeted by their eager moms with cameras and younger siblings at the corner, my mother wasn't among them. I walked the short half block home, nearly skipping, and careful to walk on the grass and not in the street as I'd been instructed.

The back door was unlocked. The house smelled like a ghost, as if it had been vacant for decades, and not merely hours. I could sense the energy had shifted. My calls echoed through the house, unmet by the clamoring feet of a toddler or the squeal of a baby. I knew. I just knew. I just didn't know what.

I could see it was my house. There was my plaid jacket, my sister's rag doll, my mother's purple flip-flops she'd worn almost daily since winter's passing. I followed the only human sound in the whole house, though I'd never heard it before. Perhaps it wasn't human. A wailing dog? Down the hall, my new pink Keds crunched on the creaky wood floor, and the distant sound registered as sobs, but I hadn't heard the manly version of them.

The heavy wooden door, with the cracking white paint and jiggly door handle, creaked open as I watched my father cry hysterically while clutching my mother's pillow. That was the first time I ever saw him cry.

That was the first time I believed my mother was dead.

My body feels tight and I'm suddenly exhausted from the memory. I want to fall into the blue beanbag chair and sleep for a thousand years. Mostly, I want to sleep away the last three hours since I slit open that letter. Instead, I feel my sister's warm arms wrap around me. I've never felt comfortable being physically close with anyone, but intimacy, at least the physical part, has never been a problem for Amelia.

When she lets me loose, I am relieved (or am I?) to see her smiling.

"I can't believe this." Amelia wipes away her tears with her forefinger before I have the chance to do it for her. Her peachy complexion glows, her bright blue eyes full of joy. I'm alarmed by it.

"I can't, either. But the way you say it makes it sound like it's a *good* thing." I smile, though it's not a real one.

"It's not just a good thing, it's a total God thing! Don't you see? He's answered my prayers! I can't imagine a better way to spend the summer. Now, come on. We've got a helluva lot of packing to do." Her long, loose, blonde hair hangs in curls around her shoulders, held off her face by a pink headband you might find on one of her students. I should've known He'd get the credit. She'd recently found the Lord, after years of believing there was no God, or if there was one, hating Him. I faintly recall a handsome evangelistic boy she'd briefly dated who had introduced her to Campus for Christ her senior year in college and now everything, it seems, is a "God thing."

"I'm not so sure," I say pensively, but in Amelia's eyes, my doubt could mean sacrilege. I want to bite my nails, but a quick look down tells me they are already gone. I don't even remember doing it.

Amelia shakes my arm. "Come on! It's what we've been dreaming of, right?"

I recall, late at night, on too many occasions to count, making up fairytale versions of a reunion for my baby sister. She preferred my stories to Cinderella or Sleeping Beauty. She has never cared about a Prince Charming sweeping her off of her feet. She prefers a mother coming to the rescue as so many real mothers do. Someone who'll meet you at the bus stop, even when you know your way.

I nod, and then watch my sister grab her oversized polka-dotted book bag. She shakes her head and frowns. "Just say it. What?"

"Something's not right. It sounds like…"

"… An amazing adventure," Amelia finishes.

"… A trap," I add.

Amelia smirks. "Don't be silly. We're all grown up now. Besides, I can't exactly go back to bartending this summer. Wouldn't be very teacherly, now would it?"

"So you're free until fall, then?"

"Broke, but free as a bird. So, what do you say? Let's fly."

As usual, her enthusiasm calms me. She latches my arm as the kids start tramping back into the classroom with their tiny legs and wide eyes. Upon seeing me, a stranger, they stop and stare, though their mouths never stop moving. The teacher greets me and I follow the yellow-haired girl with the Strawberry Shortcake backpack all the way to the pick up line and don't exhale until I see her mother greet her with open arms.

"Hell, no." Taryn jumps off of her rolling chair and it hits the cabinets behind it with a thunk.

The air is ripe with alcohol and smoke, though I'd heard through Amelia that Taryn had quit months ago. Like most vices, she never quits for long.

"What do you mean, no?" Amelia is already on the verge of tears and refuses to take the letter back from Taryn, so I do it for her.

"If you haven't noticed, I have a job here. *For starters.*"

Her voice sounds like a volcano about to erupt, the hot molten lava spewing to the surface.

"Secondly, I wouldn't waste a precious moment of summer on that bitch, and thirdly, I'm not leaving Paul for four weeks. How can you even consider leaving Shane for that long?"

I shrug and feel the sting of her foul language and the hurt behind it. Clearly Taryn doesn't believe it's a "God thing." We either go, or we try as best we can to forget that we ever received this letter. Really, life was fine for all of us before I received it, wasn't it?

Safer this way. Besides, Taryn's right. I can't be away from Shane that long, either. Especially with things already so rocky between us. Our fighting has escalated, my bad thoughts multiplying tenfold. "So we're not going," I say finally. I shove the letter back into my purse before Taryn can torch it.

"What? That's so not fair," Amelia shrieks. "We're not talking about whether or not to go to Chili's for dinner here, people. This is our *mother*. The woman who gave *birth* to us."

"Thank you, genius. We know she birthed three kids and they happened to be us. What? You think this is some kind of Hallmark slow-mo reunion?" Taryn reaches for a cigarette, her hands shaky, but she stops herself and runs her fingers through her short hair instead.

Amelia's eyes plead with me and I have to look down at my feet to the worn out sandals that needed replaced two years ago. Her voice softens. "Majority rules. Do you want to go, Marlo?"

"That wasn't the deal. All or nothing."

"The letter didn't say that," Taryn says, crossing her patch-worked arms. If she would stop squirming long enough, I could fully see what she's done to herself, but she won't stand or sit still. As usual, she's hopped up on something – maybe just an energy drink and adrenaline – though it could be much worse.

"You know I don't like to play tie-breaker," I say evenly.

"Since when? You've done it all our lives," Taryn says, raising a black eyebrow, dyed to match her short black hair. Her look is extreme, and I can only imagine what Paul the

Banker's parents think of her. She looks like a Goth pixie, though I understand Goth is no longer the term for it, anymore. Taryn has always defied explanation, anyway.

My body prickles with unease. "Fine. If I have to vote, it would be no. I'm on assignment at the paper and haven't been there long enough to ask for a leave. It might be just the excuse the paper needs to fire me. Besides, we can't afford for me not to be working right now. And then there's Shane." They don't need to know things have gone from bad to worse. Let them believe I love him too much to be away from him for that long. It could be true.

Amelia paces the concrete floor. "I can't believe this. I'll go by myself, then."

"You're not going around the world by yourself," I tell her, trying hard not to sound parental. "You've never even left the tri-state area."

"Exactly! Taryn's traveled all over the U.S. like a gypsy, and you've gotten to go tons of places with Shane. I've never been anywhere."

"I'll go on a road trip with you," I tell her, trying to sound optimistic. "We'll do Route 66 or something. A weekend in Vegas. My treat."

Amelia glares at me, her eyes small blue slits. "I don't want some petty consolation prize! I want my mother! I want my god dammed *mother*!" She screams like a child, and shakes uncontrollably.

I know, without meaning to, Taryn and I have sent her off the deep end and I'm not sure what words will bring her back to us.

Taryn glides over and puts her snakeskin arm around our little sister and from the other side, I do the same. I can't help but think of a snake shedding its skin and starting fresh. Is that possible? To leave the pain of our past behind us and move on?

Our sibling cradle calms Amelia as we sit silently on the stained concrete floor, our backs against the cabinets, staring at Taryn's accouterments of needles and crazy art samples on the walls.

Amelia returns to us and reads the letter aloud to us, certain I have not read between the lines accurately. Just because I am a wordsmith, I am told, *does not make me a mind reader.*

"What the hell is a Keeper?" Taryn asks as she bounces her head against the cabinet door. "It's really creepy."

Amelia shrugs. "Maybe she's rich and has people that help her all around the world. Wouldn't that be cool?"

"Or she's in an insane asylum." I may not believe in much, but I do believe in karma. As many ways as I imagined she'd died or that she'd been locked away in a dark dungeon and unable to come back to us however much she wanted, I never imagined her as wealthy. Amelia figured she had married well and had little princes and princesses and lived in a castle far, far away. Too many fairytales growing up, though at the time I thought they were better than the black truth.

My asylum explanation has to be far closer to the outcome, though we would never know if we didn't go.

"You two are trouble," Taryn says and sighs, shuffling to a stand. "I can't say I haven't been curious. What's the headline, writer? *'Mother Ditches Kids and Becomes Globetrotter'*?"

I shake my head. "We don't even know where these places are. They may not even be glamorous. Actually I seriously doubt they would be even close to glamorous."

Taryn huffs. "And this place is." She grabs a black notebook off the table. Used to, it would've been a little black book, but these days it's her appointment book and Amelia and I listen to the hard rock music playing in the other room while Taryn grunts and sighs flipping through the calendar. Business, it seems, is booming.

"I have four thousand dollars worth of business scheduled in the next month," Taryn tells us. "My clients are particular. They don't just pay for a tattoo; they pay for a *Taryn* tattoo. I can't just give them to Rafeal or Simone."

I don't know what to say. I wouldn't give up that kind of money easily, either. It's a lot more than I make.

"Is meeting our mother worth four thousand dollars to you?" Taryn tosses it to my sister like a grenade.

Amelia stiffens. "You know it's priceless. I don't know how, but I'll make it up to you." Amelia looks up with her crystal blue eyes. So hard saying no to her.

Taryn grunts. "On a bartender's salary? You haven't even been hired as a teacher for the fall yet. What about you?" She jabs a pencil through the air like a sword.

I feel it piercing the question like a balloon. "I'd like to talk it over with Shane. It's not just the time off, which is a *huge* if, but if it's really good for us. I'm worried that this won't end well."

"When have you not worried?" Taryn nearly smiles.

I ignore the remark. "My boss likes me. Maybe the magazine can give me an assignment I can work on from anywhere. Travel stuff gets a lot of hits in the summer. I suppose it won't kill me to ask."

Amelia claps her hands and stands on her tiptoes. "Does this mean what I think it means?"

Taryn stomps her foot and moans. "Let me just go on record here that I think it's a terrible idea. The woman is a stranger. With questionable morals and totally effed-up relationship issues. Even if we meet her and she looks like Glinda the Good Witch, she's likely to get bitch-slapped."

I nod. "Taryn's right. I don't want you to get your hopes up. All we know is that she left and we never heard from her again. Until *now*. Did it really take her twenty years to get her act together?"

Taryn crosses her arms. "How hard would it have been to drop a postcard from these places just to let us know she was alive?"

Amelia shakes her head. "I think we need to have an open mind about this."

"Just knock off the sweet teacher voice, will ya?" Taryn says. "If you want me to come along for the ride, you get what you get."

I sling my purse strap over my shoulder as a burly black Harley rider peeks his head in. "Yo, T."

"Be with you in a minute, Bones."

Amelia and I look at each other and conceal a laugh. Most tattoo shops really are like you imagine.

"Shut up. Most of these riders are just big old softies."

"Okay. Whatever you say, *T.*" Amelia wraps her arms around Taryn so I must do the same.

I can't resist adding, "If I think things are getting weird, I'm pulling the plug and we're coming back home. We don't have to see this thing through to the end. What if the knowing is worse than the not knowing?"

My question lingers in the air, the one I'd asked myself a thousand times as I drifted into sleep. What if reality is even worse than my darkest fantasy?

"That won't happen. I just have a feeling about this," Amelia says.

Before she can tell me she thinks it's divine intervention, I add, "I do, too. But it's not a good one."

"Let me talk to my clients and see what I can shuffle around," Taryn says. "I don't know what kind of wild goose chase we're going on, but I suppose I could use some creative inspiration. See what the inkers in other places are up to. Think your paper would pay me to take some photos for your stories?"

Taryn is also an amazing photographer. Her inability to stick with one thing very long means she's pretty damn good at a lot of things. "That's a great idea. I'll do a proposal for my boss and let you know."

A professional mission. Much easier to say yes to that. She had just called our mother the c-word an hour earlier.

What I don't tell my sisters is that while adoptive children are curious about their biological parents because they don't remember them, I do remember my mother and I don't like what I recall one little bit.

DESTINATION 1: KAUAI, HAWAII
"HAWAII'S ISLAND OF DISCOVERY"

"Northernmost and oldest geologically, Kauai is the fourth largest of the major Hawaiian Islands. Nearly circular in shape, Kauai's land area encompasses 533 square miles, 25 miles long by 33 miles wide at its furthest points.

Only 3% of the land area has been developed for commercial and residential use leaving the remaining 97% divided between agriculture and conservation. The majority of the island's approximately 52,000 residents live and work in the coastal areas leaving the interior of Kauai spectacularly beautiful and pristine.

Kauai's weather is near perfect year-round, with daytime temperatures ranging from the mid 70s to the mid 80s, slightly warmer in the summer. The northeast trade winds provide refreshing breezes. Rain showers usually fall in the evening and early morning hours, predominantly over the mountain ranges. The temperature of the ocean ranges from 68 to 80 degrees Fahrenheit." – Kauai Information Center

3
AMELIA, THE BABY SISTER

"*Mahalo!*" The beautiful, bronze Hawaiian flight attendant puts the flower lei around my neck as we step off the Hawaiian airline. I make a joke about just getting "lei'd," but Taryn and Marlo are too busy drinking in the scenery to get it.

We're greeted by a drizzling rain and lush tropical landscape straight off a glossy postcard. I'd never flown before – I know, crazy, right? —so when Marlo handed me an Ambien to sleep through the flight, I refused it, even if it was a long flight from Kansas to California and then over the ocean. I experienced lift-off for the first time, my stomach clear up in my throat, soaring in this amazing metal bird. Only after we'd passed over the awesome Grand Canyon did I doze off and dream, even with the turbulence: a memory of being tossed up into the air by my faceless mother. Only I'm not sure if I really remember it or just *want* it to be a memory.

"This is freaking paradise!" I yell and have to pinch somebody to believe it. I pinch Taryn and Marlo and they both scream and pinch me back. Real, all right! None of us, even Taryn, who treats cities the way I treat lovers, has been to Hawaii. I won't tell my sisters, but I think my mother must be pretty smart to start off our trip this way.

The key our mother sent was for a post office box that contained further instructions on getting our flight information and destination, so we knew to pack shorts and swimsuits and flip flops. Since we didn't fly here in a private jet, Mom must not have married an oil magnate or created a multi-million dollar makeup empire like I'd thought. Still, this ain't too shabby.

My legs wobbly from the flight, I still manage to swing my bags around and yell into the sunshine rain, "Hello, gorgeous!"

Taryn and Marlo look back at me, no smiles. I know they think I've set my expectations too high, but I had a feeling we'd go somewhere gorgeous while Marlo thought we'd be sent to a dump so a little positive thinking didn't hurt, did it? "What? You sourpusses need to look around. This place is freakin' magical!"

"There goes the kindergarten mouth again." Taryn says.

"Can you imagine what would happen if I taught all those precious little minds all of my favorite curse words? I'm not about to lose my teaching certificate before I even officially get one."

Taryn shakes her head and looks at me through her oversized bright orange sunglasses. "Life is too short not to cuss when you need to."

Marlo stops, puts her sensible brown carry-on on the ground and waits for me to catch up. She inhales and relaxes her shoulders. "It is beautiful. I wish Shane were here. Would've made a nice honeymoon."

I catch up and slap her on the back. "Well, I'm sure the screwing was still divine at the Motel 6 near Six Flags."

Marlo ignores me and walks on. She's never liked talking about personal things, and I hope I can crack her shell on our four-week journey. Taryn, on the other hand, is raw, her shell long gone; she wears her insides out, her emotions as obvious as her tattoos. She tells me everything, or so I like to think. I'm not judgy like our big sis.

Taryn wears ripped jeans and hugs her black leather bag to her chest. "I forget I even have a brother-in-law as little as I've seen of him. In fact, I almost forget I have sisters."

I smile and chew at my bottom lip. I'm not going to let Taryn drag me into a fight so soon.

Inside the small airport, a tall black man wearing sunglasses and a black suit carries a sign with thick black writing: **The Barnes**.

"That's us!" I race up to the man, who only nods and begins leading us down the rows of shuttle buses, taxis and limos. I hold my breath as we pass each one. I want to tell him to skip this whole thing and get us to our final destination. I'm ready to meet Mom right now. But we're in Hawaii, and it sounds like she's not, so I try to relax. Can't. I look around, wondering if she could be watching us from the periphery. I reapplied my make-up on the plane, just in case. What if her Keeper is snapping pictures of us like some sort of paparazzi and e-mailing them to her in her secret hiding place? I don't want her to be disappointed.

He opens the car door to a shiny stretch black limo. I squeal and turn to my sisters who are finally smiling. About damn, I mean darn, time.

"Isn't this fantastic?"

"Are you going to act this way the whole trip?" Taryn hands the limo driver her bag and a ten-dollar bill, then hands him mine. It annoys me how my sisters are always doing things for me like I'm still five years old.

"You mean, uh, *happy*?"

"Eager beaverish," Marlo offers.

"Yes! Yes, I am! If I have to put up with your attitudes, then by God, you can put up with mine. I swear, from the looks on your faces, you'd think we'd just been taken hostage."

Marlo shrugs. "It's fine, sweetie. We're just nervous is all."

"Speak for yourself, Mar," Taryn says. "I'm hungry as hell. Let's get this show on the road and get some grub and hit the beach before there's a downpour."

We slide into the back of the limo while Bane (according to his name tag) pulls away from the curb and drives us slowly down the winding streets of Kauai. We don't need to ask if he's the Keeper. I imagine this keeper person is much more congenial. Through the limo glass, I can see Bane answering a phone and speaking with someone and I wonder if it's Her. It has to be, right? I want to kick through the glass to hear her voice. Of course she'd want to know if we'd arrived. Isn't that what mothers do?

I can't help but roll down the window and stick my head out. I inhale the smell of the blooming hibiscus and pungent eucalyptus trees. Nothing like the smell of suntan lotion and aloe vera that I expected.

"She is a puppy!" Taryn asks, opening a bottle of Scotch from the limo bar.

I don't even want to close my eyes to blink. I hear the waves crashing against the shore and see the white tips of the waves in the distance as the smell of the salty ocean fills my nose. I know we're close.

We pull up to the Kaha Lani resort and I scramble out of the limo as if it's on fire. An ocean view! The turquoise waters and miles of white sand scream to me, and without a word, I take off, kicking off my sandals and running until I reach the ocean and fall into it, the cool water rushing over me.

It reminds me of a picture book that Marlo used to read to me when I was little.

When you look up, I am the moon, said Mother.
When you look down, I am the grass, said Mother.
And when you swim, I am the water all around you.

"The luau is at sunset," the Keeper says with a small smile when I return. She's short and mature, sixty or seventy, maybe. I'd never met a Hawaiian before, but I've heard they age slowly. Something about the magic of the islands or something. She could be ninety for all I know. Her eyes crinkle when I ask her if she is "the keeper," and she nods. "I have what you need," she tells us, handing us an itinerary that includes resting all afternoon before dinner on the beach, and she's just as quickly gone. I want to chase her, to beg her to tell me everything she knows about my mother, but I know there is a Plan and I'm not about to be the one to screw it up.

But my sisters don't know the meaning of "rest." While I beg them to see the island with me, they choose to be by themselves. Seems just that long plane ride was too much "togetherness." I know God has a plan for us and a part of that is to bring us closer together.

Taryn sketches on the beach and Marlo began her first article for ionKansas. Her employer was thrilled they could get exclusives on travel articles around the world without having to pay for the travel itself. They trust her. Everybody does. She even convinced them to pay Taryn for photographs after they saw her impressive portfolio, so now we don't feel as guilty about her losing so much tattoo business while we're away.

I go for a run along the shoreline, a slaphappy grin on my face the whole time. So sue me.

Neither sis will join me at the bar after, either, so I go alone, comfortable territory for me as I'd bartended the last year at various taverns back on campus since turning twenty-one. I got good tips, thanks to my big smile, big tits and tight jeans. I suppose I can thank my genes for my great memory, too. I can mix a drink once and remember the recipe, and take an order for a party of eight with eight different drinks and not have to write it down. I learned quickly how to make good money, enough to get me by one week with just a few hours' work. I'd have to figure out a way to make some money on this trip, too. My checking account balance of $23 isn't going to cut it for long. Credit card bills will be swarming my mailbox soon (what? I couldn't *not* buy vacation clothes!) and I vowed to not take any more money from him. This was the last month I let him pay my rent. I mean it this time.

I'm thankfully far away from the problems back home, though my phone vibrates again and I know it's him. The nameless him I removed from my contacts so that when he calls I won't have to look at that pretty-boy face and be suckered in to answering it. I even turned off my voice mail so I don't have to hear his sexy voice begging me to return to him. I've listened before. I've returned before.

The bar sits just off the beach in a tiki hut and the bartender isn't even Hawaiian. He looks just older than me, tanned and blonde, your typical surfer dude, though I'd only seen them on TV. I'd assumed there might be a few of them around. I'm immediately attracted to him, his bulging biceps wrapped in tattooed barbed wire, and I imagine him squeezing me in his grasp. He'd take my mind off the one back home nicely.

"What's your pleasure?" he asks and from the way he says it, I know he knows how to make good tips, too. His lop-sided smile shows off sparkling white teeth and a crooked bicuspid. His voice is low and deep, but as I order a Blue Hawaiian (what else for my first drink?), two other men down the bar catch my eye.

The first looks familiar, though I can't place him. The airport, maybe? Same flight? He's tall and slim, a swimmer's body, with brown hair and a fair complexion marked by faint freckles. When he turns to me, I see his eyes, shocking blue, as blue as the ocean, and I feel a gasp escape my lips. Yes, he was in the airport, waiting for his ride while we were searching for ours. The man doesn't strike me as the Hawaiian vacation type of guy, and he'd look like a lobster in no time flat if he ever left the shade of an umbrella.

The man doesn't smile at me in return, which frankly is odd, and his neck reddens. Perhaps I've stared too long, and he's not interested, so I move on. Happily married or super shy is my guess. Two seats down sits another man, a broad-chested, handsome Samoan businessman. He would crush me under his weight, and all at once, I feel like being crushed.

"You've been running all afternoon," he says, flicking a big bill at the bartender to pay for my drink.

"Pent up energy," I say, sucking my drink through the thin yellow straw and walking toward him, in a familiar trance I rely on all too often.

"I can help with that," he says, as he puts his large palm on the small of my back and leads me back to his room. He becomes my official welcoming party to the beautiful Garden Island. He wants me, and I so desperately need to feel wanted.

4
TARYN, THE MIDDLE SISTER

"Your charms," the Keeper says, placing a sterling silver bird charm in each of our waiting palms at our own private luau. I turn it over in my hands, the eagle's wings spread wide in flight. Marlo and Amelia immediately clip their charm on their bracelet, but I'm not playing along. The only jewelry I wear is a tongue stud and a brow and belly ring. I slip the bird into the pocket of my cutoffs instead.

The flames lick at our feet, and I almost want to get burned. The heat is so intense that eventually I scoot back, but relish the flush to my face. It makes me feel alive, much like the prick of the needle when I get tattooed.

The Keeper's name is Iolana, and she gathered us just after the shower passed over and the sun began its descent into the ocean. She feeds us an endless buffet, of pork and red potatoes, fresh pineapple and coconut pie. Mother must not know I'm a vegetarian. What a surprise. I eat the potatoes and the pineapple and push the rest aside.

A sexy bartender brings us tall, fruity drinks, and he leans down and whispers something into Amelia's ear that causes her to giggle. Obviously they're already acquainted, and I'm certain, after Marlo slips into sleep, Amelia will spill the details of their liaison to me. I don't judge her the way Marlo does. She always makes me promise not to tell Marlo, but I know that doesn't go both ways. As soon as I told her Paul proposed to me, she was on the horn with Marlo, and the two were relentless about an answer. Even worse than Paul. No answer yet. What kind of goof asks you to marry him before you've even told him you love him? We're not even exclusive, by my choice.

"What does it mean?" Amelia asks the Keeper as she studies the charm.

Iolana crosses her short legs and sits before us, the ocean and starry sky her backdrop. "After your tour tomorrow, I've been instructed to give you her journal, which she has kept here in a lockbox, along with your charms. How I came to know your mother will also be revealed after the tour. Before I knew her, she was broken, strolling the island like a drifter, finding hourly work to pay for a place to sleep. She waitressed, but wasn't cheerful enough for the job. So she bartended, where a happy facade wasn't a pre requisite."

Amelia smiles and looks at us. I can tell she's pleased that she and our mother have something in common. Perhaps they share the language of mixology. But I waitressed for years, and I feel nothing in common with her. Not a damn thing.

"She got her freedom," I said, my throat constricting. "Free as a fucking bird."

Iolana doesn't flinch from my language, but Marlo and Amelia shake their heads, admonishing me.

"Sleep well," she says, and leaves us with our drinks and the faint sound of the palm leaves slapping the resort walls, like a bird's wings flapping in the night air.

"What? Are we supposed to ooh and aah every god dammed time we're handed a charm?"

"You don't have to take your anger out on the Keeper," Marlo says, gathering up our plates. "That's all I'm saying."

Amelia sucks down her drink and hands it to the bartender with the barbed wire around his bicep. Amateur ink. Not nearly as good looking as the guy himself.

"But how did she get here, I wonder?" Amelia asks. "I mean, we're not exactly in Kansas anymore."

"If you were running away, wouldn't you want to step into a fairytale? Looks like one to me," Marlo says.

I slide my bare foot in the sand. "Must've drained Dad's bank account just to get here."

They don't say anything because they know I'm right. Elizabeth wasn't working. She was a stay-at-home mom, with no income and no inheritance.

"She was overwhelmed," Amelia says softly. "I mean, I can only imagine. Three kids under the age of four. That had to be exhausting in every way. And she was so young – your age, Marlo. Can you imagine having three young kids right now?"

"Is this where you start defending her?" I snort. "Save it. Lots of moms are overwhelmed. It's just a part of the job description."

"Iolona was right," Marlo says. "She was broken before she got here. We're here to find out why she snapped and what she did about it."

"You mean besides not returning to us. Ever." The bitterness sits vile in my mouth. Why do I care? Dad did just fine without her. We all did. Trust only yourself. That's my motto.

"She's returning now," Amelia says with a shrug. "And none of us are mothers yet, so we really have no idea. That's all I'm saying."

I lie back in the sand and stare up at the smoke swirling up to the black sky with chandelier stars. "The better-late-than-never defense. Good one. What about you, Marlo? You and McDreamy gonna pop out any kids soon?"

"I don't want children."

"No way!" Amelia slaps the sand with her palms and nearly topples off the log. "You guys would have the cutest kids, *ever*. What does Shane think about this?"

"He thinks I'll change my mind. He wants three kids, but …" Her voice trails off.

"But if our mother couldn't handle three kids, then how could you?" I answer.

Marlo nods, but Amelia shakes her head. "We're not genetically disposed to be bad mothers."

"How can I risk finding out?"

"Life is risk." I slurp down the rest of my pineapple mango daiquiri and accept a fresh one from Barbed Wire. I feel the buzz coming on and wish it would stay like this a while longer.

"Is that why you haven't said yes to Paul yet?" Marlo asks.

"I haven't said yes because I don't want to make a promise I may not be able to keep." I raise my brow.

"You told her," Marlo snaps to Amelia.

"Told me what?"

"About the marriage counseling," Marlo says, *"as if you didn't know."*

"I *didn't* know." I laugh, though there's nothing inherently funny about marriage counseling. "These things must be a truth serum."

"Way to go, Mar." Amelia laughs. "Why don't you two think I can keep a secret?"

"Because you can't," Marlo and I say at the same time.

"Then again, why do we need to keep secrets from each other? Protect our sensibilities?"

"Lecture avoidance," Amelia answers.

"And love," Marlo adds. "I think sometimes we keep secrets to protect each other."

"From ourselves? The truth?"

"More harm," Marlo says, and I wonder what she knows that she hasn't been telling us, specifically about our mother.

"Fair enough. On this trip, I'll be an open book. You can ask me anything, and I promise not to curse you out. But first I want to hear about the counseling."

Marlo tips her head and looks me over. "First, tell me why all the tattoos? You have twice as many since the last time I saw you."

"What's to tell?"

"If you want to hear about my private marital affairs, you've got to do better than that."

I weave my fingers through the sand, then draw a large heart, but resist putting Paul's name in the middle. "I like them, okay? They make me feel whole. Well, no. Not whole. More complete."

"Like covering yourself with Band Aids?" Amelia asks.

I shake my head. "No. Like you've been searching for something. Something important. Like a treasure. And you found it, and so you're putting it on display for the world to see. Only you don't care if people understand what the treasure is. Or even if they can see it."

Amelia scoots over on the log to peer at my inked skin in the firelight. "Kind of like searching for our mother?"

"Hell, no. If you'll remember, I wasn't ever the one that wanted to find her."

Marlo puts her chin on her hand and peers closer. "But hasn't the idea of her been inside you? Even if you don't remember her?"

"Her half of my DNA, at least." I hate how Marlo tries to make everything poetic and Amelia tries to turn shit into sunshine. I'm not sure I'll survive this much sibling togetherness.

"I don't believe that you don't care about meeting her. I think she will be like your greatest tattoo. That no matter what you find, she'll make you more whole."

I clap. "Aristotle speaks. That's about enough philosophy for one night. Now it's Marlo's turn."

Marlo shakes her head. "I packed my bags last week to leave Shane."

Amelia's mouth drops open. "Is Shane hurting you? Hitting you?"

Marlo flinches. "No, nothing like that. I don't know what it is. Sometimes I think I love him too much to stay. I think he deserves better."

I shrug. "All marriages have a fifty-fifty chance. In our case, it's probably only about twenty-five percent considering our childhood." Marlo nods. She knows I'm right. But sunshine girl doesn't want to admit it.

"Shut up, Taryn," Amelia warns.

"Come on, Amelia. Let's face it. Some marriages stay together because one spouse is getting his willies elsewhere."

"Screw you."

"Where's the teacher voice I like so much?" I laugh.

"What's going on?" Marlo asks.

"Hey, I said I'd be the open book, not her."

"It's nothing!" Amelia says, her eyes brimming over with tears.

Fine. Let her get her skeletons out of her closet in her own time.

Marlo stares off beyond the fire. "He thought he could change me. Make me happier somehow. But then maybe I thought that, too. I don't know. And he's not happy about the no kids thing. And I'm not happy he's looking at fellowships all around the country. I don't want to move away."

"So, what then? He might take a fellowship in another city and you won't go with him?" Amelia's voice goes all Minnie Mouse, and I feel sorry for her, I really do. She still believes in the White Knight bullshit. Even if her own White Knight is a married cheating asshole. What a fool.

"Kind of blows the whole 'you complete me' crap out of the water, huh?" I saunter over to the liquor stand where Barbed Wire has left his mixing agents and grab the tequila off the second shelf and take a swig with my back turned to my sisters. This kind of bare-boned honesty requires booze. Lots of booze. Maybe even innocent Amelia will confess her sins. "Shit, you're twenty-five! Your ovaries are eons away from expiration. And it's not like you didn't have plenty of experience changing diapers."

Marlo looks up at me. It had been a joke for a long time, Marlo changing Amelia's poopy diapers, but maybe it's not so funny. Maybe I don't know my big sis the way I thought I did.

Amelia smiles. She doesn't get it, either.

"Why *did* you change Amelia's diaper?"

Marlo shrugs. "Somebody had to."

I try to swallow the knot in my throat, but that too will require tequila. So what if Marlo wasn't trying to be all grown-up on purpose. What if she did it because she had to?

I take the tequila bottle again but find it abysmally low. I excuse myself to find Barbed Wire for something a little more palatable. "Save any good gossip 'til I get back."

"I want to hear more about Paul the Banker!" Marlo yells after me.

"Yeah, yeah." I leave just in time. I'm not ready to share Paul with them yet. I'm not even sure I'm ready for him myself. He's smart and sexy and an incredibly sweet, and I'm none of those things.

Hours have passed since Iolana sat before us, but with the help of the alcohol, I feel like I'm in a dream. I stumble down a path to a lighted tiki hut, where the lights blink off and I hear the sound of footprints coming nearer. The half moon provides enough light to see the silhouette of a man.

I feel the surge of attraction as I recognize Barbed Wire. "Anyone there?" He calls out.

"Taryn," I say, my voice sounding cloudy, though it's probably just in my head.

"My little fairy," Barbed Wire says, and his muscles arm wraps around my bare waist, just above the sarong. My skin prickles from his touch. "What can I do for you?" He emphasizes the *do*.

"Just looking for another drink." I realize I still have the near empty tequila bottle in my hand and must look like a complete drunk.

"I don't think another drink is what you need." He takes the tequila bottle from my hand and presses himself against me and I shudder. His mouth brushes my ear, and he whispers, "Let me show you my favorite spot."

I wonder if he means on the beach or on me, but in either case, I'm willing to find out. He smells like salt and sand and coconut oil. "I thought you were flirting with my sister," I say.

"I flirt with everyone. Part of the job," he says.

I like his honesty. So rare, really. "What did you say to her?"

"I told her the Samoan couldn't have been half as good as me."

"Samoan?"

"I probably shouldn't tell tales," he said. "Bartenders are expected to keep secrets."

I smile in the dark. The island is full of more secrets than I realized. She didn't waste any time.

His favorite spot is a rock twenty feet out into the ocean. We wade through shallow water to get to it and when we climb it, I feel like a mermaid on her first journey on land. The moon has lowered into the ocean and I feel the compulsion to swim to it.

"How is your vacation going with your sisters?" Barbed Wire asks.

"We've never gone away together, so we'll see. We're not what you'd call tight-knit. Marlo is bossy and controlling and Amelia is unreliable and you'd have to ask them what my problem is." I laugh, but he doesn't.

"So it must be pretty weird, then."

"Weird is a great word for it. Why didn't you go back and try again with Amelia?"

He leans his face in closer, so close I can see the stubble on his jaw line and the tenderness in his eyes. His breath smells only of mint, no alcohol. "You are far more interesting."

He kisses me, and though I hear something deep within me rise up to revolt, to resist his warm kisses covering my body, I say nothing. I push the thoughts of Paul away and replace the aching numbness of missing him with the very real presence of a stranger. If I say yes to Paul, then this arrangement, to openly be with whomever we want to be with, will end. I would no longer let the winds of chance guide my life. I would be a normal person. I can't see the future Paul has whispered about in the dark after hours of lovemaking.

I haven't actually *been* with another man since I'd made that rule. If he knew that he was my only it would give him all the power. And I hate to feel powerless. I hate to feel like I have everything to lose.

As Barbed Wire pulls up my tank top and kisses the swell of breast above my heart, I envision my tattoo there, a half of a flaming heart, only full when the other half lays naked against me.

Feeling the sting of my betrayal, I push him off of me as he sails back and off the rock, and out into the dark night as he goes down, down and finally lands with a splash below. I hope to hell we were on the only rock in the near vicinity and that his head didn't find one on his way down.

I doubt he hears the faint "sorry" I send down after him.

5
MARLO

I can't sleep. The whole tossing, turning, pathetic insomnia commercials you see, pushing magic sleep-dust pills? Been there, worn the nightshirt. Only the next morning I still look like the before pic: puffy, swollen eyes above black hammocks. No late nights banging rock stars (or rock star doctors) or getting high. Only a trippy parade of bad-to-worse thoughts that keep peaceful sleep at the end of a very dark and scary tunnel.

While Taryn and Amelia fall into a deep, alcohol-induced slumber, thoughts of Shane's imaginary indiscretions consume me. I have no right, no reason to think these awful thoughts— that he would cheat on me with smart, put-together interns at the hospital, or give in to the nurses who are forever flirting with him. My jealousy is reason number eight, or is it ten, for Why We Need Marital Counseling, according to Shane. I can't seem to keep track. The paranoia has gotten so bad, I only half-listen when he recounts his days, so I don't insert my own twisted storyline into his otherwise clinical timeline and replay it later on my nightly insomniac slide show.

I hadn't told Shane my bag was already packed before this trip, but I had *sort of* confessed with, "Maybe it would be easier if I left."

"Leaving is the easy way out," he'd said.

Maybe he's right. Which is why a ball of hate sits tight in my gut. My mother left, easy or not.

Our phone conversation hours earlier hadn't gone as I'd hoped, either. "I wish you were here," I told him too quickly.

"You'll be fine," he said, in a soothing, but perhaps condescending aren't-you-a-big-girl-yet tone. "You'll have a great time with your sisters." (He's met my sisters. He should know better.)

"Right." I pushed away the image of another woman lying beside him in bed, rubbing her hand over chest, waiting for him to get off the phone so she could get him off. Why hadn't he said he wished he were here, too? Because he doesn't. Because he wants to be there. Without me. With *her*. It's so obvious I could puke.

"Any clues so far?"

I told him about the failed waitressing and bartending and the eagle charms and our hike the following day. So far I could not imagine her here, or feel her footsteps. It didn't feel real, yet.

"Better turn in, babe," Shane said, adding a yawn. "Early rounds."

I bite my tongue from asking if he's alone. I'd done that once before, when I was on assignment in New York and he was home for three days. I'd convinced myself he'd found a companion in my absence and I finally accused him of not wanting to stay on the phone with me and straight out asked if he'd been with someone else, though I had no proof. Deep down, I knew he was as loyal as a German shepherd.

"You need help," he'd said then, and a year later he began his quest to push me into counseling, for myself and for us. Now, he seemed to believe this trip, finding my mother, would rid the monsters in my brain once and for all.

As I lay in the near dark, my chest feels as if it will explode, tears pulsing at the corner of my eyes as I imagine Shane and my home engulfed in flames, and not even the smoke is enough to rouse my deep-sleeper from his eternal rest. My Bad Thoughts about Shane are different than they were with my mother. He doesn't save the day. He just perishes. Every time.

Before I can save him or re-route the wiring in my brain to a Happy Ending like the therapist suggested (which I rarely do), I hear a light rapping on the door, followed by the shuffle of bed linens and the clap of flip-flops. I peer out my window and watch Amelia walk hand-in-hand with a large, dark-complexioned man wearing yellow swim trunks. They disappear into the darkness, murmuring what can only be the sound of new lovers.

What the hell? My worry over Shane switches to fear for Amelia. It took all my strength not to follow them into the night, to watch from a distance, just to make sure he didn't rape her or murder her and dump her into the ocean. Perhaps journalism was not the best career choice for me. Bad things are always on the wire, and keeps me assured that they could, at any moment, happen to my loved ones or me.

I haven't shared my insomnia with Shane or told him about the Bad Thoughts. I should, I know, but I prefer to watch him sleep, safe in our bed, and besides, the sleeping pills give me weird side affects. If I ask his opinion, he would begin treating me like a patient, not a wife. Not that I don't wonder what it would be like to get a full night of sleep; if that alone could make me happier.

Instead, I click on my computer to finish writing a piece for the ionKANSAS style section, prompted by the beginnings of the charm bracelets given to us by Elizabeth. I type it as my own dangles against the keyboard.

A Charmed Life by Marlo Thompson

"If the history of the charm bracelet were itself a charm bracelet, the charms might be the most interesting ever made. The first? An Egyptian Pharaoh. The first recognizable charms came from that period where they coveted their wrist and neck bracelets as protective shields and signs of status.

Next would hang the fish charm for the Roman Empire Christians, who identified themselves with a small golden fish amulet when meeting in secret providing identity and communion among like people of faith.

Thirdly, a Knight from the Middle Ages where bracelets represented things like family origin, profession, and political standing.

The fourth charm could be the Queen's crown because it was the regal Queen Victoria who made bracelet wearing popular in the 20th century with beads, lockets and family crests dangling from them. Charm bracelets were now considered fashionable.

Fast-forward to the 1950s and charm bracelets are all the rage again for both girls and women, noting all of the rites of passage of a woman's life – sweet 16 birthdays, weddings and the births of children. So there hangs a poodle to commemorate a rockin' era of the charm.

Our final charm brings us into the 21st century where charm bracelets again find favor, this time in all price ranges and styles, from fun and girly to chic and sophisticated.

Yet no matter the incarnations of the charm bracelet itself, one thing remains unchanged through the ages – the marking of time and events on a circle of life."

The next morning, with only a few hours of sleep, I follow closely behind Iolana and step into the waiting boat, powered by Bane, our limo driver, who is also Iolana's husband. I'd searched Hawaiian names in the middle of the night, waiting for Amelia's return, (thank God, in one piece, though her hair was a mess) and discovered Iolana means "to soar like an eagle." I wonder if the eagle charm is meant to pay homage to this woman.

"Kipu Kai beach is only accessible by boat," Iolana tells us as we put on our life jackets and peer into the misty morning. My hands shake from too many cups of coffee, and Amelia, full from a big breakfast of bacon and eggs and biscuits and Monster energy drinks, fills the silence with a jillion questions for her.

The jagged Hoary Head mountain ridge hugs the beach in the distance, and besides Amelia's constant chatter, the air is quiet. We are alone, and a terrible tingle crawls up my spine as to why we would travel out to a desolate mountain for our history lesson.

Bane kills the engine and helps us out of the boat. Taryn grumbles about a headache, but I can think of nothing but the raw beauty of this island. If I were to run away, I think, this is where I would run. *No one would ever find me.*

Iolana pulls a journal from her backpack and hands it to me, but speaks to all of us. "Your mother had been here for two weeks when she hired Bane to bring her to Kipu Kai early one morning. She said she wanted to read and have a picnic, yet her small bag she carried looked empty. No book, no lunch. He told her he would return in four hours, and she only smiled and nodded. I'll wait at the camp site while Bane leads you up the mountain and there you can read the journal."

"I thought I heard you get up in the night," I ask Amelia when we're halfway up the mountain. I'm already huffing and my lungs feel ready to burst. I don't want to lecture her, but I do want an answer and what she's thinking being with a stranger. STDs! Hello?!

"Just got a drink of water," Amelia says, not even looking back at me.

Taryn snorts. "Don't look at me," she says. "I slept like a baby."

I'm not sure whom I'm madder at. Amelia for lying to Taryn or me for getting the sleep I so desperately desire.

We reach the top and the view is so breathtaking, I have to step back to brace myself from the impact. The kaleidoscope of brilliant hues makes me dizzy.

"Paradise," I hear Amelia say, but she sounds far away and I feel sucked in to the landscape, as if I'm floating just above those trees, or skimming the stream or inches from the exotic flowers.

"Stop!" Taryn screams, and I feel her nails dig in to my arms. I shake my head and realize I'm at the edge of the mountain, less than a foot from drop-off.

"What the hell are you doing besides trying to scare the shit out of us?" Taryn says.

"Damn, Mar," Amelia says, with a laugh. "I thought you were afraid of heights."

I look back at them, and Bane's eyes seem to be assessing me, looking straight through to my soul. I shudder and fall to my knees. I *am* afraid of heights.

"Hoary Head can put a spell on you," Bane says. "This is why the island put a zip line in down the mountain. To soar like an eagle."

I see the zip line just a hundred feet over, and a worker setting out the suits for the day's adventurers. Amelia is right. I'm still afraid of heights. Just one of a long list, really. I've given up keeping track.

"I'll leave you here to read the journal where Iolana marked it. When you are ready, we'll proceed." Bane retreats about fifty feet and spreads out a blanket and sits down and opens a novel, the very thing he'd said our mother had come up here to do. I'm not sure if he thought this was as bizarre as I did, or if Bane regularly acts like the Ghost of Christmas Past.

I try to pull up the image of her, but all I see is a tattered, yellowed 1980s picture of her. I can't make her 3D no matter how hard I try. She had no blanket. No book. Perhaps the noise in her head could only be quieted by coming out here. Up here.

"This is Heaven," Amelia says, her voice cracking. "Don't you feel God's presence right here? And Daddy's?"

My throat constricts. I feel so much sometimes that I feel nothing.

Taryn plops on the ground and goes into Lotus position and closes her eyes.

"I had no idea you did yoga," I say with dismay. I expect many things from my sister – late night hard rock music at smoky clubs, new piercings in unexpected places and weird Facebook posts, but this seems out of character.

"There's a lot you don't know about me," Taryn says, then closes her eyes. "Sit. Marlo, you do the reading."

Amelia puts her hand on her hip. "Just because you're the oldest doesn't mean you should get to read it."

"Tantrum at twenty-two. Nice," Taryn says. "Sit down and shut up. She's reading it aloud."

We sit facing the view, myself between them, and open the journal to the yellow sticky note Iolana marked, my charm bracelet jangling against the pages. I clear my throat and begin.

September 5th, 1989

My Beloved Girls,

When you read this letter, I will be gone. I have tried for so long to make things right, to be the kind of mommy that you deserve, but I now realize it is beyond my control. I have only one choice, because I cannot stand living a life without my precious angels in it. I know this is hard to read, but someday, when you're older, you'll understand that life can be so rough sometimes. So hard! The two weeks without you have been torture for me. It's as if someone ripped out my heart, only to discover that it was my soul. I am so young, and yet how do I feel so old? So spent? Used up? My only consolation is that you will live on, that I will live within you and that you will be able to live out beautiful lives. Your father, for all his shortcomings, is a great father, and I know he will give you better care than I ever could.

Know that you have done nothing wrong. It's not because of anything you did or didn't do. How could it possibly be? You are perfect as God intended. I miss your sweet little kisses and pudgy little arms and legs all tangled up with me in bed and the sound of your laughter. My favorite times were when you all laughed at once, like when Daddy came home and tickled you and then you begged him to tickle me and we would all end up on the living room floor, our laughter rising up together. I wish I could hold on to that chorus, that it alone would be enough to keep me going.

I thought if I left that my pain would go away, but it has only sharpened.

I leave you with this: I love you, I love you, I love you. I could say it a million times over and it would still not be enough. So close your eyes and let it echo through. Feel it, know it, and carry it with you.

Love, Mom

We sit in silence, though of course it's not really silent because Amelia is sobbing to my left and Taryn is picking at the ground, cutting the earth with a sharp rock. Then I see it, just above the mountain range to my left, an eagle soaring down and over the beach and above the water. My body feels numb.

"That was beautiful," Amelia says.

"For a suicide note," Taryn adds.

"That's not what it was," Amelia argues. "She's alive."

"Taryn's right." I turn the page. "She had to have tried. And failed. She wanted to jump off this cliff."

We stand and lock hands and walk to the edge, though not as close as I had done earlier. We look down and see that just below there is not much beach, only water. I don't see rocks protruding from the water, but we have no idea what is beneath the glassy surface. Things are not as calm as they seem.

"Read on," Taryn says as we back up, but this time we don't sit down. She picks up the journal, and turns the page. We are all relieved there is another entry, yet only one entry, the rest of the journal is nothing but blank pages, slightly discolored from age. "There's more." Taryn hands the journal out for Amelia. "Here. You read it."

Amelia crosses her arms. "I can't. I don't even know if I want to hear it. I've never imagined that she would try to kill herself."

Funny. Death had been my only answer for my mother. So I take the journal and begin reading:

October 9th, 1989

My darling daughters,

I wish I could say that I don't remember what happened. As I re-read my last journal entry, the one that was supposed to leave you knowing how much I loved you before I took my own life, shame washes over me. What a fool I was to believe that death was the answer. And yet, even writing this, I know, if given the right circumstance and the right trance that this island puts on me, I could do it again. What does this make me? Whatever it is, it is not good. I know that I am not in my right mind. No one who attempts suicide is. It is a way out. A final door to walk through and bolt behind you so no one can try to rescue you.

And yet that's just what happened. I wasn't scared when I stood on my tiptoes, barefoot, my arms above my head, because I imagined I was diving, like I had so many times in high school when your father and I would spend hours at the community pool, betting each other who could do the cleanest high dive.

When I came to, I truly believed I was in Heaven. I was lying on a cot in a cottage with only three walls, the fourth wall the Paradise I had dreamed of for so long. The palm trees lined my view of the white beach and endless blue ocean. Not a person in sight. When I tried to stand, I realized I couldn't move. Every muscle in my body ached and my head pounded like all the sounds of the world boomed inside my brain.

I looked down at my legs, one leg in a cast, both arms in casts, a brace around my neck and something wrapped around my head, which turned out to be gauze from an open wound on my head. I have no idea how I survived my dive and instantly I was disappointed I had failed at death, too.

My sobs brought Bane and Iolana to my bedside. Staring up at Bane, it came back to me, in bits and pieces. Bane's strong arms carrying me from the surf. Doctors working on me. Iolana's Hawaiian prayers constantly in my ears. She sang to me every day, and fed me.

You would think I would've been grateful for them, but I wasn't. Not at first. I was angry Bane hadn't left me to die, to leave me with the ocean to have its way with me.

I was just as angry with Iolana for not letting me starve. I figured this was my only option since I couldn't reach for anything to get the matter over and done with in a quicker manner.

I know I deserve to die. I left my girls. I can't even manage what millions of mothers throughout the centuries have managed to do. Mothers should be able to mother. I know for certain I don't deserve a second chance. Second chances are for winners, survivors, not losers like me.

Now in my fourth week of recovery, I've begun watching the trees, the beach, the ocean. Do you know how miraculous a grain of sand is? With just one piece, you think, "It is nothing, just a tiny grain of sand. What difference can it make?" But without each grain of sand, you wouldn't have the beach.

I can't say why or how, but I can say that I am starting to feel something like the stirring of a soul within me again. Where had it gone? Had it been there the whole time? I do have a spirit, no matter how crushed.

It is hard to put this into words, but I can only describe it as being similar to the experience I had of quickening when each of you were inside of me. You wonder at first, "did I feel something? Was that real? Is that my baby, living inside of me? And the moment you decide that it is real, you feel important, like God has given you such a special gift, a miracle."

This is not to say that I still don't think about dying. But today is Independence Day and I know how much you love the fireworks, Marlo. I hope Daddy found the matching red, white and blue outfits I picked out for you to wear before I left.

Oh God, it's too much. Even if I wanted to, I could not get up from this chair and return to you. I long to hear your voices again. I wonder if I should call. I want to call, but your father would convince me to come home or more likely just scream at me. No, I would be even worse off than I was before I left. I would now be the "mother who tried to kill herself, but failed."

My new wish is that your father will remarry soon. You all deserve that.

I am tired now. The mid-day sun always puts me to sleep. I pray when I wake up that this has all been a bad dream.

Love, Mom

"I remember," Taryn says. "I remember the first 4th of July without her."

"How can you possibly remember that?" I ask.

"Because of what Daddy said. He had tears in his eyes, and he said, 'Mommy bought these for you.' I asked him where Mommy went, and he said, "she went somewhere to get better.'"

"You think he knew where she was then?"

"She didn't seem to think so."

"It's not fair you two have memories of her," Amelia says, brushing off her bottom.

"Be careful what you wish for," I warn. "The memories I have of her are mostly bad ones."

My sisters stare at me. I debate whether or not to tell them that this dive from Hoary Head was not her first attempt to end her life. That I had a front row seat at the first one, if in fact it was the first one and not a string of failed attempts throughout her life. But Bane sees that we are done and walks toward us.

Amelia awaits no permission and runs up and wraps her arms around Bane. "Thank you for saving her."

He pats her on the back then peels her off. "It is time," he says. "To soar like an eagle."

6
MARLO

"I'm not going on that thing." I watch the worker strap Amelia in to the safety harness of the zip line, but my mind keeps screaming *death trap*. And people actually *pay* for this experience? Complete lunacy.

"Come on, scaredy cat," Amelia says, looking over her shoulder. "You've come this far. Mom wanted us to walk in her shoes, so that means flying, too."

My arms and legs feel like Jell-O and my forehead is covered with sweat. "Well, that's ridiculous. I think Dad's saying about someone jumping off a bridge, would you do it, too has never been more appropriate. Even if those idiots are your sisters."

"Look, I'm not buying in to the sappy shit," Taryn says, stepping in front of me since I won't budge. "It doesn't surprise me that Elizabeth tried to off herself. She was mentally unstable."

I inhale through my nose and exhale through my mouth and try not to think what my mother could've been thinking as she jumped off the edge. Did her life flash before her eyes as she sailed through the air? Was she scared? Relieved?

Taryn shakes my arm. "Think of it as a theme-park ride, a fast way down after walking our asses all the way up here. And Bane said lunch is waiting down at base camp with Iolana. So if you want lunch, this is the way to get it."

Hunger gnaws in my gut. Goose bumps cover my flesh. On the upside, at least I can use it for my article. I hear Shane whispering in my ear, "What do you have to be so afraid of?"

So many things, I had wanted to tell him. Afraid of love and more afraid of losing it.

Shane had taken my head in his hands and quoted FDR. "The only thing we have to fear is fear itself - nameless, unreasoning, unjustified, terror which paralyzes needed efforts to convert retreat into advance." He'd kissed me and I'd let him drag me on the most terrifying roller coaster in California. This—ohgodIcan'tlookdown—is much worse than a roller coaster.

I must not retreat.

"Fine. I'll do it."

The sound of Amelia's screams turns to laughter as she flies through the air, followed moments later by the sound of Taryn's raucous laughter. I hadn't heard her laugh in so long. The greatest surprise of all is my own feeling of weightlessness as I leave the cliff, no net below yet held up from above, like God's fingers clasped the harness. With the wind at my back, I soar over the trees, my laughter mixing with theirs, filling this heaven with our chorus. I wish she could hear it, if it might fix her.

The exhilaration overcomes me as I speed down the line, fear peeling away like a useless second skin. I've never felt so free, so unhitched from my thoughts, pushed out by the air so I get a glimpse of what's beneath them, deep inside of me.

7
AMELIA

"Don't cause a scene!" Alofa, my Samoan lover, the one who just the night before had told me he'd never made love to a woman as beautiful as me, wipes the margarita dripping from his chiseled face.

I'm not sure what I regret more. Wasting ten bucks on the margarita I'd just thrown in his face or that I'd slept with him three times in two days only to find him rollicking in the sand with a gorgeous blonde definitely as pretty as me though ten years older, and two half-Samoan children jumping on his back.

Amazing how they find their wedding ring *just* before their family arrives. I hadn't even thought to ask. Had I cared, or was I too afraid to hear the words, that it would officially make me the "other woman?" Again.

"Fuck you and the high horse you rode in on." I push him back with all of my might, but he doesn't budge. He's twice my size, easy. He pulls my arm so we are even farther away from the perfect beach scene with his wife.

Had I really thought a beautiful island would change human nature?

"I'm sorry," he hisses, grabbing for napkins at a nearby table to wipe his face. "I never meant to hurt you. I thought we were just having fun. And for what it's worth, it was the most fun I've had in a very long time."

I stare up into those big brown eyes, and realize it's not him I hate. It's me. *Fun.* It's always about fun with them, isn't it? Why should screwing be anything but a good time? I'm the idiot for thinking it was romantic, that we were making love, that the sheer act of our naked bodies together under the Hawaiian moon meant our souls gave a shit.

"I'm keeping your number, Taryn," he says as I turn away, and feel a stab of guilt. I'd used my wild sister's name in vain, but I was beginning to get the feeling she only *looked* wild. I am the true wild child of the family, and it suddenly makes me sick.

I look back over my shoulder and see his wife take their children's hands and lead them into the surf. "Yeah, you've got it really rough. Poor you." I force a smile. "Actually, I figured you were married all along. I was just hoping we'd get one more screw in before they got here." I'll not be a sniveling dumb blonde he can tell his work buddy assholes about. If he hasn't already.

Alofa smiles, his large shoulders relaxing. He cocks his head. "We could sneak into a bungalow," he whispers.

I stare up into his eyes, and see what a stupid cocksucker he really is. A soulless bastard. Why am I such a magnet for them? "Not interested anymore," I say with a shrug, which I know is like a machete to his ego. He walks away, and jogs to his family, while I watch, fighting back the tears, then feel a cold slim hand on my shoulder.

"That sucks," Taryn says. "Jerkwads, every one of them."

I wipe away my tears and laugh. "I blame using the F-bomb again on you. I was being *so good.*"

"Were you?" She pauses long enough for me to feel another prick of shame. "Looks like the kindergarten teacher has lost it. Come on. You need a drink."

"I'm sorry I used your name."

Taryn shrugs. "Better than using your own. You must've known that he couldn't be trusted."

"I dunno. Maybe the one I can't trust is me. Damn. Did you see how toned his wife's abs are? And you could bounce a quarter off her ass. She definitely looks like she's trying to keep her man."

Taryn grimaces. "Who knows why men cheat. Come on. Marlo rented some bikes for us, but I'd like to check out some local tattoo shops."

"Where the hell would you put one?"

"Oh, you'd be surprised."

The story of the Good Samaritan is one of my favorites in the Bible, yet I hadn't ever met one in real life, until now. Iolana and her husband Bane are workers on the island, catering to the tourists, not at all the wealthy Keepers I had imagined. They had helped my mother because that's the kind of people they are. You don't let someone die. You don't abandon a sick person. You heal. You love. You bring them back to life.

Iolana, who works as a maid during the day at a ritzy resort, mapped out the directions to her house so I could see where my mother had recovered. I see Marlo through the window of our cottage working on a story, but I know she'd be able to tell I've been crying. I don't want a speech.

Just as I doubted Taryn had room for more tattoos, I have no more room for Marlo's speeches. My mind is full of them, yet she would try to cram another one in there!

I quietly take the bike without her knowing. Alone, I bike down the winding streets of Kaui, where the speed limit is never over thirty five, and breathe in the fresh air and forget all about my lover, and all the ones that came before him.

I find the bungalow, which sits just in front of the couple's small island house, and it's just as my mother described it in the letter. I see the cot, kick off my flip-flops and walk through the sand to sit in the shade. I close my eyes and ease onto the cot, then open my eyes and stare at the view, my whole body electrified.

There. The same trees. The same ocean. The same sand. My mom and I hadn't been this close since I'd last nestled against her bosom twenty years earlier, which I couldn't remember no matter how hard I tried.

My body convulses, the sound of my own howling cries filling the otherwise peaceful morning. I crawl through the sand, one hand, one knee at a time, pulling myself forward until I collapse and become one with it. We are all just a grain of sand, I think, but what am I without the others?

Iolana wakes me sometime later. My skin is hot, and I realize I must've slept for hours. I'd lost so much sleep sneaking out to be with Alofa. I seemed to put men above all the other needs for my body. What the hell is wrong with me?

"Your sisters are looking for you," she says, handing me a glass of iced tea. I drink it down, then wipe my mouth with the back of my hand.

"Tell me what happened. After. How long did she stay? What did she do? Did she try to kill herself again?"

Iolana is never quick to smile, and I admire her for it. I am always too ready with a smile, to set the other person at ease, to win them over. I want her to heal me like she did my mother. I want to lie on that cot and make the rest of the world go away.

"Your mother got well, physically," she says, sitting cross-legged on the sand. "She bartended and knew enough to stay away from drinking it. Said slopping it all night made her sick of it. She enjoyed the work, the late hours. Her Dracula hours, she used to call them. She'd work all night and sleep half the day. Then she would run. Running allowed her to reconnect with her spirit and the spirit of the island."

I can hear Taryn's voice in my head making a comment about my mother being very good at running, but I don't say it. "The island has a spirit?"

"You've probably heard of it. The Aloha spirit."

"I thought it just meant hello."

"The deeper meaning of Aloha is passed down for generations. It is our code of ethics. Aloha is being a part of all, and all being a part of me. When there is pain, it is my pain. When there is joy, it is also mine. I take only what I need, and cherish all."

"So when you and your husband found my mother, you also shared her pain."

Iolana nods. "It is not something you question. You just know. You *do*. The code makes it so. Here, I'll teach you.

A, *ala*, watchful, alertness

L, *lokahi*, working with unity

O, *oia'i'o*, truthful honesty

H, *ha'aha'a*, humility

A, *ahonui*, patient perseverance

To the Hawaiian of old, Aloha meant, 'God in us.'"

I run my fingers through the sand, nodding. "So you're saying that we aren't separate from each other? We're all one?"

Iolana stands and helps me to my feet. "If we see ourselves in others and others in ourselves, than how could we possibly harm each other? We are all manifestations of aloha."

I bend down, hug her and feel her enormous energy. I never want to leave.

"As for the rest, I think that your mother should tell you," she says. "She wanted you to know that she struggled. That she fell down many, many times on her way to walking a more righteous path. My wish was that she returned to you, and now it's happening."

"But it's been twenty years," I say, my voice cracking. "I'm all grown up now. I needed her when I was a child."

Iolana looks at me, and I can see she is not studying me, not judging me, only being with me, feeling my words. "Of course you did. And you still do. It took twenty years for the cycle of life to come around again."

My heart feels heavy. I want to kick the sand and scream that it's too late to make things right, that I'm already too screwed up to make a difference, when my sisters pull up on their bikes.

"So this is the place," Taryn says hopping off the bike. "If a picture is worth a thousand words, this one is like, a million." She takes her camera and begins snapping pictures.

Marlo folds her arms, her body a bucket of nerves as she looks over at me. I can see she is angry with me for leaving without word. I know how she worries. I try for the first time to understand that she hasn't been preaching and scolding me all these years. I have to consider she has been feeling my pain, too and took it on as her own. Though I've never given her credit, - and she can still be a bossy pain in the ass - she's had many Good Samaritan moments with me at the other end of it.

We drink more iced tea while we make plans for the evening.

"We're hula dancing," Taryn announces, no question.

Marlo rolls her eyes and I shrug. If I needed someone to push me to try something new, I'd go to Taryn. Marlo groans, as her editor Ken had suggested she do that very thing for a story. How can you go to Hawaii and *not* hula dance?

"Research for the story," Marlo says.

"Just go with the mofo flow!" Taryn responds.

I grumble but even though I'm exhausted, I wouldn't miss seeing Marlo hula dance for the world.

An hour later, the hula instructor tells us that hula is story through dance. The outspread arms of the dancer represent the swaying of the palm trees gently blown by the wind. The dancer is supposed to coordinate the facial expression and the eye movements with the graceful movements of the fingers, arms, wrists, hips, knees and feet.

I'm pretty sure bursting out laughing at how seriously Marlo is taking the whole thing is not cool.

"Shut up," Marlo mouths, and Taryn exaggerates her hip movements even more, to try to outdo me, but when her face freezes, I follow her stare to Alofa's wife and beautiful daughter who have joined our circle. A circle, I'm afraid, I have to break. Guilt overcomes me, and I think I might be sick.

I grab my bag and rush inside to the bathroom and fall to my knees. I don't get sick, but instead fold my hands and pray the *Our Father* fervently. When I get to one part, I say it over and over, like a record skipping. "And forgive us our sins, as we forgive those who have sinned against us."

I fall back against the wall, sweaty and spent, wondering how I can pray those words and then go out and sin again. I have held every sinner up - my married lover back home, even my mother - like a crucifix on my wall.

The water feels good on my face. After I dab it dry, I reapply mascara and lipstick and rub lipstick into my cheeks for color, ready to face them again.

After a glass of water and a shot of tequila, I'm feeling much better. Through the sliding glass door, I see them gliding on the sand, my sisters and the one I've sinned against. Should I approach her? Tell her I'm sorry? I know how that works out: it doesn't. Instead, I leave her to her fantasy of being married to a faithful, successful, loving man.

"Mind if I share the bar with you tonight?" I ask Tommy, the bartender I'd met in the tiki hut the first night.

"You any good?"

He has a bandage on his forehead and I instinctively reach up and touch it. "Burn yourself flat-ironing your hair?" He isn't exactly a pretty boy, but he laughs at my joke.

"Your sister pushed me off a rock. Banged my head on the way down."

My mouth drops open. "What the hell did you do?"

"Hey, I thought she was into me."

"She's practically engaged!" I playfully slap him on the arm. I swivel on the barstool and adjust my swimsuit wrap, feeling the eyes of a half a dozen guys in the bar on my body. Business types trying not to look like stuffed shirts, wearing garish Hawaiian shirts and khaki shorts. Like wind up toys that would march to my orders. Then I see him. Blue Eyes is sitting in the corner, a straw hat on his head, laptop on the table in front of him, deep in work. Still pale and handsome and alone. I contemplate getting up to go meet him, to find out his story, but Tommy taps me on the arm.

"They look like they want to order you for dinner," Tommy says as he dries off a glass.

I shrug. "Yeah. A little quickie while their wives are out on the beach with their kids? Assholes. And, yes, I'm a great bartender. I've even concocted some pretty good recipes of my own."

Tommy leans over the bar. "My boss leaves in a few minutes. Boss being my dad. You can bartend with me as long as you'll split tips fifty/fifty. I imagine you rake it in pretty good."

I push my breasts together, by far my best asset, and lean over the bar and kiss him lightly on the lips. "How'd you ever guess?"

"Just don't bring your sociopathic sibling along, okay?"

"No problem. I'll be sure and tell her that she didn't kill you, though."

"Why spoil her perfectly good vacation? Hey, there's my dad now. He wanted to meet you actually. He knew your mom."

I've never been known to be tight-lipped about anything. Everyone within a mile radius of this place knew we were on a quest to meet our mother. I spin in the chair and study the man who looks more like Tommy's older brother than his father. His salt and pepper hair and rugged good looks take me off guard. His looks are nothing compared to what he knows. *Who* he knows.

"Mark Fulton," he says, sticking his large hand out for me to shake. "You're the spitting image of your mother."

I stand, nearly tripping over my own flip-flop, and try not to choke. No one has told me that before. But it makes sense. She was just a few years older than me when he met her.

"Amelia."

"The angel baby," Mark says. "That's what she used to call you. I think it still applies."

I nearly forget to let go of his hand. "Can we talk? I mean, I know you're just now getting off work and all, but I'd love to hear about my mother."

"Let's walk down on the beach. I need some fresh air. You've heard of cabin fever? I get bar fever every day about this time."

My sisters are still hula dancing by the firelight in the distance as I walk off with Mark. I know what they'll think if they see me with him, but I don't care. I've never been picky about age.

We walk along the water's edge, leaving our footprints in the sand as we walk only to have them washed away with the next wave. The night is calm and cool. Goose pimples cover my arm.

"My mother worked for you?"

"At first. Before she broke my heart." He smiles but I can hear the pain in his voice.

I nod, and feel my whole body turn white. I wonder if I'm glowing under the moonlight. I wondered if she fell in love again after my father, but I hate to hear the words.

"I'm sorry. That didn't come out right. I guess seeing you just brought up some old feelings I thought were long buried."

"It's okay. As my therapist says, you have to let people feel their feelings. That's what used to upset me about my big sister Marlo. She wanted to tell you how you should feel. But you know my mother better than I do. It's not fair."

"It is. I'm sorry. I really don't know what to say. Or where to begin."

"What was she like?"

He sighs and looks out into the water. "She was beautiful, but so sad. Like if you said the wrong thing she just might break in two. I learned to handle her like china. Slowly she trusted me. She told me all about you girls."

I try to hold it together, but it's darker now, and I let the tears fall. "What did she say about us?"

"How happy she was when you were born. Said she gave you a huge first birthday party that she'd spent weeks planning."

I have pictures at least. Lots and lots of pictures of my first birthday. It's almost as if my mother knew she might leave and took extra care to have someone besides herself snap all of them so she's actually in a fair number. Holding me. Kissing my icing-covered face, icing herself in the process. Giving me a bath after. From those pictures I would've never known she was just months away from attempting suicide.

I stop and grab him by the arms, planting myself in front of him. "Why did she leave us? What did she say about *that*?"

Mark placed his hand on my shoulder, landing like a rock. "I'm sorry, princess. She never told me why she left. Only that she didn't feel that she had a choice. I respected her privacy. She told me the good things, which made it hard for me to understand why she couldn't go back. But we all carry demons. Some are small and we can crush them easily. Others I imagine are like big dragons that chase us no matter how fast we try to escape them. Believe me, in my line of business I've seen more than my share of them in my customers. I'd say you've got some demons of your own, eh?"

"You obviously don't believe in the story of David and Goliath then, do you?"

Mark leans down, his face half-lit in the darkness. "Your mother was no David. How many of us really are?"

"But where did she go? Did she leave without telling you, too?"

He shook his head. "I suppose she wasn't ready to land yet."

"Another man?"

He walks into the ocean, where the waves hit our ankles, then looks up at the moon, half-full, much like my heart. "I served him at the bar off and on for about six months. Don't even recall his name. Never talked much. Just kept to himself, you know. I never thought your mother would be someone I, or any man for that matter, could hold on to."

A part of me is glad she left him, but I feel sorry for him all the same. A broken heart is universal. And it wasn't just the stress of having another baby that sent her over the edge. Believe me, feeling guilty that my mother left because I was too much to handle has never completely left. I suppose I want to hear someone other than my father and my sister say it: that I didn't give my mother post-partum depression, that I didn't make her feel so crazy that running away was the only answer.

There's more, and I'm determined to find out what it was. I clear my throat. "So you're convinced she wasn't a monster?"

"A monster? Good lord, no. Look, when I say we all have demons, let me say your mother was putting up the good fight. She fought hard. She wanted to change. When I first met her, she hated everything about herself. Iolana helped her. This island helped her. I tried to help her. But it wasn't enough."

I choke back a tear. Bartending wasn't all we had in common, then. Of course I have my own demons. And it seems one of them is trying to reach me. My phone vibrates from its place in my bikini top. I say my goodbyes to Mark, thanking him, and pull the phone out. The screen lights up like a firefly in the dark. Sixteen missed calls. I have the feeling he won't stop calling until I give in, because I normally do. He's trying to wear me down, but I'm stronger than he thinks. He's an anchor I have to cut loose.

I hold the phone tight in my fist, remember my daddy's specific instructions on how to pass a football, and stretch my arm way back and hurl the phone into the air and watch it soar a good fifty feet before it lands in the ocean with a tiny plunk. His next call will vibrate in the belly of a reef shark, as it should be.

No surprise, Marlo and Taryn aren't talking to each other when I return, but instead both are on their phones, talking to their men. I push aside the feelings of jealousy and go inside the bar to work off some steam, promising to meet them in the hot tub later. I don't want to talk about Alofa or Mark or speculate about the rich man my mom could've left the island with. They would ridicule her, pick her apart. I want them to *want* to meet her at the end. I believe she's a good person. I have to believe it, even if they don't.

I know without a doubt I can get lost in my work, and desperately need to get lost. Busy bartenders don't have time to chat you up, but we know what to prescribe for what ails you. When an adventurous-looking group of recent college grads (you can spot a sorority girl a mile away), want something "Hawaiian" that they'd never had before, I jump in.

"You girls need a Lava Flow," I tell them, and their perfectly lashed eyes widen. "It's sweet and delicious, and you'll fall in love with it way more than any jerk you ever loved in college."

The women whoop and holler, and just like that, I sell six Lava Flows at $14 a piece versus the traditional Mai Tai that sells for just $10. It's easier to convince someone to buy one pricey drink than two cheap ones. And I have a knack for knowing what people like. Even the women.

I gather the ingredients and get to work. I blend the two rums and the strawberries in a blender to form a smooth paste and pour the mixture into a tall Hurricane glass. Next I blend the banana, the coconut cream, and the pineapple juice with crushed ice until it's smooth. Then I very slowly pour it into the glass and watch as the strawberry mixture oozes its way to the top along the sides of the glass creating the flowing lava effect, which gets more excited woos from the girls. I finish it off with a pineapple wedge and paper umbrella.

"You are good at this," Tommy says, two hours later, as we split the tips and I get ready to join my sisters. The knot in my stomach is small now, the demons the size of ants. I can see why both of my sisters prefer to stay lost in their work. No time to feel your feelings. Easy to pretend you're this perfect, put-together human being.

"If you decide you want the island lifestyle, I bet I could convince my dad to hire you," Tommy says as I take a wad of cash.

I toss him my best smile, head tilted. "My future is a mystery. Mostly I want to get married and have a carful of kids. A normal family, you know?"

"Doesn't sound unreasonable."

I feel my eyelids fill with tears and bite my bottom lip. "Yeah. We'll see." I touch his bandage. "And I'm sorry about my sis and the bump."

"I probably deserved it. Karma or some shit." He hands me another fifty-dollar bill. "We sold more tequila tonight than we have in months."

I nod, wiping the spilled tequila from my chest with a clean, wet rag. "Works like a charm every time."

Next, I wipe off my belly button, where two-dozen men's tongues had plunged that evening for a salt lick before picking up the tequila shot nestled in my cleavage. Sadly, Blue Eyes wasn't one of them. He'd watched the first few, and then looking uncomfortable, took off into the night. Not many men would turn down a chance at a body shot. Especially off of me.

I tuck the bill into my bikini top. I'm not sure if I'm happier about the money, or the fact that it was the first time in a long time that I'm not leaving the bar with a man.

8
TARYN

"I could fly out in the morning and be there by the afternoon," Paul says on the phone as Amelia brushes past us on her way into the bar.

"Don't be an idiot." My stomach flutters. I go from feeling like *is this guy for real?* To *THIS GUY IS FOR REAL!*

"This idiot misses you," he says, and my heart thumps in pain.

"Tomorrow's our last day, anyway," I say, instead of *I wish you could. I miss you.*

"Well, maybe we could go back there for our honeymoon."

"Paul, you promised."

"I know, but dammit, Taryn. I want to marry you. What's so difficult to understand about that?"

I roll my eyes though of course he can't see it. I want to tell him my dad's first marriage (to my Mom) sucked. I don't remember much about them, but I do remember their fighting, late at night, as I fell asleep.

My dad's second marriage blew chunks. He married Cecelia two years after Elizabeth left. She tried to make things work, like all step moms do, I guess, but just when I decided I didn't completely hate her, she left us, too. Then I hated her most for breaking Amelia's heart.

Our family was an active volcano and there was nothing I could do about it. Marlo tried to make things normal for us, dinner on the table, laundry done and sorted, but no matter of goodness on our part kept Dad from getting cancer. He fucking died. DIED. Left me. The only thing I know is that people leave. They don't stay. How could Paul be any different?

I clear my throat. "I thought the 'where do we stand' speech was strictly girls' only? You know I'm crazy mad for you, ya big dope."

We'd been dating off and on for six months before Paul started dropping hints about a "future." Future? My future is what I see right in front of me. And I see right now that … I need another drink.

"I know. But I'm ready to settle down. But not with just anyone. With *you*. I've known you were the one since our first date."

I smile, remembering the cheap carnival I'd thought a guy like Paul, dressed in his Polo shirt and madras shorts and sandals, wouldn't be caught dead at. He'd looked scared when I mentioned it, but he agreed to go, and the kid in him emerged immediately. His mom had never let him go to the traveling carnivals for safety sake, and because she thought the carnies were escaped convicts, with their tattoos and poor dental care.

I had made him ride all the rides, the Tilt-A-Whirl, Death Winder, Egg Beater. We ate corn dogs and cotton candy and he won me a cheesy stuffed animal, a Garfield like I'd always wanted when I was little. The kind with suction cups so it sticks to your car window and annoys all the passersby. It's back home in my Prius, guarding it until I return.

He tells me I'm fun incarnate, but what if I wake up one day and I'm not fun, anymore? What then?

Why the hell did I fall in love with an old-fashioned guy who doesn't believe in moving in together first? He's twenty-eight, successful, owns his own house already. I get that he's ready to settle, but ... yeah, there's always a *but*.

My heart thumps again, remembering where I am, that I'm on a mission to learn about a woman who could stand to be away from us for twenty years. Does Paul mean he wants me *forever?* How could he? What if he hits thirty and changes his god dammed mind after I've given him my tiny black heart? And if I believe *him,* then how can I not hate my mother for staying away?

"Marriage is a dying institution," I tell him, knowing full well it will hurt his feelings. There must be something wrong with this guy. He doesn't even believe in divorce. Who talks like that these days? "Even Mr. and Mrs. Perfect are in marriage counseling." I look over to make sure Marlo can't hear me, as she's on the phone with her Mr. *Nearly* Perfect.

"No marriage is perfect," Paul says. "Not that I've gotten to meet them yet." Hint like a bomb. Ka-pow.

"Trust me, you don't want to. They're *nothing* like me."

"I want to meet your family. I want to *be* your family."

"Look, I know you're under the 'distance makes the heart grow fonder' spell, and I do miss you like hell, but I'm not any closer to saying yes, K?"

Paul pauses, then sighs. "Have you been with someone there?" No accusation, just a question, like, *can I get you cup of coffee?* An unfair question even in an open relationship. Don't ask/don't tell.

"I kissed a guy, but that's it. It was nothing. Maybe I wanted it to be something, but it wasn't. It felt nothing like you, and I thought of our heart tattoos and it drove me insane. You happy now?"

"Hell, Taryn. I'm sorry I asked." I hear him punch something, but it's not like a banker to punch a hole through a wall, is it? Even a very tattooed banker?

"Settle down, Paul. Shit, I said it was just a kiss."

Marlo looks over at me, alarmed. Her convo doesn't look to be going too well.

"Even the prostitutes don't let their johns kiss them." I hear something break, like glass, and I imagine it might be the pricey wine glasses his mother gave him for Christmas that sit neatly in the upside-down glass rack underneath his kitchen cabinet. I've never dated a guy who drinks wine, let alone has clean wine glasses hanging around.

"Prostitute? I'm going to ignore that you said that. For chrissakes, did you just cut yourself?"

"Dammit, Taryn." He sighs. "Dropped my glass."

"Shit, babe. Look, I'm sorry. I gotta go. Marlo's off the phone. And if it makes you feel better, I pushed the guy off a rock. I thought I killed him for a minute until I saw him swim to the shore."

"Wow, that does make me feel strangely better. He okay?"

"I can see him through the glass. His head is bandaged, but unless I caused some brain damage, I think he can still tend bar."

"I need to confess something, T."

I close my eyes and wrap my right hand around the arm of the chair, bracing myself, but try to keep my voice light. "What did you do?"

"It's what I haven't done."

"For shit's sake, Paul. What did you *not* do, then?"

"Since we've been together, I haven't been with anyone else. Not even a kiss."

I want to be angry with him, but I find myself smiling and tiny bubbles are popping in my brain. I exhale, pretending to be upset with him. "What are you saying? That you don't want an open relationship?"

"If you'll recall, I never did."

"Is that why you asked me to marry you? Hell, why didn't you just say, *can't we go steady*?"

"Obviously if you said yes, that would put an end to the open relationship."

"I see. So if I agree to not be with any other guys, can we drop this whole marriage proposal bit and just date for a while? No pining over wedding bouquets and three-tier cakes when we go to the bakery?"

"A guy can dream, T."

"Dammit, Paul. I'm serious."

"*Exclusively* date?"

"Yes, exclusively, dipshit."

Marlo is laughing at me now, but I swear to God I don't see a damn thing funny about this love business.

"You don't know how happy that makes me. I love you, babe."

But all I can say is, "I know," and hang up.

Marlo pinches my arm. "Taryn's got a booooy-friend."

I punch in the arm as hard as I can. That'll teach her.

I have to prop my bandaged ankle up and out of the water in the hot tub to keep from getting an infection. Akela is the best inker on the island, and it only took him an hour to fashion the beginnings of my trip around the world tattoo. Small tattoos are tough, requiring the steadiest hand.

"So can we see it, or what?" Marlo asks, sipping on the Piña colada Amelia brought her.

"It's still red. It'll look better in a few days," I tell them.

"After it scabs over and heals, you mean?" Amelia asks, scrunching her face in disgust.

"When will you let me ink you?" I ask, taking a swig of lime beer.

Marlo turns to Amelia. "Hell freezes over work for you?"

"Pretty much," Amelia says, clinking her glass with Marlo's.

"Pussies. Now are you going to tell us about that man we saw you walking with on the beach, or are we going to have to beat it out of you?"

"Oh, nothing," Amelia says, playing coy. "Just a former boss of Mom's."

"Nothing, my ass."

"So what did he say?" Marlo asks.

"That she was a nice person."

I throw my head back and laugh. "The guy must have a memory like a steel trap then!"

"I knew no matter what I said, you'd make fun of it," Amelia screams.

"You're right there, sweet cheeks. If you think I'm gonna buy into an idea that our mother was nice, then you've got another thing coming."

"Girls, please," Marlo starts.

"I don't get what Paul sees in you," Amelia says. "You're just mean and cranky and spiteful. Or do you just save that behavior for when we're around?"

I stick my face within inches of hers. "Oh, I'm pretty restrained right now. Actually, I've been on my best behavior."

"God forbid!"

"Guys! Cut it out," Marlo screams, then lowers her voice, noticing several onlookers around the pool have gotten up to leave. "See what you just did? You just ran them off. Can we not have one civilized conversation?"

"No!" Amelia and I answer at the same time, and then laugh. Finally, Marlo does, too.

"You guys are incorrigible."

"What the hell does that mean?" I ask.

"I don't know. Thank God kindergarteners don't use that word." Amelia smiles.

"Marlo's kids will if she ever decides to have any." I wink to show I can play along.

"Too bad. I want to be the cool aunt," Amelia says. "Every child needs a cool aunt to take them shopping for clothes and corn dogs at the mall like Aunt Darla did."

"Every child needs a mom first," Marlo says, matter-of-factly.

"It's weird though, don't you think?" I ask. "That Elizabeth *wanted* our dad to get remarried and we got Cecelia of all people."

"No comment," Marlo says.

"What was wrong with Cecelia? I think she was a great step-mom," Amelia says.

I point my bottle at Amelia. "You were the one she loved. You were only four when they got married so she still had a chance to get you to love her like she wanted to be loved."

"I did love her. You were the ones that made me stop calling her mom. Every time I said it you'd correct me. Do you know how much that hurt her feelings?"

"Let's see. I think her yelling at us that you *did* have a right to call her mom pretty much gave it away," I say. "She tried, I'll give her that. I didn't make things any easier for her."

"Well, you were a daddy's girl. Jealous as all get out when Cecelia moved in and took some of his time," Marlo says.

I take another swig and try not to think about Dad, but the memories rush back in. I wasn't a natural tomboy, but I became one to please my father. I was the son he never had, playing softball and soccer so he could be the coach though I'm not a natural athlete and was always the smallest kid on the team. We went fishing though I hated the smell of fish and cringed when Dad made me touch them. I tried not to girlie-scream when he cut them open and we cooked them on an open campfire. I hate the taste of fish, too, but I stomached it with a smile so I'd get the atta-girl.

"I wonder what she's up to now," Marlo muses.

Amelia sits her drink down on the ledge. "She's still in Kansas City. Her twins are in middle school now. Can you believe it? I used to babysit them when they were younger."

"You what?" Marlo asks. "I never knew that."

"Don't look at me like I'm some kind of traitor just because I don't give up on family so easily. She loved us and took care of us. I don't think I'd marry a man who already had three kids. Especially with one who kept putting dead frogs in her bed and replacing the sugar for salt with her morning coffee."

"Unbelievable how many times she fell for that one," I laugh. Yeah, I was a bit of a hellion. Figured I'd make her work for it. She wanted a ready-made family, by God she got one. Maybe I regret telling my sobbing little sis that we didn't need a mom after Cecelia left and that she didn't need to visit Cecelia every other weekend. Cecelia even fought for sole custody, but only wanted Amelia. Over my dead body. I may have thought my little sis was a pain in the ass, but no way I was giving her away. Amelia loved her and needed her—I shouldn't have messed with that, but I was ten. What the hell did I know about anything? I sigh. "She knew that going into it. Did she tell you why she and Dad split?" I ask.

Amelia shakes her head. "You know she wasn't a gossip. She made it a point never to say anything bad about him, which is why I still liked seeing her. Besides, I never had the guts to ask."

Marlo finishes her Piña colada and raises her finger in the air. "Infidelity."

"What?" Amelia turns off the hot tub bubbles, quieting the space.

"She said infidelity. Are you shittin' me?"

"I'm positive. I heard Cecelia and Aunt Darla talking about it one day. They were arguing actually."

"Aunt Darla never liked Cecelia," Amelia says.

"She blames Cecelia for our mother leaving."

Amelia leans forward in the water, her chin touching the surface. "What? I'm confused."

Marlo sighs, puckering her lips in an o. "Dad was having an affair with Cecelia when you were a baby. They worked together at his office. She was his sales assistant."

"I knew I didn't like that woman for a reason!" I used to call her Sexy Celia, which drove her batshit crazy. She tried way too hard with the overdone make-up and skintight clothes that might've been fine for the office slut look but didn't bode well on the playground. None of the other moms liked her. Now I guess I knew why.

Amelia's eyes gloss over. "No. I don't believe it. Cecelia wouldn't do that."

"It's true," Marlo says. "As I got older, I kind of put two and two together. It wasn't long before Elizabeth left. I was sick in bed and Aunt Darla had you both for the day so you wouldn't be around me. I woke up in the afternoon to a terrible crashing sound. Something breaking in the kitchen. So I go in there and see our mother pulling dishes from the pantry and throwing them on the floor. I was out of my mind, of course. I'd never see her act this way. The floor was covered with broken pieces and our mother was barefoot. She didn't even see that her feet were bleeding."

"Finally I scream for her to stop and she just looked at me with such a blank face. She didn't even look like our mother anymore. Her eyes were puffy and her skin was blotchy. I was crying and said, 'why are you breaking our dishes?'

"In this matter of fact voice, she said, 'Because your father gave them to me.'"

"Then bloody feet and all, she took me back to bed as if the whole thing didn't happen. But when she got to my door, I said, 'what did Daddy do to make you so mad?' She said, 'he broke a very big promise.'"

My whole body feels suddenly cold, even in the hot tub. I look over and see Amelia's tears mingle with the water. Always was Daddy's princess. As hard as I tried to please him, she was the cute one, the one who got all of his praise. Of course she doesn't want to believe he's done anything wrong. I don't want to believe it, either, but as good a man as he was, he was a man. And human. And apparently, a big-ass cheater. Dammit.

"I'm sorry, Amelia." Marlo says. "Why do you think I didn't tell you? I only bring it up now because if we're going to see what Elizabeth went through after she left, it's pertinent to know what happened before."

"Then I bet there's more," I say. "You haven't told us everything. How many Piña coladas does it take?"

Marlo shakes her head. "I don't know that much more about it. But years later, just before Cecelia moved out, I heard her tell Darla that she found him with another woman, and our aunt said something about not being able to change a zebra's stripes. And you know how Darla feels about karma."

"That it'll bite you in the ass when you least expect it," I say. "Did you ever confront Aunt D about it?"

"No," Marlo answers. "I guess we still can. If we're cleaning the skeletons out of the proverbial closet, we may as well get all the old bones out."

"I just can't believe daddy would *do* that," Amelia says quietly.

I look her in the eye. "Come on, Amelia. Are you saying that you've never known a good man, a decent man, to cheat on his wife before?"

Amelia shoots up out of the water and grabs a towel. "I don't have to listen to this."

"What's going on?" Marlo asks, flustered.

I shake my head. "I can't believe you don't know, Mar. Our sis is the teapot calling the kettle black."

"Shut up, Taryn. At least I don't have to make the pain go away by covering my body with tattoos so the world will leave me alone."

"Oh, you bare all every time a guy gives you a sideways glance, sweetheart. Hate to break it to ya, but it's far safer to use needles than dicks."

"Stop it!" Marlo rises out of the water. "Whatever is going on with you two, just cut it out. Taryn, you're goading her. Obviously she doesn't want to talk about it. Amelia, we don't give you hell about your cleavage, so let's lay off the tattoos, okay?"

Amelia and I look at each other and then back at Marlo. Silence laps around the pool before we finally speak. "Yes, Mother!" Amelia says in the singsong way we have since we were kids when Marlo would give us one of her speeches after a fight. Truthfully, I'd like to dunk her head in the water, but that would mean getting my bandage wet.

Marlo gives us the finger. I want to tell her that I think she'd be a great mom to little runts, but I have no business giving anyone advice. I can't even tell my own boyfriend that I've been faithful to him for fear he'll love me like a parasite. I don't need love that bad. If my dad, the guy I loved most in the world, was a serial cheater, how can I trust a man to love me of all people?

"We look like wrinkled old ladies," I say, swinging my legs out and grabbing a towel.

"Let's come back here when we're old," Amelia says. "Just us, you know? A sister reunion. In forty years."

Marlo smiles and I can't help but laugh. "You really think we'll still be speaking to each other then?"

We pass the lighted palm trees on our way back to our room. Marlo puts her arm around me. "I'll come just to see your tatts turn into a Dali painting."

Amelia bursts out laughing and I elbow Marlo.

"Hey, saggy tatts are better than saggy tits," I tell them.

"I'll get those fixed," Amelia says, pushing her already high bosom even higher.

"Oh, we don't doubt that one bit," Marlo says. "Count me in."

After our showers, we converge on Marlo's bed because she's popped the popcorn. Just like when we were kids. Dad would be on a date with Cecelia, or on a date with God knows who after she left him, or at a work conference, and the babysitter would let us pop popcorn and eat it on our bed while she talked to her boyfriend on the phone in the other room.

Marlo's laptop is open and I plug in my camera to upload the pictures of the island I took that day. I get fifty bucks for every shot they use in the magazine. I would've done it for free, so it's a pretty good gig.

Amelia tells us about her tip money, and I think I have the easier job. At least I don't have to bat my eyelashes at pot-bellied old men to make a living. I ink them up on a regular basis, though.

"Please can we see it?" Amelia asks, batting her eyelashes and sticking her bottom lip out. Hell, it works on me, too.

"Fine. You two are so impatient." I gently remove the bandage and stick my leg up in the air.

"It's amazing," Marlo says, lifting her arm up, placing her bracelet with the eagle charm next to my ankle.

It's a perfect replica. Maybe even better than the original. The tattooed ankle bracelet goes around my ankle just above my ankle bone (yes, it hurt like hell), and the eagle charm is the first charm, centered on the front of my leg.

Amelia puts her charm next to it on the other side, her skin brushing against mine, causing me to wince in pain. "I can't believe it," she says, tearing up. "We can take ours off, but you can't. You really do care."

I roll my eyes and put the bandage back over the tattoo, and toss some popcorn at her chest, which conveniently sticks in her ample cleavage.

9
MARLO

ionKansas Travel
Mahalo from the Garden Isle
by Marlo Thompson

"When I was a child, we had a blue station wagon that had long gone out of style. In fact, its only unique character was the left fender, askew from my mother backing in to a parked car she didn't see on the street, a rust stripe along the right door that I had once tried to color in with a blue marker, and a dashboard hula dancer that swayed her hips as we drove along.

I hadn't remembered that hula dancer until I arrived on Kauai and saw many hula dancers just like her. I wonder if the presence of that dancing doll in our car made Hawaii the first place my mother wanted to escape to when she finally ran. Now that I'm here, my first trip off the contingent states, I will admit the word "paradise" somehow doesn't do it justice. Hawaiians don't believe nature is separate from us – we are all one with it.

Sitting among the majestic beauty, you feel yourself soak in to the scenery and the scenery soak up within you. It will be hard to pack my bags this afternoon. This place naturally strips you of the material world: what is left is whatever you are feeling. You may feel a renewed sense of peace or happiness, or quite the opposite. I can't think of anything sadder than being lonely in a place that begs for you not to feel anything but joy and oneness with life.

Besides the coconut drinks and fruit and fish and miles of beachfront promoted by the travel magazines, a deeper culture runs through the land. The hula dance, performed poorly by this writer, began as a sacred ritual before it became entertainment for people like me. The heart of the hula dance is poetic text with meaning in every expression and hand gesture. It is an ode to life, nature, plants, trees, water, wind, fire. Besides the sacred Native American dances in the lower 48, our gyrating dances seem grotesque compared to the simple beauty of the hula dance.

Likewise, words are sacred. Mahalo means, "May you be in divine breath." The wind here feels like the breath of God. I've never been a spiritual person, so this gentle awakening was even more refreshing than the fruity drinks my bartending sister keeps handing me.

What started as a trip to paradise quickly became a journey to something so much more. So when I wish you, 'Mahola,' know that I mean it."

I click the publish button to put my first blog entry on our web site back home. Our sales director sold four weeks of advertising to a travel agent. One blog and one print article per week. My main story would cover the adventures on the island. The touristy stuff. I imagined a few Kansans might even attempt the zip line if they ever ventured across the ocean to Kauai.

Besides not knowing our second destination beyond that it required a passport, a greater feeling of unease rattles my bones – not with where we are going, but where we have been. With the charm bracelet on my arm, it's impossible to stop thinking about the eagle and soaring through the sky, and wondering when, *if,* I'd ever get to do it again. Would I go back to Kansas, repair my ailing marriage, agree to a future of kids and the PTA, never to return again? Or would I do as my mother had done and break things off, saw my life in half, and wander the earth, writing as I go along? Would one life be better? Worse?

I am still very much afraid of heights, and yet the rush of the zip line was like nothing I'd ever experienced - the closest feeling to recapturing the adrenaline on my wedding day. Overpowering. Raw.

While Amelia and Taryn lounge on chairs on the beach outside of our rooms, I tell them I'll be back in an hour and to have their bags packed when I return. I can't bite my tongue before the reminder slips out. Taryn calls me Sister Mother for a reason.

I ride the rented bike all the way up and around the winding two-lane road, not caring to stop the tears streaming down my face and hoping that along with the tears, the memories will spill out to make room for better ones.

Just weeks before my mother left, a heated argument in the middle of the night brought me tumbling out of my bed and into the lamp light of the living room where my mother sat on the couch and my father stood over her, his hands on his head, the clearest look of desperation and pain on his face.

At first they didn't see me, yet I didn't try to hide. I stood in the doorway, my flannel pajamas suddenly too hot for the spring night.

"What's wrong with you?" My father screamed, grabbing at my mother's arm. He tried to take something from her.

It was a few weeks after the broken dishes incident, and we'd been using paper plates ever since. I wondered if the argument had something to do with the promise he had broken and if I might find out what it was.

I held my breath, afraid it would give me away, and looked at the coffee table, littered with small silver pieces of metal, then back to my mother, whose face looked distorted with puffy eyes and red cheeks and more tears than I imagined anyone could ever cry. "Let me do it!" My mother wailed, and then I saw it in her hands, the sliver of a razor pinched between her fingers.

"Stop!" My high-pitched scream seemed to bounce off the walls and I held my hands up to my own ears to block it, but I couldn't stop screaming.

"Baby, go back to bed!" My mother says to me, choking back tears.

My father, his face red and hard as stone, waved me over. "No. Come here, Marlo. If your mama wants to kill herself, she can do it in front of us," he said. I was shocked by his monstrous expression, the weight of his ugly words. I'd never seen him talk or look that way before. I didn't understand "kill yourself," but I knew that our cat Cali had killed a bird the week before, and tried to bring it in the house. Amelia had screamed, "Birdie! Birdie!" and tried to take it from Cali's mouth when our mother explained to us that the bird would not fly again. She was dead. Cali had killed her, and death is final.

"Go back to bed, now!" My mother's eyes pleaded with me, but all I wanted to do was run into her arms, but I wasn't sure she was safe anymore, if in her arms was where I was supposed to be.

So I ran to Daddy instead, even though he's the one that broke some promise and caused my mother all this pain, turning her into someone I no longer recognized.

"You ready?" The zip line operator says as my turn approaches. I smile, this time feeling more confident as I push off the mountain and sail through the air, vowing to let go of that memory, too, leaving it high on the mountain top, before I've shared it with my sisters or my husband, because it is the past and should bear no witness to who I want to be.

All I know is that I will not turn in to my mother.

Iolana serves us mint tea that afternoon as Bane gets the car, a white Lincoln, from the rental car company. I assume my mother has paid for this. That she has compensated Iolana and Bane for watching over us during our four-day stay.

"How can we ever thank you?" I say to Iolana, kissing her on each cheek.

"Your presence is thanks enough. Mahalo." She hugs each of us, then squeezes my hands, looking up into my eyes. "Give my love to your mother, will you?"

My throat constricts, but I nod, blinking back the fear that the word conjures.

Bane stands before us, his hands folded in front of him. Amelia jumps up and hugs Bane. "Thanks again for saving her." Bane blinks hard to keep his composure.

Taryn and I shake his hand. "Where are we going?" Taryn asks, as she steps into the car, our passports tucked safely in my purse, where I'll keep them for all of us.

"Mexico."

DESTINATION 2: MEXICO CITY

"History and culture dominate Mexico's capital city, where you'll find the ruins of Aztec temples, the murals of Diego Rivera and the paintings of Frida Kahlo. Connecting the 21st century to the city's vibrant past, local dancers and drummers perform at the Zócalo, a public plaza surrounded by famous landmarks such as the Metropolitan Cathedral and Palacio Nacional. Chapultepec Park, with its popular anthropology museum, and the ancient canals of Xochimilco offer endless family activities."

— Trip Advisor.com

10
MARLO

"Our Keeper is a real estate agent?" Taryn stares at the business card Rialdo Conzeulo handed each of us in the back of the limo.

Rialdo, a short, affable man with a Cheshire cat smile and one gold bicuspid, folds his hands over his sizeable belly.

"Aye, Senorita. Long time friend of the family," Rialdo says as we wind through the streets of Mexico City on our way to Merida. Everything I've heard about Mexico is not good, yet Rialdo assures us we will be staying in the finest of accommodations.

Rialdo makes an animated tour guide pointing out landmarks along our route. "Mexico City is the intersection of the first and third worlds," he tells us with the lilt of a game show host. "Where glamour and poverty co-mingle. Eighteen million people, mostly poor. But we are a proud city, historic, with some of the most beautiful architecture and art in the world."

"I see you do okay for yourself," Taryn says, eyeing the gold rings on nearly every one of his pudgy fingers, and Amelia jabs her.

"Si. We are nearly there." He taps on the glass behind him and the limo driver rolls down the window. They exchange words in Spanish, but I have no idea what they are saying, and I feel like I've stepped in to a Spanish version of the Sopranos. How had we trusted our mother so blindly after what she did to us? But then she'd never been around to tell us not to get into a car with strangers. Lame excuse.

"No way," Amelia breathes, as we all roll down our windows, and the rancid smell of the city disappears behind us, like the click of a slide, to a beautiful tree-lined road within iron gates that seems to go on for miles.

"The Santiago Mansion is a 17th century hacienda on eighteen acres," Rialdo begins, his tone changing to his perfected real estate pitch. "The Santiago family lived here for nearly two hundred years," he says. "I've listed it for $18.5 million American dollars."

"I won't go a penny over sixteen," Amelia says, faking a rich American southern accent, her hands folded on her knees.

"A sense of humor," Rialdo says with a snort. "Just like your mother."

I flinch and look at my sisters, who stare blankly at him. "What does this mansion have to do with Elizabeth?" I ask. "And why don't the Santiagos live here anymore?"

"All in due time," Rialdo says, as the limo stops in front of what looks like a church with two bells in a tower above the front entrance with ropes hanging down on each side. I haven't been inside anything older than a hundred years old, and that was a Kansas one-room schoolhouse we'd visited in third grade.

The Spanish-style architecture with curved arches goes on forever, surrounded by breathtaking gardens with more than a thousand rose bushes, give or take.

We tumble out of the car and Amelia bounds for the bells and yanks on the rope on the right, the resounding clang filling the afternoon air. "Now that's what I call a doorbell."

The noise is so loud that Taryn and I hold our ears, but the bell does the trick in opening the massive wood and metal doors. An old, round woman wearing an apron and black dress greets us. "Hola, Senoritas." She waves us in, and Rialdo continues his pitch as we step into the massive foyer with cathedral ceilings flooded with colored light from the stained glass windows. The story of the judgment, the crucifixion, and the resurrection are told in eight ten-foot high windows around the room.

"Nothing says welcome home like Jesus on the cross," Taryn says, rubbing her hands together. A bevy of Mexican caretakers surround us, taking our bags up massive spiral staircases, and offering us water with lemon, which we take from a silver platter. No, we are definitely not in Kansas, anymore.

In fact, Jesus is there, and the saints, too. Everywhere we look, figures from the Bible peek out of the woodwork, from paintings on the wall, sculptures on stands and more crosses.

"At least we're safe from vampires," Taryn cracks.

"I think it's beautiful," Amelia says, staring up at a metal and crystal chandelier about the size of my first car.

"Ninety percent of the population is Catholic," Rialdo tells us, before launching back in to the tour. "The estate boasts a chapel, a library, six bedrooms and three living areas. And a gourmet kitchen to die for," he says, pausing because, I'm certain, most women swoon at the mention of the kitchen. But women who live in estates like this don't cook themselves, do they? I spend so much time in the kitchen growing up that it's my least favorite place in the house. I've never been a good cook, but a proficient one.

On days my mother couldn't get out of bed, I managed to pull together ramshackle meals of uncooked hot dogs and potato chips or cereal with or without milk, depending on whether or not she remembered to buy any. I'd thought my mother would be proud, but she barely noticed.

After my mother left, Aunt Darla brought us meals for awhile, much like one does after someone has died, but soon the casseroles stopped and Dad thought it would be easier to eat out every night. When he and Cecelia got married, I was thankful for home cooked meals again. She was a better cook than my mother, though I hated to admit it, and it was the one thing my father thought she did well, besides behind the bedroom door. They were always kissing and pawing at each other in front of us, which made my hatred for her grow with each public display of emotion. He should've been kissing my mother, not her. God I hated her. Do I hate her still?

After Cecelia left, I'd just finished fifth grade, plenty old enough to cook for the family, though I didn't especially enjoy it. Somebody had to do it. Cecelia's recipes had been too complicated, each day trying to outdo the meal before, to snag the compliment from our father. She could've cared less if we liked the food or not. (Gourmet meant we usually did not.)

I managed scrambled eggs and bacon, was hailed queen sandwich maker, and routinely roasted chicken and baked potatoes, and daily doses of salad. Lots and lots of salad.

Iceberg lettuce, a few chopped carrots and plenty of ranch dressing, the only way I could get my sisters to eat anything green growing up. After Dad got the promotion at work, he didn't even eat with us at all. I'd make us dinner and leave a covered dish for him in the microwave. Often I'd hear the whir of the microwave as I studied in my room, late at night. He's home, I'd think. Safe and sound. I could never fall asleep until then.

"Show me to the bedrooms, Rialdo," Taryn says, clearly getting a kick out of our princess status. "I call first dibs."

"They are all magnificent, senorita."

"Thank God we won't have to hear Marlo snoring." Amelia hikes in front of us, passing even Rialdo.

"I don't snore." Hell, I barely even sleep.

"Do so. But not until about 4 a.m.," Taryn adds.

With the long flight, where I was the only one of us who couldn't sleep, I longed for a comfortable bed, but soon even a concrete floor would suffice for my exhaustion.

Taryn plops on an oversized bed with gold bedding and buries her head in a king-sized pillow with navy embroidery and peacocks. Our eyes sweep the room, taking in the built-in hot tub, which overlooks the valley, marked by other historic homes, though none as opulent as the one we are in.

"Who's up for a jog around the estate?" Amelia kicks off her sandals and wades on the step of the tub.

Taryn and I groan in response. Taryn begins snapping pictures. "Look at that view. It's a different kind of beautiful than Hawaii, but it's magnificent, isn't it?"

I let Amelia take my hand as she shows me to my room, just down the very long hall, a blue room with white bedding and sheer organza curtains blowing like friendly ghosts from the three open windows. "I'll take it," I say, flopping my tired body on the bed, while Amelia notices the century-old desk.

"What if our mother wrote letters to us right here?" she says, running her hands over the desk.

"It's a possibility," I say with a yawn. "But if she had, we'd have seen them."

"Enjoy your siesta." Amelia kisses me at op the head as I wonder if I'll dream of Jesus if I ever sleep.

The chill of the evening wakes me from my deeper than deep slumber. No Jesus. Not even Shane made his way into my dream-free sleep. The ghostly curtains still as Rialdo shuts the windows. Thank God we haven't been killed. It wasn't a trap, and we are safe. I exhale. I know I need to trust more and fear less, but I've had twenty-five years of practice on the latter. So damn good at it.

"I am sorry to wake you, Senora." He faces me, the plastered grin still on his face. "Are you hungry?"

The waft of authentic Mexican food fills my nose. "Starved. Are my sisters already downstairs?"

"In the kitchen with the cooks. They insisted."

"Figures."

Rialdo hands me a gray sweater, and I'm surprised it's my size, though I shouldn't be surprised by anything by now. Our mother has left no stone unturned. Even feeling rested physically, however, I'm not sure I'm strong enough to find out whatever the secrets of the Santiago mansion hold. I am eager to reunite with my sisters, and wish I had taken Spanish instead of French in high school.

The mansion is even more majestic at night, lit not by electricity but by a thousand candles of all sizes. The figures of Mary and the saints provide a creepily romantic ambiance to the mansion. Shane would love this place.

Spanish music fills the halls as my flip-flops clack on the stone floors. I reach out and touch the cement walls, cool as expected. A chill runs through me.

The kitchen is alive with the buzz of Spanish music and the sight of my sisters twirling and dancing around in the center of the room. Three cooks, the woman who had answered the door earlier, Esmeralda, with her two daughters who are just older than us. They greet me and hand me a plate of hot tortillas and my stomach growls in anticipation.

"There you are, sleepyhead." Amelia hands me a Mexican beer in an ice-cold glass rimmed with salt, with three wedges of lime floating in the glass. I'm so thirsty I gulp half of it down, followed quickly by the authentic tortillas and chunky salsa.

"Have I died and gone to food heaven?"

"Food and good beer heaven." Amelia begins to pick up one of the entrees but the daughters shake their heads, refusing to let us help. We are not used to being served, and are promptly shooed out to the corner table.

"I don't know a word they're saying, but they seem nice." Taryn pours herself another beer when Rialdo sticks his head in the kitchen doorway. Amelia, the only one of us who can speak Spanish, thanks the cooks for us, but even I know gracias.

"The table is ready. We eat in the formal dining room."
Rialdo leads the way.

"As opposed to the eight other kinds of dining rooms
here," Taryn scoffs.

The dining room table is twenty feet long with eighteen
chairs around it, and set for just four people at one end. The
candles flicker from the centerpiece, which extends the full
length of the table.

We snicker at the sheer opulence of it. "Isn't there a
smaller place we could eat?"

Rialdo looks disappointed, but after a moment, snaps
his finger with a solution. "A-ha! We'll dine in the library in
front of the fire," he says, and a small Hispanic man who
has taken our bags up earlier begins moving our place
settings as we follow Rialdo down a long darkened corridor
with double doors.

"Okay, now I've died and gone to book heaven," I
exclaim staring at the thousand tomes filling the room from
end to end in the built-in bookshelves.

"This is the most animated I've seen her on the trip
yet," Amelia says, following me inside the library. Six five-
foot portrait paintings provide the only non-book décor in
the room.

"This is the Santiago family, going back two hundred
years." Rialdo leads us around the room, explaining the
Santiago heritage, how Diego Santiago was a general in the
Mexican army and made his fortune in tobacco crops,
which the family still owns to date, and ending seven
generations later with a family of four, Rocco and his
gorgeous bride Lucia and their children, Dimitri, Peyton and
their baby sister Karina.

"And who's this hottie?" Taryn stands in front of the final portrait, a male in his late twenties, wearing a suit and bolo tie. He looks like a Mexican soap opera actor.

"This is Dimitri, the good son." Rialdo makes the sign of the cross. Isn't the good son the one who dies young?

"A doctor, very passionate about his life's work. You will hear much more about him."

The library is centered around a grand limestone fireplace, nearly big enough for me to walk in without crouching. We sit on the rug around the large square antique coffee table with legs as thick as thighs, and the food keeps coming – trays and trays of it carried by the staff.

Rialdo is such a skilled conversationalist that he keeps things light and pleasant throughout our long meal. I feel so stuffed, and slightly inebriated, that I am honestly surprised when he switches the subject to our mother.

"I came to know Elizabeth in the summer of 1991," he begins. "The Santiagos were widely known for their parties, which usually lasted for days. On the second day of one such summer celebration, in comes Dimitri from a business trip in Hawaii, with a young beautiful American girl on his arm. They were so in love, one could plainly see. His father Rocco was outraged, for he had planned for Dimitri to marry the daughter of a wealthy business partner in Mexico."

"Lucia had never liked the family Rocco wanted him to marry into, so she was kinder to Elizabeth than everyone expected. She took her to church with her every day, let her stay in a guest room, and Elizabeth began working at the clinic that Dimitri ran against his father's wishes."

"Medical clinic?" I ask.

"Si. A free clinic. People tried to pay what they could, sometimes with chickens and eggs. He didn't work for money. Some say he was trying to make up for the sins of his fathers. The familia business."

"Which was?" Taryn leans her head back against the sofa.

"Tobacco. *Officially.*" Rialdo doesn't smile, and a tingle crawls up my spine.

I wonder if the place is bugged, if armed men sent by Rocco will come take us away.

Taryn has no inhibitions. "So the Santiagos are drug lords? Jesus Christ."

I wrap the sweater around me tighter, still cool even in front of the blazing fire.

Amelia scoots closer to me. "I don't think I like this story."

"You have no reason to be fearful, senoritas, senora. You will learn why the Santiagos no longer live here, soon. The staff is no longer the Santiago staff. They have only come back and cleaned this place and worked here again because your mother asked them. Your mother holds a special place in my heart. In their hearts."

Taryn rolls her eyes. "Not you, too."

"Not as you think. I owe your mother my life." Rialdo's eyes go soft, but he blinks any tears away.

Taryn can't think of a smart-alecky reply to that, and we wait for more, but he is done with sharing, at least for now. The fireplace cracks and whistles and the wind outside blows fierce against the window. Rialdo reaches into a bag and pulls out three boxes, wrapped in gold foil.

"Our charms!" Amelia opens the lid and holds the thick charm up to the firelight. "It's a bunny."

"A rabbit." Taryn turns it over, then puts it back in the box while Amelia and I add the charm to our bracelets.

"Do you know what it means?" Amelia asks.

Rialdo shakes his head. "I didn't even know what was in the boxes. They've been in a safety deposit box for a long time. Along with these."

He opens an elegant shoebox and gently places a stack of folded letters, tied with yarn, in the middle of the paper. I see a journal, but he purposely leaves it in and closes the lid. "I've been instructed to give you those for your first night, and the journal in a few days. Don't stay up too late. I have much to show you of Mexico City tomorrow."

This time Amelia grabs the letters as Rialdo excuses himself for the night.

September 1991

My darling daughters,

I decided to address this journal entry to you, as a way of explaining how I got to be here.

I no longer want to die, and yet just as I have found the will to live, I find my life in danger.

The world I left behind has already become fuzzy, like a dream, and I wonder if this is why I am able to sleep at night. When I force myself to remember, to count the days, I am alarmed that so much time has passed. That you, Marlo, are in second grade, Taryn learning how to read in first grade, and Amelia learning her numbers and alphabet in pre-K. I catch myself wondering if you've learned to ride a bike, if your father makes you home-baked cookies, if he has found another woman to love and to help care for you.

I have requested photos from your father each year. I'll admit to holding my breath each day when the mail is brought in, hoping to find a letter with photos of you, but I know this is a selfish request.

I find myself gazing out the window at the long winding road and daydream about that old station wagon pulling up to get me. I don't deserve a second chance from your father, or you, and I can't imagine how I would make it work after all this time. I still haven't forgiven your father for his transgressions, and yet, isn't mine a thousand times worse?

When you are older you may understand this, but it still won't take the sting away: I fell in love with another man. I really doubted I could ever trust another man again after the pain I endured with your father.

Dimitri made several trips to the island before he told me what he was doing, and by then I was already in love with him. By then it may not have mattered what he was doing — I was already in too deep. Every bit a fool in love.

Sometimes helping people means that you have to go about it in a way that seems wrong at first. The same could be said of my leaving you.

I know I am not wanted in this house and must find a way for us to leave without turning our back on Dimitri's work. His passion has become mine. These people need to be fixed and in fixing them, I am slowly healing myself.

Love,
Mom

"Mom became a drug trafficker?" Amelia looks up from the letter.

Taryn climbs up on the couch and folds her legs. "No. Rialdo said Rocco was upset that Dimitri wouldn't go into the family business. It has to have something to do with medicine, yet something that was illegal."

"What about trafficking drugs for medical reasons, then?" I begin clearing the plates, but upon hearing the clank of the dishes, the staff enters the room to clear them away, and bring us sopapillas.

"She did care about us. Think about us," Amelia says, hugging her knees closer. "She wanted pictures. Why didn't Daddy ever tell us that she wrote?"

"We were little," I say. "He knows it would've upset us more. Besides, she didn't tell him to come get her. She only hoped for it."

Taryn slams down her tequila glass. "The guilt made her write, not love."

"That's not fair." Amelia shouts.

"Oh, please, princess. Give it up." Taryn growls, then gets up.

The tension in the room is thick as smoke, and I pat Amelia on the knee to comfort her. "What about the other letter?"

Amelia opens the next one, scrawled on what looks like a torn piece of brown paper bag. She hands the scrap to me. The scrawl is hurried, the words small and uneven, as if written in the dark. I have to lean in closer to the fire to read it and notice the dark brown spots on the paper, which look like dried blood.

My Girls,

This may be my last letter. I have a feeling they will kill me either way. In this last moment I can only think of Dimitri and you. I am remembering our last Christmas together, how I let you add the sprinkles to the sugar cookies and Taryn, you poured the whole shaker on two cookies and claimed those were yours. Oh, Amelia, how you cried! Then we heard the noise outside, your father dressed as Santa Claus pretending that he had fallen off the roof. He asked if you'd been good girls this year and Marlo gave a long speech about all the good things you'd done, including taking care of me, and you were so right. It's funny. When I feel I have nothing left to believe in, I marvel that I can still believe in Santa Claus and you girls. Always my girls.

"No signature." I hand the paper to Taryn.

"Think she was kidnapped?"

I shudder and see that Amelia is crying, that no matter how painful, she believes our mother has given her a small gift more precious than the charm; another memory of them together.

The fire ebbs and I see my father in the flames, the fake Santa's beard crooked on his face as I tried so hard to believe that he really was Santa Claus, even if he sounded an awful lot like my father and reeked of cheap beer. I wanted to believe then, but I couldn't. Yet I think how much this says about our mother. When her world was falling apart, over and over again, she still held on to the goodness of a magical man who would bring joy to children when she couldn't do it herself.

"Your phone," Amelia says, handing me the cell phone.

Shane's kind face appears on the screen. He is the closest thing to goodness I have ever known next to my father. I wonder if I can ever replace my fear with hope. If I can hold on to him without suffocating him. If I can believe in us, in our marriage, and our future.

Or if he'd be better off if I leave.

11
TARYN

The Mexican hulk sits to my right, scanning the crowded sidewalks as the black Escalade SUV takes us to our next destination in Mexico City. Fortunately, the giant is quiet and smells faintly of soap, but Rialdo is chatting as usual, as if having to hire personal security to go into the city is a normal thing.

He tells us that kidnappings are all too frequent, for ransom or for drugs, so anyone of wealth must hire bodyguards. "Isn't driving with a caravan of luxury SUVs a bit obvious, anyway?" Rialdo hadn't even removed his gold jewelry for our journey.

The SUV in front of us and behind us ensure we have power in numbers, four hulks in all, but I can't imagine the waifs along the road could do us much harm.

As we pull up to the deserted building with the big sign reading "*Clínica médica gratuita,*" Amelia tells us it means Free Medical Clinic.

If the hulk steals one more glance at my sister's bare legs, I may have to … what? He's carrying a gun and is at least two hundred pounds heavier than I am. I decide to let him get away with it, *this time*.

"Why do I feel *less* safe traveling with loaded guns in the car?" Marlo asks, eyeing the machine gun in Hulk's grasp.

Rialdo assures her the safety is on, but Marlo only shrugs.

A black Mercedes pulls up, and two more hulks greet the car, and I realize all these bodyguards aren't just for us, but for her. She's gorgeous, thirty-something with a Salma Hayek figure, tight blue dress, big round sunglasses, and silver high heels you might see in glossy designer ads. She's like a diamond among pebbles.

Stick-thin, grungy kids surround our SUV, and even the machine gun men don't scare them away. I've never especially liked kids, but I don't like to see them hungry, and these tykes look famished. I wish I'd brought along the contents of the well-stocked pantry back at the mansion. These little ones need it way more than we do. I begin snapping pictures of them and the tiny, hungry mob smiles for my camera. I bet some of them have never seen a camera in person before.

Rialdo opens the trunk of the SUV, pulls out a cooler and starts throwing out dozens of foil wrapped tortillas into the group. I'm relieved he's thought of it. The kids cheer and their hesitant mothers and fathers approach to get some, too.

After dispensing the food, Rialdo greets the woman in the Mercedes warmly, air-kissing both cheeks before introducing us, but the woman interrupts him, preferring to do it herself.

"I'm Karina Santiago," she says in English. "It's been so long since I last saw you."

Crazy much? I don't smile, but let her hug me as if I have a choice. She smells like wildflowers. Expensive wildflowers. She couldn't have seen pictures of us because our father hadn't sent any, and rightly so. My birth mother didn't deserve a damn thing from us, not even an image.

"Let us talk inside," Rialdo says, opening the three locks on the back door of the clinic. The windows are boarded up and graffiti covers the exterior. More Spanish I can't read, except for the name Dimitri Santiago, with an exquisite painting of him, older than the one in the library, topped with a halo above his head. Great. The sinner falls in love with the saint, is that it?

The clinic is musty, and Rialdo opens a couple of windows to let in some fresh air. Three hospital beds line the wall, and what used to be a prescription cabinet has been emptied out, with only a stray mouse scurrying along its edge. I resist a sissy scream.

"This is where your mother and Dimitri spent most days," Karina tells us. "Your mother became a skilled nurse in no time. But let me begin at the beginning."

"I met your mother the day she arrived with my brother. My father and I had just had a huge fight. I was eighteen and wanted to go to America, to attend college. He wanted me to stay in Mexico, attend University here and marry a wealthy, older man. He was fat and ugly, along with being old. Besides, I had no intention of staying in Mexico."

"Elizabeth heard me crying in my room and comforted me. I couldn't speak much English back then, but we understood each other. She became the big sister I never had. She helped me convince Dimitri to help me get to

America. Anyway, my father was livid with Dimitri when he found out what he was doing with his private planes."

"The trips to Hawaii?" Marlo asks.

"*Si*. My father has three planes used to smuggle drugs into various countries, mostly the United States. My brother paid off one of the pilots to take him and a patient to Hawaii after the regular stop."

"So he was on the plane with the drugs then?"

"*Si*. Because the planes have a weight limit, it meant delivering fewer drugs to make room for my brother and the child. The patients were all sick children who needed surgeries or transplants that my brother could not perform. He paid surgeons in Hawaii a modest fee for doing the procedures. He would spend a week or so in Hawaii while the patient recovered. That's how he met your mother. He was staying at the hotel where your mother bartended."

"They fell in love. He told her the truth, and she understood."

"But if your daddy is so Richie Rich, then couldn't your brother just have paid for the surgeries in Mexico City?"

Karina shook her head. "Unfortunately, here everyone knows the Santiagos. They would bribe him for too much money. And there is a terrible black market for transplants. You would think Rocco would give his children anything they desired, but he used our family fortune to control us, only doling out money if he felt we deserved it—if we respected him and his wishes. Because Dimitri didn't go into the family business, Rocco cut him off. Which is why he wouldn't pay for my college, either. My mother had to sneak me money."

"Your dad sounds swell," I say.

Karina continues. "The only reason he and Elizabeth were allowed to live in the *hacienda* was because my mother Lucia begged Rocco, and he loved his wife too much to say no to her."

"So how did Dimitri get money for the surgeries then?" Amelia asks.

"He stole drugs from his own family to pay for it."

Rialdo adds, "Everyone in Mexico has a price. *Dinero* is thicker than blood."

"Shit," I mutter under my breath. Now I knew we were in the middle of a Mexican *Sopranos* episode. My knees begin to buckle and I lean against the counter.

"It worked for about two years," Karina continues. "My brother would steal the drugs, pay off people along the way, but then one of the workers tipped off my other brother, Peyton, and he wanted to get his brother kicked out of the family for good, to prove loyalty to my father."

"So he ratted him out?" I ask.

"You have heard of Cain and Abel from the Bible?" Karina asks, and her eyes spill over with tears. Rialdo takes her hand and squeezes it.

"Who was Cain and who was Abel?" Marlo asks. Karina's tiny shoulders shake, and the cross on the gold necklace around her neck glistens in the sun. I guess the drug thief who steals from his warlord family is supposed to be the good guy?

After a moment, Karina regains her composure. "Come. I would like to take you to your mother's favorite place." Karina accepts the tissue from Rialdo and dabs at her eyes. "There is still so much to tell. How I got to Kansas and how my family fell apart."

Marlo and I exchange wide-eyed glances. Kansas? As in *my* Kansas?

Karina smiles. "Yes, but one place at a time. First, to the Pyramids."

Karina takes Rialdo's seat in the SUV, so we can talk the thirty miles to the ancient ruins of Teotihuacán. Our new passenger is full of more questions than answers. More than once, she seems to know more about us than she should, though at first it seems superficial. Amelia's bartending, and then student teaching. Marlo's job at the weekly. My tattoo parlor and new interest in photography. I get the feeling she has been checking up on us, or that she and my mother are still in contact. I had assumed that my mother knew nothing of us until that letter. Had she known about our lives from her place in the shadows all this time? The thought sends hot prickles up my spine.

"Tell us about Kansas," I say finally, as we near the ruins.

"Your mother and I had a deal. She would convince Dimitri to help me get my passport and student visa if I would go to the University of Kansas and periodically check up on you girls, until she could visit herself."

Amelia's face goes white. "I think I'm going to be sick."

"So you spied on us?" I say, feeling the red-hot heat in my face.

Marlo closes her eyes and exhales through her mouth. "I can't believe this."

"It's not like you think. I didn't follow you around all the time. I had my classes, and really lived like a regular college student. I had boyfriends, tests, and for the first time in my life, a job. But about once a month, I would drive to Wichita to spend the day there. You were eight, seven and five at the time. I would watch you playing at the park with your father, riding bikes in your neighborhood. I had the unfortunate news to report that the woman your father married wasn't what your mother had hoped or *whom*, I should say."

"Serves her right," I say, crossing my arms.

Karina's eyebrows shoot up. "So you know how Cecelia and your father met?"

We nod and shift uncomfortably. "Did you take pictures of us?" I ask.

"Yes. Your father refused to send pictures or any news. Your mother wanted to see that you were okay. That you could still smile."

"So that makes it alright for you to invade our privacy like that?" Taryn spits.

"Calm down, sis," Marlo says to me.

"Come on. You're just as pissed as I am about this. She didn't have the decency to hitch one of those drug planes and come see for her own damn self that we were okay? Would a visit have been too much to ask? No, she's too busy saving all the *other* children to give a flying fuck about her own."

Karina leans forward. "She had written your father repeatedly, asking him if it would be okay if she came to visit. She didn't want to just show up. After she found out about Cecelia, she was more determined than ever to get back to you. As soon as they got the word about a transplant for another sick little girl, Elizabeth was coming to see you."

The SUV screeches to a halt, and my breath is taken away at the sight of the Pyramids before me, nearly, but not completely, dissolving my anger. I hop out of the car and don't wait for the others, especially not the hulks. Back home, I'm used to being alone, which is one of the reasons I doubt I'd be very good at being married. Having someone there all the time. Hovering. Needy. I know I can only depend on one person. Me.

The place smells like dirt and sweat. Three buses flank the periphery; swarms of people walk through the ruins and buy tchochkes at the stands.

I get stares, I always do, as strangers scan my skin, but I look past them and take off into the crowds alone. I don't acknowledge their curiosity or disdain, and pass by the big tour group as the guide tells them about the smaller pyramid, the Pyramid of the Moon. Going to the moon sounds like a great idea.

I snap pictures on my way up, and instinctively turn around and take one of my sisters and Karina as they head up the larger pyramid, the Pyramid of the Sun. An elderly man near me tells his wife the street below is called the Avenue of the Dead.

I hate myself for feeling anything for my mother, even hate. I want ambivalence. How much easier it would be if she really were dead. If she'd managed to kill herself jumping off Hoary Head or if her kidnappers had done the job for her. Now all I can think about is how she could've escaped, and what happened to the Santiagos. Screw it. The only person who can answer my questions is on the opposite pyramid.

My thighs burn from the rapid ascent on the steps. I stop to take pictures of the Avenue and ponder what I want more—a stiff drink, a tattoo, or Paul in the flesh telling me everything will be all right. The fact that I think of him at all tells me more than I want to admit. I need him. I want him. Though I have no idea for how long, or if I can give myself over to him completely. And if as soon as I do, I'll feel the compulsion to run again.

Right now, though, I need the Spy to give up her secrets.

12

AMELIA

"Your mother loved this place because it is a lost civilization," Karina explains as we sit at the top of the Pyramid of the Sun. Karina swapped her stilettos for sandals and Taryn just raced up the steps of the pyramid and pants beside me. I knew she would come back.

"In 500 AD, the population here in Teotihuacán was as large as Rome, but no one knows where the huge population went. It's as if they vanished," Karina explains waving her fingers through the air.

I close my eyes and imagine that we live among the indigenous people thousands of years ago, walking among the temples and the bustling avenues. There are lavish ceremonies and human sacrifices made in the name of the Sun, the Moon and the astronomical events.

I shudder. To believe in something so much that you'd be willing to sacrifice another human for it? For that matter to sacrifice *anything* in the name of faith? I couldn't even give up anything for Lent, and that only lasts 40 days. I don't want to believe that my mother sacrificed her years away from us because we would be better off without her, but what if she did?

Marlo hands Karina my mother's note scrawled on the brown paper bag. "What do you know of this?"

Karina studies the paper and frowns. "After I'd been in Kansas for six months, your mother was kidnapped by a Mexican gang. They had intended to kidnap Dimitri, but he was on another trip to Hawaii, and your mother was working at the clinic alone one afternoon. The security guards outside had been paid off. This is the problem with hiring security here. Like we say, everyone has a price. They took Elizabeth, hoping she would still have value to Rocco, or at the least that they could get a ransom from Dimitri."

"Don't tell me. Rocco said kill her and feed her to the birds, right?" Taryn interjects.

"Not quite so awful. Rocco told them he refused to pay anything. The gang searched high and low for Dimitri to collect a ransom from him, and they finally found out through sources that he was in Hawaii for the week, with no way to be contacted. Your mother refused to give him up. That's how much she loved him."

"So our mother was held captive for a week?" My lips quiver.

"*Sí*. She was in a cold basement, with only a small window to see the sunlight. She was given bread and water each day. On the fourth day, she became very ill and her captors feared she would die before they could collect their ransom, so they brought in a doctor to give her medicine and provided her warm clothes and blankets. Still, her fever raged on."

"On the sixth day, when she awoke, she was sure that she would die. She had the chills, and the medicine she'd been given didn't seem to be working. But she managed to stand and look out that small window and instead of seeing despair, she saw a tree, like she had meditated on when she was recovering in Hawaii. So she meditated for what seemed like hours just gazing at that tree, no longer feeling the pain of her sickness, and a rabbit appeared near the tree, looking right at her. And she knew it was a sign from God that she would live. See in Mayan culture, Rabbit represents the 'struggle to overcome the material state.' She remembered that while her body was suffering, her spirit was still strong. And so she fought."

Karina stops, and looks out at the mountains before us. I feel my chest cave in and the tears drop onto my folded hands on my lap.

"They say the pyramids have an energy," Karina says, "beyond the energy of all living things. If you are still enough, you can feel it." I try to concentrate on the energy, just as I do in church every week back home, hoping for enlightenment or that Hallelujah moment I see other people get. I raise my hands in praise, hoping like metal in a lightning storm that I'll be struck by God's love, but even after church, I still feel empty.

Nothing.

I open my eyes and Marlo is standing, though this time she isn't close enough to the edge to jump. Taryn sits still, breathing deeply.

"Look." Marlo points down below, to the entrance of the city, where a group of men dressed in traditional costume have gathered around a tall pole and begin to climb it.

"They are the *Voladores de Papantla*. The *Papantla* Flyers," Karina says.

One man sits on the top of the pole playing a flute and four others "fly" down the pole in an anti-clockwise direction, supported only by a rope connected to their ankle.

The *voladores* descend to the tune of the whistle player at the top of the pole, then reach the bottom as onlookers begin throwing *dinero* into a hat.

And I thought doing body shots for extra tips was a bit much. This is crazy.

Now we all stand, watching the crowd below us disperse. "Is this where you tell us the white knight came and saved the damsel in distress?" Taryn asks, sarcastically.

Karina flinches. "I understand your skepticism. And I'm sorry that it must hurt to hear about your mother and my brother when he returned. Dimitri had little money to give the gang, not even one tenth of what they were asking. So he gave them his car, an old Cadillac Seville my father had driven when we were children. Now he and Elizabeth had no transportation, and they were in even more danger. Rialdo insisted that they take a jeep of his, so they could get back and forth to the clinic."

"And our mother got well?"

"*Si*. She had a staph infection, but when she was given the proper antibiotics, she recovered within a few days. Come. You have been through much. Let us celebrate tonight, because the worst is yet to come."

"I hope you mean for Elizabeth and not us," Taryn says dryly.

"Grow a heart, sis," I tell her.

"Grow some balls," she growls back, but winks to show she means no harm. "But, come on, what if these drug dudes are still around? And I'm not sure I want to hear anything worse than what we've already been told."

Karina leads us back down the pyramid. "When you retell the past, it's like living it again. Come. We'll swing by the church for evening prayer and confession."

"Pass!" Taryn says. "I didn't sign up for a holy stop."

"You can get some great pictures," Marlo says matter-of-factly. "The cathedrals in Mexico are among the most beautiful in the world. We'll include them in our article."

Taryn sighs. "Look, you guys are the only confessional I need, so I might as well spill it."

We stop and stare at her. I hold my breath.

"Jesus, don't look so petrified! I was just going to tell you I've gone to church a few times with Paul and I did not combust when I walked through the door."

Marlo and I burst into laughter. "You scared me for a second." I wrap my arm around her tiny waist.

"What did I say about PDA?"

"That you hate it. Which is why I'm going to squeeze you even tighter."

She pushed me away, but not for long. I'm way stronger than my scrawny sis.

Karina claps her hands. "If we hurry, you can get the tour before mass begins. Tonight I will treat you to an amazing feast."

"Now you're talking," Marlo says. "Eating is the one thing we've always agreed on."

I find myself seated in the dark, the smell of incense and old wood all around me, as I swallow hard and make the sign of the cross. The priest, a male (well, they're all male, aren't they?) speaks to me in Spanish. It's been so long since I've spoken much of it that I stumble and he starts speaking to me in English.

"How long since your last confession?" he repeats, his profile shadowed through the screen.

"It's my first time," I tell him, my mouth dry. Boy, it's been awhile since I've said *that* line.

"Are you Catholic, *senorita*?"

I grab the door, wondering if I could be locked in and the priest could hit a button and send me straight down to Hell, but I don't try to turn it. I don't know what I was thinking. Karina says confession is good for the soul, a spiritual cleansing, so when she got in line, I got in step behind her. It seemed like a good idea at the time.

The tour got the best of me, placing me in some sort of spiritual trance, the centuries-old cherubs peeking down at me, the saints with their Good Acts, beckoning me to do good. Do *better*. The fruit carved into the wall, like the pomegranate representing Christ's blood. If there is a place in the world to feel holy, then this is it, right?

The cathedral was built five centuries ago, in the 1500s, and I can't help but think about the women who must have worshipped here back then. Had they gotten on bended knee, as I'm doing now, and confessed similar sins? Times change, but sins really don't, do they? Murder. Adultery. Coveting your neighbor's husband. (Over and over again.) Taking the Lord's name in vain. This place even has an Altar of Forgiveness. I figure if there can be altar for it, it has to be open to people like me, too.

"Yes," I say to the priest, who sounds pretty young, with a deep, soft voice. "Shit!" I say, aloud. I've just lied to a priest, and I hold on to the edges, sure the kneeler will drop out and I'll be sent to the glowing embers of Hades. "I mean no. Sorry, Father. I'm just nervous. Is it okay if I still confess?"

I blame my sudden need to confess my sins on the art on the left-hand portal in the church depicting Jesus handing the keys of the Church to Saint Peter. The image made me think of the Keepers handing us the charms. They were keys, too, weren't they? They mean something, and I know I'm not supposed to just sit idly by and let them hang on my wrist without doing something. I can't go back in time and rescue my mother, but I can ask for forgiveness and really, really mean it.

"All are welcome in the House of the Lord," the priest says. "Please continue."

I rub my sweaty palms on my shorts and close my eyes. My mind goes back quickly, like an old tape being rewound at top speed. So many sins. Where to begin?

"Marlo's favorite sweater went missing her eighth grade year. She looked high and low for it, but I knew where it was all along. In my backpack. She wouldn't let me borrow it, too afraid that I'd spill something on it. I can't blame her. It was our mother's sweater, and because our mom was petite, it fit Marlo when she turned 13. I was so jealous that Marlo had the sweater that I'd begged her every day for it, but she only let me touch it once—until I stole it. I slipped it over my regular clothes each day when I got to school. The arms were way too long, so I rolled them up. The teacher never said anything, nor did my classmates, until one day we had spaghetti at school and I got sauce all over the front of it. My teacher found me crying in the bathroom. I had no idea how to get a stain out. Marlo did all the laundry after Cecelia left."

"My teacher, Mrs. Schneider, knelt down in that bathroom, both knees on that cold tile floor, and wiped my eyes. 'We can't have sauce on your favorite sweater,' she said to me and pulled the sweater off over my head, leaving my thin T-shirt underneath. She went to a supply closet in the corner and pulled out some stain remover and gently washed it in the sink and handed it back to me. It was like a miracle. A bonafide miracle.

"She said to me, 'Now do you think it's time to return the sweater to your sister?' I opened my mouth to speak, but was too dumbfounded to say anything. How had she known it wasn't my sweater? She smiled and told me that Marlo had called her a few weeks before asking if I'd brought a sweater to school, but she'd said 'no.' I couldn't believe she'd lied for me.

She goes, 'You have to weigh your options. Is being truthful more important than protecting someone's feelings? I haven't seen you more content than when you're wearing that sweater. But I bet you won't need that sweater to feel that way anymore.'

I was confused. 'Why not?'

She gently folded the sweater and placed it over my arm, and pointed to my chest. 'Because the sweater is in here. It's always with you.' And that's the moment I stopped wanting my mother so much. But I never stopped wanting what I never had. I never stopped wanting or seeking love. You know that country song, "looking for love in all the wrong places?"

He doesn't answer so I go on. "Of course not. Well, it all makes sense now. I realize you haven't even said a word but obviously you have some type of voodoo power. Okay maybe voodoo is the wrong choice of words, but some sort of magic, well it's not magic, either, is it?

"It's fine, child. I understand; go on. Maybe no one has ever really listened to you and really heard you."

"Yes, that's it! On this trip I'm realizing my sisters and I had very different feelings about my mother leaving. Sorry, Father, long story, but Marlo's role was to pretend it didn't matter. Taryn's role was to hate her. And mine was to miss her because I was the baby. And I just realized that not much has changed in twenty years. But maybe it's all mixed up. Maybe I'm the one that hates her and Taryn misses her but pretends she hates her and Marlo really does need someone to take care of her instead of being the one who thinks she has to take care of everyone else."

I blink open my eyes to see the priest patiently waiting for me.

"It sounds like this trip has already been good for your soul, child. But it doesn't sound like a confession. Would you like to confess other than the sweater?"

"Oh, Father, sir, I was just getting warmed up. That was just the earliest sin I could think of. How long do you have?"

"I'm here for...well, eternity, perhaps."

I couldn't tell if he was joking, (Do priests do that?) but I decided to make the most of it.

"My step-mother got remarried when I was eleven. She asked me to be a flower girl, as if it would be a compliment. She was already pregnant with the twins. She'd told me that as a secret. Most people didn't know it yet. She thought I'd be happy for her, but I wasn't. She left my father and was starting a whole new life. I knew what would come next. I told her I wished her babies would die. She slapped my face."

The priest clears his throat. "You were a child. You didn't mean it."

I pause and think hard. "No. I knew better. I think I meant it. But I apologized and she forgave me. At first I thought it would be fun to be a big sister, even though I just saw them every other weekend, but it became more like a chore. She was so wrapped up in the babies that we didn't do fun things together anymore, like going to get our nails done or shopping. I sometimes made up lies about my weekends so I wouldn't have to see her. I was jealous of the boys. And I think her new husband thought I was a nuisance. I started understanding how Marlo felt being the big sis and having to help out around the house."

Father laughs. "This is all normal. Feelings of guilt over childish ways are nothing to be sorry about."

"Wow, okay, I've confessed to dark thoughts and stealing so I'm going for broke. Daddy was diagnosed with cancer just after Cecelia got re-married. He was sick and puking his guts out from chemo and radiation and there Cecelia was with her happy, shiny new life. I went from hating the babies to hating her for not coming back and taking care of us. I became your stereotypical hateful teenage girl. I bet she was thankful she had boys instead of girls."

"I'm sure she didn't feel that way. Divorce is very hard on families, then to throw cancer in on it. That's a lot to go through. Acting out is natural."

"I didn't help Marlo with my father. Before he got sick, he was so handsome and muscular. All the girls loved him. He dated a new girl every week, each one more beautiful than the last, but I was angry with him, too, for whatever he did to make Cecelia leave and my birth mother before that. But then he got so thin, and his hair fell out. At first he looked like Mr. Clean, but then he got frail. At the end, Marlo fed him baby food."

I squeeze my eyes shut and remember Marlo at sixteen, who broke in her newly minted driver's license chauffeuring our father to and from chemo. She'd asked me to bring in the groceries, which I did with a chip on my shoulder.

"What's this?" I pulled jars and jars of strained carrots and peas and chicken goulash baby food from bags.

Marlo had forced a tight smile. "It's all he can eat now."

I clear my throat. "Suddenly no home felt like home. I knew the baby food was the beginning of the end. So I spent as much time away from home as a I could."

"I lost my virginity when I was fifteen. In Chad Davis' El Camino. He was eighteen and the quarterback. I craved the attention, even if it was only short-lived. I figured if I slept with him I'd be popular and all my problems at home would melt away, but it only made me popular with the rest of the football team. And the basketball team. Then baseball. Basically, I kept up with whatever sports season we were in. I guess I can count myself lucky that my school didn't have golf or soccer." I smile, but of course this isn't funny, and I shouldn't expect the priest to laugh at my promiscuity.

"I see," the priest says, but I'm not sure if he does. "You sought solace in the arms of men."

"I never thought of it that way. Escape. I wanted escape, and partying and boys seemed the best way to get it. Taryn, that's my middle sister. She changed her look about that time. Like she started her year of mourning before Daddy even died. She wore black every day, dyed her hair black, too. She got her first tattoo, but Daddy hated it. He hated her new look and told her. He liked his girls blonde and gorgeous. I guess on the outside he thought I was doing okay because I looked okay, but inside I was more messed up than Taryn."

I take a breath and feel relieved that my admission hasn't caused lightning to strike. I'm still in the God box. The priest doesn't seem shocked that I've just confessed to sleeping with athletes on every team in my high school, so I go on.

"Daddy died just after Taryn graduated from high school. He was holding on, you know? That meant a lot to him. He made me promise I'd do my best in high school and go to college. He wanted me to find a career I loved as much as he loved sales. He was a director before he died. But all I wanted to explore in college were men. You know, older, wiser men, though they weren't too old, and didn't end up being too wise, either. My junior year, I took a sociology class with Professor Younger. Alex Younger. He was thirty and a full professor. Handsome, and too nice, you know? I'd never really dated a nice guy before. And he did all these charity projects. Helping the poor and stuff, you know? I'd just joined a local church group at the college, and Jesus talked so much about helping the poor that I decided to join Alex on some of his charity work. I spent the weekends building houses for the poor and feeding the homeless and reading to kids in the bad areas of town. I felt better than I had my whole life. Like I was finally doing something to contribute to making the world a better place. I didn't feel quite as empty. As useless."

I open my eyes, but the memory is still there, shining brighter than ever. I can feel Alex's skin on my skin to this day. I crush my face against the screen, letting the tears fill the tiny holes, and then I feel the cool hand of the priest on my forehead. I pray he can make it all go away. Erase Alex from my mind, from my heart.

"I'm so sorry, Father. He was married, but he didn't tell me until we'd already been together for three months. He never wore a ring to class; never talked about family. He told me I was his soul mate. That he would leave his wife and we'd get married. Then one day his wife and the cutest toddler I'd ever seen came to see me at my dorm room. She cursed me. She made me look at that baby. She screamed, 'do you really want to be a home wrecker?'"

"I was devastated. So I broke it off and told Alex to stay with his wife. But after a month, he came back to me. And I know I should've been stronger, Father. I know I should've slammed the door in his face, but I thought of everything good about him. How I couldn't stop thinking about him, and I let him in."

"Are you still having relations with him?"

I choke back the tears. "It's complicated."

"It's a yes or no question."

"When I took him back, I pushed his marriage out of my head, even though we rarely went out of the house. Or out of the bed. But one weekend I just happened to see his wife at the grocery store. And she was very pregnant. I felt so sick. I didn't think he was even sleeping with her anymore. He'd lied to me and I believed him. Seeing her, I was filled with shame. And you know what she did when she saw me? She comes over and thanks me for breaking things off with her husband. She tells me how wonderful things have been for them. I'm standing there dumbfounded, my whole body on fire. I watched her walk away, knowing inside of her was my lover's baby, but it was never meant to be for me. I left my grocery cart right there in the store and ran out as fast as I could. I know it was fate that brought us together that day; that God or the Universe or something needed me to see her. When you don't listen, God will hit you over the head with it."

"So you ended things with him then?"

"Yes. I avoided him on campus and moved on to other men. But none of them made me feel like Alex. I think he really loved me. I know that sounds crazy, but I think he loved both of us."

"*Senorita*," the priest interjected. "A man can have both lust and love in his heart. But if you are asking for forgiveness for this sin, then you know you must be willing to break things off with him, for good. You must repent and stay away from him. You are both living in mortal sin."

I wipe my eyes. Can I live in a world that doesn't have Alex in it? Or will I just replace one sin with another? "I thought if I was with another man, it would help. Without realizing it, I slept with a married man in Hawaii."

"What can you do to break this cycle?"

"I threw my cell phone into the ocean. Does that count?" My knees burn, so I lean back against the wall.

"It's a start. All I can offer is God's love and grace and forgiveness. But you must also forgive yourself, and love yourself. Seeking love in the arms of men is not the answer. I would like for you to consider healthier ways of feeling good about yourself– such as your charity work."

The priest gives me my penance: say twenty Our Fathers and consider a period of celibacy. I nearly choke. Can a priest do that? The bigger question is, can I be celibate for *any* amount of time?

As I step out of the confessional, I spot my sisters sitting in the back of the church in a pew, waiting for me. But something else catches my eye, behind them, moving slowly in the shadows. I swear it's Blue Eyes, the one I saw in the bar in Hawaii. He's even easier to pick out here, a white beacon among the brown sea. I try to catch up to him, but the church exit is crowded, the next tour about to begin, and as I hear my sisters calling for me, I scan the crowd for him, but see nothing. I wonder if he is a mirage, or perhaps my angel, but decide I must be imagining things. This place can do that to you.

13
MARLO

The *Papantla* Flyers soar on the page of my article, the laptop on my chest, my body stiff as a board back at the mansion. I imagine what it might feel like to fly down the pole, if it's anything like flying off that mountain, if it feels like your stomach is stuck in your throat even after you've done it a thousand times, the same falling feeling as being in love.

The Skype button pops up on my screen, and there it goes. My gut bashing right into my brain as I see his username: DocShane. He seems to always know when I'm thinking about him. I hit "accept" and his freshly-shaven face fills my screen.

"Hola, señor," I say with a sleepy smile.

He ruffles his hair, one of the jillion things I love about him, as he leans closer to his web cam. "How's my Mexican adventurer?"

"You definitely didn't marry a hiker. You would've loved the pyramids, though."

"Make any sacrifices to the gods?"

"Only virgins need apply, so I guess I have to thank you for saving my life."

He laughs and my heart does a victory dance. When all else fails I can still make him smile. "Happy to oblige, m'lady," he says. "I'd take a virgin sacrifice to rounds any day. Bloody damn day. Literally."

I know how much he loves rounds, and that I'll get to hear about every single patient he saw that day, what their conditions were and how Shane can fix them. He knows I can't handle the details. I always had an aversion to blood, beginning with the time my mother cut herself throwing plates in the kitchen. And hospitals? I could go the rest of my life without ever stepping into one of them again. I'd spent my adolescence in waiting rooms and next to my father during his chemo treatments, reading him business books like Covey's *7 Habits of Highly Successful People* and Dale Carnegie's *How to Win Friends and Influence People*. He told me he needed a refresher course, but it was only after he died that I realized he wanted me to read them because he wouldn't be around to spout them off anymore. He wanted me to be a success, like him. But I'd take good health and a whole family to business success, any day.

I show Shane the new charm, holding it up close to the web cam, and explain how the rabbit came to be. My voice strains, and realize in the retelling I'm feeling much more than I had the first time I heard it. When I'm finished, Shane shakes his head. "I'm sorry, Marlo."

"For what?" *You were right. You should leave. Since you never unpacked your bag, it's in the foyer, ready to be picked up. I've realized how much easier my life is without you.* I shake the thought.

"That stuff can't be easy to hear. But I think it will be very healing."

I swallow hard. Okay. Not giving up on me yet. I nod despite wanting to argue – she would never have been kidnapped if she hadn't left us. It's a fact, but it's moot. Shane is compassionate, a big reason why I fell in love with him. Of course he would feel my mother's pain – just as he's so keenly felt mine. As for the healing, how would we know? Would I feel better? Be able to love Shane more easily? Or what if it only gets worse?

"You studying tonight?" I ask, hoping to wipe out the thoughts of kidnappers and dungeons.

"Whole gang's coming over here," he says, his shoulders rising. "Ordering pizza."

I smile, though inside my gut twists. The whole gang is comprised of his fellow interns, four guys and three girls, much more attractive than I feel comfortable with. He spends endless hours with them at work and then ends up spending more all nighters studying with them, often leaving me to fall asleep in bed alone, worrying about him.

My jealousy feels like a caged tiger ready to pounce. I can't say anything, because I know where that road leads. Fights. Talk of more meds. Fodder for our next counseling session. Now that Shane knows every drug known to man, he things he can prescribe away my problems. What kind of cocktail would it take to make me a better wife, a more pleasing human? What could make me something more than Anxiety wearing bones and muscle?

He's given me no reason to doubt his fidelity. And yet nearly everyone who knew my father would be surprised that he'd been unfaithful to my mother. And then again to Cecelia. So I'm transferring my father's sins to my husband—which isn't fair, I know. But wouldn't a no-strings-attached affair be just what the doctor ordered?

I snap back from the dark thoughts and mutter, "That's nice." I can't think of anything else to say, but feel like I'm going to be sick. I want Shane to myself, but I know that's impossible. In the space of a heartbeat, I picture him with a much bigger, better life with Renee, the prettiest intern.

They speak the same language, know all the medical lingo and share witty banter about the older doctors and annoying patients. They can save the world together. I can't even save myself, save my marriage.

"My mom sends her best," Shane says, his green eyes gleaming. "She's been bringing over meals."

"I'll bet she has." I don't mean for this to sound condescending, but of course it does and Shane rolls his eyes. Why should I be bothered that his mother can care for him while I'm away? Like I said, making a decent grilled cheese sandwich is a stretch for me.

My annoyance is not unjustified. The woman hates me. In the two years that Shane and I have been married, I've picked up on nearly all of her passive-aggressive messages, which she *calls "wishes."*

I wish you were more outgoing.

I wish you would invite us over more.

I wish you could afford to hire a housekeeper.

I wish you enjoyed cooking.

Why not just come out and say, "I wish my son had married an entirely different person altogether?" It's obviously what she means.

Shane blames my inability to connect with his mother on the estrangement with my own, but I wonder if she should get all the blame. What if I'd had a mother all those years and still didn't get along with his mother? Isn't that what spawned a thousand mother-in-law jokes?

"I've got to go," Shane says. "Tell your sisters hello."

He looks tired and I'm anxious about an argument we haven't had yet, but can't stop myself from bringing on. I feel my lips quiver and blink back the tears. "Amelia asked me if we're getting a divorce."

"There's nothing wrong with going to marriage counseling. I don't care if you tell your sisters we're having problems. That's what families are for. I've told my mom, and she thinks it's a good idea."

"Hallelujah!" I shriek. "By all means, if *she* thinks it's a good idea. I can't believe you'd tell your parents."

"For chrissakes, Marlo. Calm down! Look, I'm sorry you don't have parents, okay? For the thousandth time, I'm sorry! But my parents love me and they want to know I'm happy."

"And you're not, right? Not happy with me? That's what this all boils down to. I just don't make you happy anymore."

Shane grabs a fist of hair and stares down at the desk. From the sight of his pulsing temple, I can tell he's had enough, but I have to know.

"What if it doesn't work, Shane? Do you want to divorce me?" I whisper it, but he can hear me. You'd think I slapped him.

"Dammit, Marlo. I love you! But you don't get that. Whatever is going on in your mind, you refuse to hear it! You can't believe that I could possibly love you or want to spend the rest of my damn life with you. When I said those vows, I meant it. I'm here for you, for better or for worse, but you've got to meet me half way. For us to work, you've got to stop thinking the sky is going to fall. You're making our marriage worse just by thinking it, but you can't see it! You piss on any semblance of happiness we have. You complain about everything. You obsess over minutia. My hours. My friends. My parents. You won't tell me about your childhood or talk about your parents. You don't want to share in counseling and by God I know you have things to share."

That's not good. My mouth is glued shut.

He bangs his fist on the table and inhales, then closes his eyes. When he opens them again, he leans in closer, his eyes pleading. "Baby, please! Listen to me. You need to use this trip to figure out if you're willing to meet me halfway here. It's not about my family. It's about creating a family together. I don't want kids for years, but I do want them someday. I just need to know that it's possible for us to function as a happy family who has regular struggles not a struggling family who is rarely happy."

My head is in my hands and I can't stop myself, even if I wanted to. Which I don't. Because seeing Shane, so close and yet so very, very far away, brings it all out of me. My tears drop into the keyboard. I know if I don't stop I'll short-circuit the computer, but my brain is spinning so fast, I couldn't stop it if I tried. I want to tell him to please not let one of those girls seduce him. I want to tell him that I'll be the happy, secure wife he deserves when I return from this trip. But I can't. I can barely muster, "I love you," before his face clicks off the screen.

Love wasn't enough to keep my mother with us or keep my father from straying. I have to believe if I find out why, I'll know the answer.

"You're not even going to try it?" Taryn asks with a spoonful of *rabo de toro*, a deep, dark, rich stew with bull's tail, inches from my face.

"You can't lie in the article and say you've tried it if you haven't," Amelia says from her position behind the ultra-cool bar at D.O, short for *denominacion de origen*, in Mexico City where Karina is treating us to Spanish cuisine.

Karina sweet-talked the bartender to give Amelia access behind the modern orange, frosted-glass bar to make us a drink to go along with the tapas bar. Tapas is a fancy way of saying appetizers, though I'd never eaten squid tapas before, even at Shane's cousin's wedding a year earlier. Every time I attempted to pop a piece in my mouth, I imagined it living, and threw it back on the plate. Now I understand Taryn's aversion to meat. I stick to the olives and cheese.

"You don't see me sticking the Jabugo ham in your vegetarian face, do you?" I slap Taryn's hand down, sending the bull's tail down on the bar.

Amelia sweeps it away with a cocktail napkin and hands us our drinks. Karina sits on the other side of Taryn, wearing a fitted purple dress and huge gold necklaces.

"Sangria," Karina coos. "My favorite."

Amelia raises one brow, waiting for us to taste it. I take a sip, expecting to be blown away by alcohol, but instead it's fruity and sweet. Amelia hands me a white cocktail napkin with the recipe scrawled on it.

"For your readers," she says. "Wouldn't that be a great sidebar on your story on Mexico?"

I glance at the note. Rioja red wine, oranges, lemons, red apples, confectioners sugar, orange juice, and, ah, yes, the spirits: rum and cognac. The last bit gives it the kick. I smile in appreciation. "Before long, you'll be doing my job for me."

"We make a great team," Taryn says dryly, toasting

each of us.

Amelia's eyes dance. I haven't seen her this happy in a long time. "What gives?" I ask, after I've drunk half my Sangria and finished off the Camembert and anchovy, just to show I'm trying.

She throws her arms out and looks up at the antique chandelier above her. "You mean besides that fact that my sins have been forgiven?"

The way she says it, you'd think she won the lottery. I try not to laugh.

Karina claps her well-manicured hands. "I told you you'd feel better."

"More than that. I feel so weightless that I could fly around the world. But, wait; we're already doing that, aren't we? Then I'll keep flying. Who says my traveling has to be over when our trip is through?"

Taryn high-fives our baby sister, but I clutch my chest. "What about your student teaching? You're so close to getting your degree."

Amelia's smile disappears. "I can get a teaching certificate anywhere. Besides, I think maybe the world has more to teach me than I have to teach the world."

"Word," Taryn says, but I elbow her.

"Stop encouraging her! You really want her traveling the world alone?"

All three of them stare at me, unblinking, so I raise my hands in defeat and turn over the napkin. "Fine. Forget I said anything. I'm just going to take Ms. World Traveler's advice and add a few Spanish entrees to the sidebar as well." I scribble, *Jabugo ham, croquettes, lomo canapés and piquillo peppers.*

Amelia puts her hand over mine as I'm writing. "It's okay, sis. I do appreciate your concern. I always have. But maybe the only way for me to break the cycle I'm in is to leave."

I press my lips together. How do you know when leaving is the answer, and when it's not? I can't keep my mouth shut this time.

"If it's about money problems, the debt will still be there. If it's about guys, there will be men to sleep with everywhere you go. Your problems will go with you because they're in here." I point to my chest.

Taryn grunts. "Amelia. You have to tell her."

Amelia looks small again. I can still see the child in her.

"Yes, for God's sake, tell me."

"You asked me earlier where my cell phone was, and it's in the bottom of the ocean in Hawaii. I threw it in because Alex kept calling me."

"Who's Alex?"

"My married lover. Ex-married lover. No, he's still married. I mean he's *my* ex-lover. I broke things off with him before we came here, but he doesn't take no for an answer that easily. I've been with him off and on for two years."

I feel the knot in my throat, but even another sip of the sangria doesn't help and I nearly choke on it. My sister, the other woman. Her kind, my worst nightmare. I know I should be proud of her for breaking things off, but then I remember her going off into the night with the stranger in Hawaii and suddenly I look at her and don't see the innocent child, but someone I don't recognize. I knew she'd been hurting, struggling with her ups and downs ever since our father died, but I had no idea it was this bad.

I scoot off the sleek black and white chair and look down at my feet. So she's been seeking love in the arms of men because she doesn't feel loved enough? *I* haven't loved her enough. After Dad got sick, I spent so much time taking care of him and trying to keep up with my college coursework, that I didn't pay close enough attention to what she was going through.

Even before he got sick, I tried to keep everything perfect to keep Dad off our backs. House, spick and span. Cupboards full. Laundry done and folded, just the way he liked it. I remembered everything he'd yelled at Cecelia and my mother about, and made sure I didn't make the same mistake. If my sisters slacked, I made up for it. I cleaned up after them, often re-cleaning what they'd just done when they weren't looking. But in the process, I'd become a bickering big sister whose little sisters never did anything good enough. Not good enough for my father and therefore not good enough for me. I probably drove them both half out of their minds.

Whatever is broken within her is partially my fault. I can't stand to look at them.

"Where are you going?" Taryn asks.

"To bed," I say. "The pyramids today really wiped me out. Thanks for the drink, Amelia, and for the wonderful dinner, Karina."

Karina bounces off her chair and wraps me in a big, warm hug. As screwed up as her family is, she still manages to keep that huge smile on her face. My mother helped make her dreams come true, sending her to America. So what does my mother think she can do for her own daughters?

"The SUV will pick us up at eight a.m. to take us to the crash site."

Taryn and Amelia lunge forward to listen. I shake my head. I don't think I can handle any more bad news tonight. Karina looks at my sisters, her face screwing in to a cry. "There was a terrible accident."

14
MARLO

The still, cool morning would be perfect if I were sitting here on the patio looking out over the valley with Shane by my side. He'd be reading the paper, wearing his dark shades and Tommy Bahamas flip-flops. We'd be on vacation, our baby moon, perhaps, those trendy vacations that you take when you're in your second trimester and still able to fly.

I'd look at my successful doctor/husband and ask him if he wants a refill on his coffee and he'd say no, he was going to get a run in before our day full of tourist stops. We'd hold hands as we looked through the shops. He'd buy me a scarf and some Mexican pottery to go in the oversized home he'd bought me as a surprise after I'd told him I was pregnant. A bigger home for our growing family. Besides, doctors need bigger homes to entertain in. So I'd go to the magazine racks in the stores the first week of each month to buy all the knowledge I needed to sustain the life Shane wanted for us. I'd buy *Good Housekeeping* and *Martha Stewart Living* and *House Beautiful* and, because of the baby, *American Baby* and the truckload of baby books I'd need to ensure I didn't screw it up.

Instead, I sit with my bare feet on the rock wall, looking out into the majestic valley while my sisters sleep and I worry that Renee stayed late at my house and fell asleep on my couch. Maybe nothing happened, but when they wake up on the couch together, Shane realizes how peaceful it feels to have someone there who doesn't cause him such heartache. Someone easy.

Rialdo waves from the gardens below and I decide to join him, thankful for the interruption.

"*Buenos días, Senora,*" Rialdo says as he waters the rose garden and I walk down the path to greet him.

"Good morning," I say back. "Don't you have a gardener to do that for you?"

Rialdo shakes his head. "I am the gardener. And the housekeeper. And the maintenance man. If I do it myself, I don't have to pay it out of the commission I haven't made off the sale yet."

"Any interested buyers?"

"*Sí.* Two wealthy American businessmen. They both do a lot of business in Mexico City, but their offers have been too low. I'm almost to the point of introducing the cheap bastards and saying they must each pay half of the asking price and share it."

"Would they do that?"

"No. Rich men are greedy. I should know, because I am one. They would be too embarrassed to share a property. But I'm not going to sell this place for less than it's worth. Everything in time, *Senora.*"

"I guess you're right. What happened to the Santiagos? Why don't they live here anymore?"

Rialdo turns off the water hose and crosses his arms, studying me. "You are an anxious one, aren't you?"

"Patience really isn't my thing. I'm a journalist. I like to know the facts before everyone else. Part of the allure of the job."

Rialdo doesn't say anything. I'm sure it's hard for him to say no to his guests. He is our Keeper, after all.

"You said the other day that our mother saved your life."

"That wasn't a part of the tour."

"Elizabeth can't control all of the information."

"It's difficult for me to talk about."

He leads us to the lounge chairs near the pool and I slide the sunglasses down from my head to my nose and patiently wait. Okay, impatiently wait.

"Your mother went searching for me after I didn't show up at a house party. On the third day of the party, Elizabeth went to my house after many failed attempts to reach me by house phone and cell phone. She'd finally reached my then wife, who told her she hadn't seen me in three days and figured I was at the party, sleeping over as I often did. My wife loved when I was gone for days because she invited men into our house while I was away. Which is why I went missing in the first place. She didn't know at the time that I had caught her.

"Elizabeth even went to Rocco, a man who despised her, and told him she was worried about me, and because Rocco and I have been friends since we were small boys, he sent out a small search party. And Rocco knows everyone.

"Still, no luck. I was not in the hospitals or the jails or the morgue or at any known friend or acquaintances house. So on the fourth day, Elizabeth had the idea to search all of the empty homes of my real estate listings. There were only three. After getting copies of the house keys from my office, she and Dimitri personally searched them. They found me in the last house, sprawled out on the master bed, surrounded by a bottle of pills, a bag of cocaine and a bottle of whiskey.

"A millimeter, no more or less, from my demise. My breathing was shallow, my pulse weak, my skin a pale blue. The whiskey and pills were a terrible combination and they came back up. I was afraid my attempt had failed so I used the cocaine, something I had promised Rocco I would never do."

"Why would a drug lord care if his friends took drugs?"

"Would a distiller want his friends to become alcoholics? Or a knife maker want his friends to cut themselves? No. He'd seen too many loved ones die over the years."

Unfathomable. I'd never get that logic, and didn't really want to.

"Dimitri had brought some medical supplies with him. He placed an oxygen mask over my face and he and your mother carried me into the car and took me to the hospital. The first thing I saw when I woke up in the hospital was your mother's gorgeous blue eyes. She said, 'welcome back.'"

I think of all the fantasies I'd had where mother had saved our lives, became the hero. I never imagined she would really save anyone, and yet Rialdo, the paunchy, loud-mouthed real estate agent with the big heart, sits beside me now because she saved him fifteen years ago.

I turn my head to wipe away a tear. "Quite a story," I tell him.

"Everyone else had given up on me. Taken me for dead. If they hadn't found me when they did, I would've died within hours. I got a second chance."

"So you dropped your dope dealing monster of a friend?"

"I dropped my wife first. As for Rocco, I was in a precarious situation. If I became a rat for the government to catch Rocco, then I was also jeopardizing Dimitri and Elizabeth's work. By now Dimitri learned to fly and had struck a deal with his father. He would fly the drug plane once a month himself, as long as his cargo also included the sick child he was taking to Hawaii for surgery. This pleased Rocco, because he took it as a sign that his son was accepting the family business and that he might take over the family dynasty some day. Rocco's health was in decline. His son Peyton had started taking drugs and was in and out of drug rehab centers, so he no longer could see the drugs as simply a product. Peyton was kicked out of the house, out of the family. He sought revenge by attacking the thing most precious to his father."

"Dimitri?"

"*Si.* I shouldn't say any more. You'll learn all you want to know and more after breakfast."

"Thank you for telling me," I pat him on his arm. "Even if it wasn't a part of the tour. It helps, you know?"

"*Si.* I understand. This must be very difficult for you. Did you sleep well?"

"No, but it has nothing to do with the accommodations. The bed is comfortable. The temperature is just right. It's just me."

"Your mind must quiet to sleep. I can see it, constantly turning. You worry too much," he says. "Just like your mother."

I suck in a breath. A wonderful thing to have in

common.

"Hey, guys. Where's the coffee?" Taryn shouts from her balcony, wearing a man's tank top and boxers, which I presume are Paul's, the not-quite fiancé. I can't remember ever wearing any of Shane's clothes, and wish I would have brought a piece with me. *She does love him*, I think.

Next Amelia pops her head out of her balcony door and waves to us. "I'm starved," she yells, which I take as code for "get me some breakfast." So I do, but thankfully, for everyone's sake, someone else has cooked it.

"Peyton tipped off the authorities," Karina tells us, as we stand in the middle of a field an hour from the mansion. "He paid off the guards at my father's airport and added more weight to the plane. Your mother was going on this trip, which my brother also knew. The little girl, Tamira, was in bad shape. If she didn't get a new kidney, she would die. They had waited for six months before they got one in Hawaii, and by then it was almost too late. So when Tamira asked her to go with her, she agreed, to hold her hand on the flight."

"After the surgery your mother was going to take a commercial flight from Hawaii to the lower 48, to meet me in Kansas. She had given up on hearing from your father and decided to just surprise you."

I realize I've been holding my breath and begin to feel faint. I steady myself and take deep breaths.

Karina points to a white cross about twenty yards from where we were standing. "That is where the plane went down." She hands us the photos of the crash site. A ball of flame. A wing in one place, the tail in the other. I can only glance a moment. I've seen similar scenes in my mind, like the time we'd been studying World War I and I'd seen the plane crashing into the medical barracks killing all of the nurses and patients. If it weren't so morbid, I might think it was funny that I had ever imagined her as a nurse and that she became one.

I don't want to hand Amelia the pictures. It's my job still to shelter her, whether or not she knows it, but I'm still a little upset about her news of her married lover. She says it's over, but don't they all say that before crawling back? Reluctantly, I hand them to her, and she gasps, averting her eyes and passes them to Taryn.

"When my parents got here, they had already been carried off. They had no idea who lived and who died until later. I was told my brother and the young girl had perished. Died upon impact." Karina makes the sign of the cross. "I flew back for the funerals. It was the hardest day of my life. My brother's plan had worked. He had killed his competition, but what he hadn't counted on was that the government did not immediately go after my father. They believed the drug run was strictly Dimitri and Elizabeth's operation and that they had kidnapped the girl. The flight plans were under Dimitri's name. They needed any victory they could get, even if it was a lie."

"What happened to our mom?" Amelia asks.

"Come," Karina says. "Her broken bones eventually healed. But her heart; her heart was never the same."

"I'm not going in there," Amelia says, her eyes welling up with tears. "Is she in there?"

We're standing at the gates of the Santa Marta women's

prison in Mexico City, one of the most infamous women's prisons in the world. I feel like I'm going to be sick. As hardened as my heart had grown over the years from her absence, I never wanted my mother to spend her life in a place like this.

"Do the crime, pay the time," Taryn says coolly.

Karina has changed into sensible clothes. Nothing flashy, nothing fleshy. She's wearing baggy jeans, tennis shoes and a long-sleeved T-shirt. After lunch, she instructed us on what to wear. She preferred we looked like asexual blobs. We don't even wear makeup.

"Is this where our journey ends?" I ask her. "Is our mother here? Sentenced for drug trafficking and kidnapping, maybe? Involuntary manslaughter?" I'd written enough feature articles on crime to know they could've stuck Elizabeth with a long list of crimes for what she and Dimitri had done. And she survived. That alone could've been enough of a crime to enrage Rocco and demand she spend the rest of her life in prison.

Karina takes Amelia and my hand. "I'm sorry to worry you. Your mother is no longer here. But she did spend a great deal of time here. I have her journal in my bag. She wrote almost every day. It's as thick as a book. She wanted you to see where she stayed when she wrote it. We're not asking you to spend the night behind bars."

"Thank God for that," Taryn says. "But hey, I think if we're going to read the damn thing, it would give us a good perspective to see what the hell she was talking about."

New adventure, my ass. Flying off a mountain was one thing, but prison with hardened criminals? "Fine. Take us in. We all go."

Amelia nods. "Since I know she's no longer here, I feel better."

We walk up the sidewalk to the front door with two guards, one of our hulks, and one from the prison. In the distance I hear the sound of …. but it can't be. And yet. "Is that what I think it is?" I ask Karina, stopping and staring in the direction of the exercise yard. I squint and sure enough, there they are. Little people. Children. A baby's cry echoes in the wind.

"*Sí.* Babies born in prison are kept with their mothers until they are six years old."

Our jaws drop, but the guard keeps on moving. I don't dare stop them again. Tiny prisoners, being raised behind bars. Wait until Ken hears about this one.

For the first time, I wonder what our lives might have been like if our mother had taken us with her on her sojourn. Lots of mothers leave their cheating husbands, but pack up the kids, too. Most mothers would never dream of leaving their children. I'd reckon most mothers would choose their children over their husband in the crowded lifeboat test.

Whatever hell she made for herself, she spared us the same fate. And for the first time I'm thankful, truly thankful, that she left us behind.

The guard, Emmanuel, a middle-aged brute with a long, graying mustache and a tattooed serpent on his arm, leads us through the prison. At first, we don't see the women, and I figure Karina has planned it this way. Afternoon means time in the exercise yard, out of their cells so that we can see where our mother lived unfettered by the company she kept.

The pungent air sticks to our skin as we enter a 144 square foot cell, not unlike the ones we've seen on TV. Two beds, dressed simply with a white sheet, standard-issue flat pillow and a sink and toilet. Cement walls. Taryn plops on the mattress, but it's no thicker than six inches and has no springs. No rest for the wicked.

"I think I'm going to be sick," Amelia says, holding her nose.

Karina pulls the journal out of her backpack. "Do you want to read it here?"

My sisters eye the book in her slender hands like a prized egg at Easter, but we don't grab for it. Without saying it, I know we're more afraid of what we'll read there than anything that came before it.

Taryn begins shooting pictures, and I scribble some notes for my article. By now I can write an entire magazine on Mexico.

"Can't we read it somewhere else? As in, anywhere that's not here?" Amelia asks as I begin feeling guilty that I'm cataloging our reactions for a story. A story that I don't want to be so damn personal.

Karina puts the journal back in the bag. "Of course. You'll want to be comfortable."

I cringe at the word, "comfortable." Maybe the whole idea is that we would read our mother's prison memoir within these cell walls and feel what she felt – every ounce of pain and heartache and rage. But I can't, and not even Taryn, whose shield has always seemed much stronger than mine, doesn't want to, either.

"We'll read it back at the mansion," she says.

A horn sounds, and we all jump. Emmanuel rushes us

out of the cell, and down the long dank corridor, passing a brightly colored room that looks to have been dropped from the sky like Dorothy's house into the Land of Oz. The room held the only primary colors among the cement gray and bleached whites of the rest of the prison. "The nursery," I say, pausing at the door. Tigger bounces on the wall. Mickey Mouse holds hands with Minnie. Big blocks line the wall with a small, solitary bookshelf only half-full of children's books. I make a note to send some books when I return home.

The nursery director, a plump small woman with short-cropped hair and a slight mustache, enters through the opposite door, like a mama duck followed by her ducklings, twelve children, three-to-five-years-old. They fold their hands behind their backs, their cheeks puffed, and I'm relieved when they take their seats on the small colored dots on the floor that their hands had not been cuffed behind their backs. They were simply walking in an orderly fashion, just like kids in back home are asked to do in school. The puffed cheeks are blown out. Amelia tells us it's a game to get the kids to hold a bubble of air and it keeps them from talking.

I study the faces of these children, wearing ill-fitting hand-me-downs, either too big or too small on them. Their hair is unkempt, but they don't look like the impoverished kids you see on the Feed the Children commercials, either.

I barely hear Amelia ask if she can read a story to the children, but there she is, the teacher in her natural state sitting on the floor reading *Robin Hood* to the bright-eyed children eager to hear the tale of a man who would steal from the fortunate to give to the poor.

They don't look or act like little prisoners. Minutes earlier I'd been so sure these children were being punished, and yet after seeing the hungry ones on the streets next to the clinic, I realize these children have what so many in the world do not: food, shelter and their mother's embrace. At this age, what do they know of freedom? And what will their souls remember that their little minds forget?

The late afternoon quickly turns to dusk, turns to night. We read by the pool, only stopping for the occasional bathroom break. We hand off the thick journal wordlessly, picking up where the last sister left off, passing tissues, too. Lots and lots of tissues. Rialdo and Karina flitter silently around us, keeping us stocked with fresh tea, tortillas, fruit and grilled vegetables, but I don't recall eating any of it. My mother's words seem to be the only fuel we need to go on.

15
ELIZABETH

July 16, 1996

Death had finally found me, hovering just above by broken body.

I awoke to the sounds of men's laughter and Spanish music blaring from a car stereo. Pain seared through my body, and my eyes were matted shut. Probably for the best. I could smell him and sure as hell didn't want to see him. I smelled blood and burnt flesh, my own and something else. Sweat. Sex. Him. Bile rose in my throat, causing me to choke, surprising the bastard on top of me. I felt seeping wounds on my arms and legs and the weight of him crushing me as I gasped for a deep breath, but to no avail. My mind caught up, against my will. The crash. The fire. And now this. How did I get here? Where's Dimitri? Tamira? I can't connect the dots or find the missing piece of the puzzle that lands me inside this van. Then I heard the sound of hope: sirens.

I tried to scream, but my attacker and his buddies only laughed and he covered my mouth with a calloused hand.

Any moment now these criminals would be pulled over, and I would be rescued, I thought. I noticed the van had increased in speed. At first I thought they were trying to outrun the law. Then I realized something worse. The siren was too close— right above me. I was inside an ambulance or a police van, and either way I was in trouble. They were the law.

Another scream, met by a slap against my cheek. I screamed profanities in English and Spanish, causing more laughter. I'd turned into a one-woman comedy act, which pissed me off even more.

I tried to push him off, but my right arm wouldn't move.

Broken? I could move my left hand, balled into a fist, but the rapist pinned my arm down to the floor.

When the attacker finished having his way with me, the stinging in my chest continued, made worse with each bump in the road. A broken rib, too? The doctors would have a heyday trying to put me back together again. Then another shock sent nausea coursing through my body. What if I wasn't going to a doctor? What if it was a shallow grave in the Mexican desert instead?

The pain went away if I held my breath, but eventually I had to breathe again. I'd been around enough broken bodies to know I was in bad shape and probably in shock, which is why I wasn't writhing in pain.

I listened for details, but only heard the sounds of one man buckling his belt and another man unzipping. I wailed then. Begged. Then willed myself to leave my body so I wouldn't feel Act 2.

And I didn't. I didn't feel anything for the longest time imaginable.

July 21, 1996

Lucia came to my bedside to tell me that Dimitri is gone. She wore a black veil and a long black dress. My body was still too broken to get out of bed, and she didn't try to console me. I didn't even tell her what the men in the ambulance did to me. It seems like nothing compared to this. I silently wished she would find a black blanket, cover me from head to toe, and bury me alive.

July 30, 1996

I'm inmate number 874581. I share a cell with Maria Gonzales. Her real name is too pretty for the prison, though, for the crimes she's committed. They call her Gonz. She's my age, thirty-one, and the leader in one of the prison gangs. She's been here half of her life, caught drug trafficking for her father. I asked her if I could call her Maria, and she spat in my face. I took that as a no.

Tattoos cover only the left half of her body, reminding me of the Julie Andrews movie where she's dressed as half man, half woman. For the life of me, I can't remember the title, but what does it matter? Why only half, I asked, squeezing my eyes shut, expecting to me spit on again, but her voice softened. She said, "I want to remember what it was like to be pure."

I understand this. Pure like a child. Her right half is a symbol of the better times - baking with her mother, who was killed when she was twelve, and going to Mass with her grandmother, who is memorialized on her left arm. I'm amazed she can even remember a life before prison. In just a week it's done a number on erasing who I was before. I'm caught by surprise every time I see my reflection in the glass. There I am. Still here.

I catch myself studying her tattoos — some days there isn't much more to do than that — and eventually she'll tell me what they all mean. The prisoners wear them like a code of honor. Me? No, thanks. If I ever get out of this shit hole, I don't want to tell people on the outside — yeah, I got that tattoo in prison. I wonder if there will ever be a day in the far distant future where I can forget being here. It seems as likely as ever forgetting anything before it. I still dream of death, but not so much for escape as in the past, but for a reunion. To be with Dimitri again. I bought in to Lucia's idea of Heaven and Hell and Guardian Angels and Everlasting Life. It's the only thing left I have to cling to. What is this — these days and weeks and years in prison, compared to spending eternity with my Dimitri and making amends with my daughters that I couldn't make the first time.

Yet as appealing as death sounds, I don't want to die here.

August 4, 1996

"Endurecer."

It means, "toughen up." Gonz barks these things at me like orders, but I think it's her way of trying to be nice to me. She also told me to never smile. Not even in my sleep. No one wants to see anyone happy here. Had I smiled? I thought I'd only cried. No, she told me I hadn't smiled, but I looked like the type that might let it slip.

Lucia had brought me the letter I'd been waiting for. The one from Richard, responding to the two-dozen letters I'd written him since arriving in Mexico, asking him if I could come see the girls. I wouldn't stay long. A quick visit. Just to see them. Hug them. The letter was a single line. Three words.

Elizabeth,

Go to hell.

Love, Richard

He might be pleased to know I'm already living in Hell. But if Hell is the absence of God, I get it. My personal Hell is the absence from my daughters.

I'd felt so certain I would see my girls again, but now I wonder. Was the plane crash a sign that I should stay away from them? Perhaps I'd been selfish in wanting to show up unannounced, like some ghost from the past and expect I'd get hugs and a warm welcome. I would've likely gotten the door slammed in my face, and for good reason. I'd probably have to go to court to get permission to see them, but I would've done it. I would've done whatever it took.

Now Tamira is dead, and though she would've died anyway without the surgery, she should've had the chance to die in the arms of her loved ones, not like she did.

What irony if Richard had said I could see the girls now. I've been sentenced to ten years, five with good behavior. What can I do? Break out of prison and hitchhike to America? I'm probably crazy enough to try. If I died trying, though, they would never know. What would be the point of that? No use in writing him back with a never mind, I'm in prison, anyway. *Let him think I'm living the high life.*

As for the crying, Gonz says cut that shit out. Makes me weak. Prison is no place for crybabies. Everyone has lost her freedom. Lost loved ones.

"Todos somos iguales."

We are all the same.

Who am I to argue? Not even half of me feels pure. I feel tainted to the marrow of my bones. In fact, I envy her. However she did it, she worked her way up. She's a leader.

So I must learn to act tough. They call me, "el pálido una." The pale one. I am the lightest inmate in Santa Marta, which I suppose could make me feel more like an outsider, but since I am the pale one loved by Dr. Dimitri Santiago, I am somewhat revered. And by revered, I mean they let me live and no one is allowed to rape me, though the guards are a different story. As long as Gonz is on my side, I suppose they'll leave me alone, too. For now.

They don't know that Rocco Santiago hates me, and Gonz tells me many of the women hope if they are nice to me that I'll get them a job with the Santiago cartel when they get out. They think I have pull. I must hold on to any semblance of power I have, and though it disgusts me that I am in any way associated with Rocco Santiago, I must hold on to it for the sake of my life.

September 18, 1996

I've learned to cry silently. Do you know how hard this is? To cry and not have any tears fall? Gonz beat the hell out of me the day I cried after she told me not to. She only wants to tell you once. So now I cry, but miraculously keep the tears from falling. The sobs echo through my soul, my blood swirling in grief. I miss Dimitri, of course. But mostly I cry for my girls.

I want to transfer to a prison where there are no children. Every time I see them, I feel the knife twist in my heart. To make matters worse, Gonz is pregnant with a guard's child. She's due any day now, and the memories of my own pregnancies flood my mind. I'm sure I was matched with Gonz for a reason, but for the life of me, I can't figure it out. Guess I've got time to think on it.

Do you know why the country allows children under six to stay with their incarcerated mothers? Do you?

Mother-child bonding in the early formative years.

I know these prisoner mothers love their children and their children love them. Most of these moms seem sensitive to their children's needs. Others, not so much. But it's so much easier to judge from the other side of the prison bars.

I'm not even sure I met my children's needs when I was with them. What does Marlo remember about me? Does she remember the good times like I do? How much of my depression and anger did she feel or witness? I've blocked so much of that time out.

I really thought I was doing the best thing for them by leaving, but now all I can think about is how I've left them emotionally scarred in their formative years.

I don't think I've ever hated myself any more than I do right now.

November 1, 1996

Día de los Muertos. The Day of the Dead. Those of us who are Catholic, which is most of us, spent the morning in the church chapel celebrating All Saint's Day. You celebrate for two days, praying for your loved ones who have died.

The priest, Father Castillo, invited us to put pictures of our loved ones on the altar. The nuns brought three sugar skulls, representing the

Father, Son and Holy Ghost.

You eat the favorite foods of the deceased and leave them at their graves as offerings. Dimitri loved sugar, but I'm a terrible cook. Instead I'd buy him M&Ms. They never failed to turn his mood around. If I weren't in prison, I would go to his graveside and scatter M&Ms around his gravestone, inking the ground with red, green and orange candies.

So, I ate nothing. Catholics often fast in penance and prayer. If not eating can give me grace, then by God, I'll do it.

Last night was Halloween. I stayed in my cell, dreaming about my girls and drawing elaborate costumes for them. I'd forgotten how much I love to draw. I put the drawings in the mail today for Richard, asking him to please give them to the girls, though I doubt he'll do it. I didn't explain that I'm in prison but if he notices the return address, he'll know. But what joy I got making them.

I dressed Marlo as Queen Elizabeth in her early years, with the cinched dress and the beehive red wig and pale face with red lips. Marlo would be the most elegant trick-or-treater on the block.

Taryn was a pirate with a black and white striped top, black satin pants and a red sash around her slender hips. I'd make a skull and crossbones appliqué with rhinestones for her chest and a beaded headband. No eye patch. You'd want to see her beautiful brown eyes. This is what would make her dangerous, you see. She'd disarm them with her beauty and then defeat them with one swift swath of her sword.

And for my baby? Well, not a baby, anymore. Six years old! I wrapped her in gold organza, drew feathered wings that spanned from her neck to her ankles, then topped her crown with a golden halo, only slightly askew. I curled her blonde hair in ringlets. She'll always be my Angel Baby.

As for Gonz's baby, when Gonz can't get her to stop crying, she hands her to me. Her cries go right through me. She stops, and I start.

December 5, 1996

Karina has sent me more pictures! She kept her promise to me, even after her brother died. The best news? My girls look beautiful and healthy. All of Marlo's big teeth are in, and she wears glasses. Taryn is nearly as tall as Marlo, and Amelia is missing her front tooth. All day I haven't stopped thinking how much I would've liked to put their baby teeth in a pillow and play the tooth fairy. One of a long line of things I've missed out on. How had I not remembered baby teeth before I left?

Why had I not made a list?

I couldn't think straight enough to make a list. I know this, but what if I had?! Would everything be different?

The only pause in my lapse into happiness was seeing the fifth member of the family. Cecelia. I hadn't seen her since I'd found her in my bed—naked, on top of Richard. I'd taken the girls to the zoo, so Richard figured it would be safe, but we'd come home early because Amelia was cranky. She wanted no part of feeding peanuts to the elephants. Yet I digress; the point is that you don't forget the face of the woman in bed with your husband. Ever.

What did I expect? By leaving, I practically held the door open for her to walk through it, to take what she wanted all along. I had nearly believed him when I thought she was just an office fling. I suppose he let her take my place and will go on to fling elsewhere. Mark my words. She will catch him one day, just as I did. You can't change a man's stripes.

I scratched my arms raw thinking about that woman mothering my children. How emotionally healthy could she be to have an affair with a married man?

Yet if a picture is worth a thousand words, then this one of ice cream in the park says all I need to know for now. They are safe and loved.

March 5, 1997

Peyton is now a prison guard. I have no idea why he picked this prison, if it's because I'm here or because it was the only job he could get since being kicked out of the family. He claims it's a brother's right to take what his brother has left behind. Not all guards are bad, but some, like Peyton, abuse their authority. He uses his position to torture me on a daily basis. I can't even write the things he's made me do.

Today, the rage was more than I could take. I've been growing my nails out for exactly this purpose. When we were alone and he demanded I remove my clothing, I scratched his eye out. Blood gushed everywhere, but I didn't stop. I tried to get his left eye, too. I don't care if I have to look at his blind eye the rest of my days here or that it will go in my disciplinary report. It was worth it to prove to him that I can fight back. He'll know that I've taken away something precious of his, like he's taken something from me.

Of course he beat me to a pulp, but the other guards stopped him from killing me. You should've seen the look on Gonz's face when I told her that her idea worked. She was so proud of me. I'd been so brave. So tough.

Long ago I put my fate in the hands of God. Now I'm wondering if putting it in the hands of Gonz was a wiser move.

16
TARYN

When I awake, Paul is leaning over me, my small hand swallowed by his.

"Where am I?"

I look around, the room more familiar to me now than my own bare apartment back home. Ancient luxury. So I'm not the one out of place. My tongue feels like cotton, and I can't speak. I wonder if he's a mirage.

"There's Miss Sunshine," Paul says. Even in my dreams, he tries to rile me up.

"Screw you," I try to say, but it only comes out as rushed air. He hands me a glass of water and lifts my head to sip it. Behind him, I see my sisters hovering over me like anxious angels. Now I know I must be dreaming.

I close my eyes again, thinking back to the pool, where we'd been reading Elizabeth's journals for hours. It's like a soap opera, I'd told my sisters—a telenovella like the ones so popular here. I must've fallen asleep, and now I'm dreaming of my big biker banker. Wow. He's even better looking in my dreams. I want to dive into his hazel eyes and stay there forever. I close my eyes and dive off the Hoary Head cliff and sail through the air. I know Paul will be at the bottom of the mountain to swallow me whole.

"Hey, you still with us, Sunshine?"

"Please stop calling me that." My voice is hoarse.

My sisters laugh. My body feels sluggish, drugged. You know those dreams where you want to move, but can't?

When I try, it's like walking in water.

"She's back," Paul says.

"Back from where, dumbass?"

"And she's still bright and shiny as ever," Marlo says.

Amelia rushes to my left side. "We've missed you."

"This is the craziest dream I've had in a long time." I search out their faces. We hadn't even drunk alcohol while we'd read mom's journals. Not mom. *Elizabeth*. We'd made it to her third year in prison. I think of our photos taped to the cement wall next to her bed.

Karina and Rialdo are at the foot of my bed, too. If I didn't know better, I'd think this was my deathbed.

Marlo grabs my toe and gives it a shake. "Dirty needles. You don't remember?"

My brain is so foggy, that I can't piece anything together. I see a man, covered in tattoos, really amazing tattoos. He's the best in Mexico City. "No way. I watched him pull the needles out of the bag. They were brand new," I say. "And then just to be careful, I asked him to sterilize them again."

"He faked you out," Rialdo says with a shrug of his shoulders.

Tattooing isn't regulated in Mexico. I'd known this. Anyone, anywhere can hang a shingle, and much like the drug industry, half of it's done in someone's kitchen. Tino did so much business he had an actual shop, though it was the dirtiest shop I'd ever seen, but then not much that I'd seen here was the clean you expect in America. And I've seen a lot of shit holes.

"Dammit." I pound my fist on the bed. "What the hell are you doing here? Come to read me my last rites?"

Paul leans down and kisses me square on the mouth. *In front of my sisters.*

"God, I've missed you," he says rubbing my nose in an Eskimo kiss that makes my face redden from the neck up.

"What have I said about PDA?" The room erupts in laughter. "Get out. All of you."

A flash of hurt crosses Paul's face. I yank on his surfer T-shirt. "Except you."

He smiles. *Geesh. So easy to please, this one.*

The room clears, leaving Paul and I alone. "Why did you come?"

"You had an allergic reaction to the antibiotic. You've been sick for two days."

"So my sisters call and you hop on a plane? Just like that?" My heart hurts. Whatever they've given me makes my eyes water and my chest swell. But how does my medication affect Paul? His eyes are watering, too.

"You don't get it, do you? I love the hell out of you, Taryn. Seeing you like that was the worst thing I've ever been through."

I have to look away, feeling my eyes spill over. I've never seen him this serious before. He's hurting because *I'm* hurting? "You need to shave."

It's been at least three days since a razor touched his skin. I hate how sexy he looks. I shiver. "I'm cold."

Instead of covering me with another blanket, he lifts the sheets and climbs in next to me. I shudder from his warmth. He wraps his arm around my belly and I feel my whole body respond to his touch. I've missed his scent. Sunshine and rain. I want to bottle it and keep it with me wherever I go. He kisses my shoulder, and then lays his head beside mine. I close my eyes and just listen to our breathing. A wonderful dream, this. I don't want to wake up.

"We don't have to talk," he says. "Save your energy."

How odd to have a dream where you're lying in bed, awake, but then I get the urge to get up to go pee. I haven't peed my bed in a dream in a long time. I'm not about to risk it.

"Stay there." I get up, and slowly walk to the bathroom and land with a thunk on the toilet. When I get up, I see my reflection in the oversized mirror and think about my mother, and how she was surprised to see her image, proof that she still existed when she felt invisible. How many times I've thought the very same thing.

How often I'd hated that girl in the mirror. Too small, too bony, lips too big, eyes too large, hair too blonde. I did what I could to erase her, or morph her into something different. Working out to add muscle, dying my hair black to match my mood and carefully painting myself as a work of art. A work still very much in progress.

I gaze into the mirror and see my father, lying on his deathbed, his hair prickly as a porcupine, growing back in because the poison hadn't worked this time. He'd been in remission once, when I was thirteen. He'd said at the time, "I told you we'd kick cancer's ass," as if we'd done it together. Then, two years later, it came back with a vengeance, and he fought like hell. I was on the team, even shaved my head in unity with him, to show him I was still his girl, but he'd looked at my baldhead in horror.

What fifteen-year-old girl shaves her thick head of blonde hair?

"What have you done to yourself?" he'd asked, disgusted.

I'd made a joke about taking our show on the road, the Balding Barnes, but he hated being bald. His wavy, thick hair was a part of his perfect image. The ladies' man, the hunk of the corporate office. When mine grew back in, I died it black and began spiking it. I began getting tattoos — where Dad couldn't see them at first, but then I started not caring if he saw them. I wanted to create my own image, be my own person outside of who my father or sisters or anyone else thought I should be.

All the determination and LIVESTRONG bracelets and fundraisers and walkathons and good wishes and prayer circles and the best treatment money could buy didn't do a damn bit of good. He watched my graduation ringside from his wheelchair, pride still apparent in his glazed eyes. Cecelia sat behind him, as if she still gave a shit about him. I suppose she did. All the women loved him, even if they weren't good enough for him to keep around for very long.

He died a week later. I swore I'd never love anyone again.

I stare at the colored lines all over my body, thinking of Gonz, my mother's cellmate. Half pure? My tattoos cover sixty percent of my body, and I know for certain I'm not done yet. I lift my left ankle up to the counter and look at Tino's handiwork—the tattooed rabbit next to the eagle. I'm relieved to see the rabbit is perfect, even down to the fine rabbit ears and fuzzy tail. It better be if it nearly cost me my life.

I can't wait to show Paul. And my sisters.

I remove my T-shirt and pajama shorts and walk back

to the bedroom where Paul has his head propped up on his hand, waiting for me. He groans with pleasure when he sees me, his eyes full of want, and I think how nice it might be if it were always like this. A man who wants nothing more than to be by my side. To love me.

Thank God this isn't a dream.

An hour later, we join my sisters on the patio for mint tea. My hunger has returned with a vengeance. I eat everything in sight. Karina and Rialdo have left for grocery shopping, promising to return to cook a big feast for dinner, swearing we will go someplace quiet tomorrow—quite the opposite of the prison. It's afternoon, when a lot of Mexicans are taking an afternoon siesta. Considering I've had a 72-hour one, I'm ready to show Mexico to Paul. He's clingy, and doesn't want to let me out of his sight. For once, I see this as a good thing. Being pampered isn't altogether a bad thing.

When Paul leaves to grab Tecates and lime from the massive commercial fridge in the kitchen, my sisters practically pounce on me.

"He's the cutest thing ever." Amelia gushes.

"I can't believe you haven't introduced us before now," Marlo says. "He seems really amazing. I mean that."

Amelia bobs her head. "Sweet and nice and smart, and my God if I could get a guy to dote on me like he does you, I swear I'd never let him go." She points her finger at me. "You are sooo lucky!"

I don't want to give them the satisfaction of a smile, so I just roll my eyes, but inside I'm beaming. I'll take luck if I can get it. Marlo notices my new charm tattoo and leans closer to the lounge chair to get a look.

"Lucky rabbit's foot, indeed," she says.

"It's cool." Amelia's own charms jingle on her arm. "Maybe because it was a rabbit, like the one that Mom saw when she was in that basement, you pulled through, you know? A God thing."

My "cup half-full" sis. At least for today, anyway. I lift my ankle high in the air, the blue Mexico sky a cloudless backdrop. "Who knows is right. I'm just glad I'm here. And it doesn't suck as much as I thought it would for you to meet Paul." I look each of them in the eye, the girls I've known my whole life—the ones I played Barbies with until I ripped off all the doll's heads and Cecelia sent me to bed without supper. The girls I skinned my knees with riding bikes because I insisted we play daredevil. The girls I couldn't wait to tell ghost stories to at night, with a flashlight under the sheets. I'd never confessed anything big before. I didn't even tell them about my tattoos, letting them discover them for themselves. Kind of like Paul. I didn't have to say how wonderful he is for them to see it. But for once I feel like sharing.

"I love him. I absofuckinlutely love the jerk."

And the smiles on my sister's faces seemed to say they know he's not a jerk at all.

Bees hum nearby in the hydrangea bushes. Ice clinks in the glass on the side table. I couldn't dream up a more tranquil afternoon if I tried. My eyes close. Just for a moment, I think. So I can remember this moment forever. I won't fall asleep. The girls say they'll catch me up on Elizabeth's journals, but I'm not ready to hear about more trials. I'm ready to skip to the end, hopefully a good one, where she gets her freedom. Maybe later then.

Amelia's piercing scream echoes off the palatial wall, spearing the tranquility like a sword. I shoot up out of the chair and instinctively reach for her. A bee sting? A stray dog? What?

I spin in the direction of my sisters' stares. They are frozen.

"Buenas tardes." A strange man's voice growls.

White-hot fear floods my system. I can't scream. Marlo jumps up, in front of us, a human shield between the Mexican and us with the gun to Paul's head. Shit. I could really do for a dream right about now. Even a run-of-the-mill nightmare.

I still feel groggy, but nothing like the sight of my lover with a pistol to his brain to wake me up for good.

Paul is a foot taller than the man, and Paul's veins are pulsing, his strong muscles tense. If given the chance, Paul could beat this guy to a pulp. *If it weren't for that shiny black revolver up against his head.* I want this to be an action movie, where the star elbows the bad guy in the gut and then twists the fucker's arm off, causing the gun to fly across the cement. But it's not a movie, and one false move and Paul is no more.

I don't know Spanish, except for a few phrases like *beunos tardes*, but I do know it's definitely no longer a good afternoon. It's suddenly a very fucking bad afternoon.

Amelia slides out of Marlo's frame to see the gunman. She puts her hand up in a stop motion, as if that's going to help. She says something to him in Spanish. Whatever it is, the Mexican laughs and he takes three steps forward, shoving Paul along. As he steps in to the light, I can see the man's face, the scar running from his tear duct diagonal to his jawbone. His right eye is blind and cloudy white.

Peyton Santiago.

I understand what he says next. "No way."

"We'll give you money," I yell.

Another growl. "I don't want your money, *senorita*. I heard Elizabeth's children were staying in my house. Thought I'd stop by for a visit. I've been looking for her."

Where the hell are the Mexican Hulks when you need them? Paid off?

"Don't look around, *senorita*. Your guards are dead."

I feel like an arrow has lodged in my chest.

Marlo huffs and crosses her arms, suddenly looking inches taller and stronger. "So, what then? You're going to kill us because our mother poked your eye out, you deserving asshole?"

"Marlo!" Amelia and I yell.

"Let's not give the guy any ideas." And she's supposed to be the smart one in the family?

"I can see the resemblance," he says. "Which is going to make this a very pleasurable afternoon." He smiles and licks his lips, two silver front teeth shining in the sun. I shudder. No way that asshole is getting his hands on me or my sisters, but I dare not add, *over my dead body*.

"I just didn't plan on you having company," Peyton says, flicking Paul's ear with his tongue. Paul's nostrils flare. Any moment now he'll turn into Superman, right?

The gun. The loaded gun that just killed our hulks, pressed against the temples of a guy that's way too good for me. A guy who loves me way more than I ever thought someone could.

I want so much. If I have a fraction of a second left to tell Paul how much he means to me, he'll die without knowing. If I have all the time in the world to tell him, I still don't think I could do it justice. I want to scream, "I love you." Just so he'll know. I've never said it, though it's the favorite tune I play in my head. I've been so afraid. More afraid of that, of a real future with a really great guy, than I am in this situation.

Fact: Peyton has plenty of time to rape and kill us before Karina and Rialdo return home.

I have a strange thought. *What would Elizabeth do?*

"*Endurecer,*" I say to my sisters. They nod. Our fists pump. Our eyes slit.

"Rialdo!" Marlo yells, pointing behind Peyton, giving us the time we need. Peyton loosens his grip on Paul as he turns to look, and Paul won't budge, so Peyton trips back into the door, the gun now eight inches from Paul's head. Paul grabs Peyton's wrist and slams his hand hard against the glass door of the patio, the gun unloading onto Peyton's foot before it falls from his hand. He doubles over, clutching his knee, a wincing, pathetic flamingo dancing on one foot.

Marlo, Amelia and I jump on him, sending us all back inside the living room and crashing into a heap onto the old wooden floor. Peyton's head smashes hard, bouncing twice, and he has no chance of getting up. He's pinned to the ground, three against one, because we're not giving Paul a piece of the action.

Amelia stands and kicks him hard in the ribs, while Marlo punches his face and I take a cross off the wall, the nearest weapon within reach, and hit him on the head with it.

"Don't kill him," a voice says, and we look up, shaking, adrenaline still pumping. A pale, handsome man with sharp blue eyes stands before us, two fingers and his thumb up, his palm towards us, a hand gesture I'd seen a dozen times on Jesus figures in this house and the cathedral.

"It's Blue Eyes," Amelia says as Peyton spits blood and curls into a fetal position on the floor.

"Who the hell is Blue Eyes?"

"Frank Sinatra," Marlo answers, wiping sweat from her forehead, but smearing blood in the process.

The man smiles. Jesus. Maybe it *is* Jesus. Nothing seems impossible now.

Amelia laughs. "No. I mean I've seen this guy in Hawaii and he was at the back of the church the other day."

"Are you following us?" Marlo says, threatening. I love it when she gets angry.

Now Blue Eyes raises both of his hands. "Let's get cleaned up and I'll explain everything."

"Isn't that what they all say?" I stand with my hands on my hip, my best Wonderwoman stance. I feel like I can take anyone on now, but of course my Superman has rushed to the front of the line, in case this gentle-looking man is really a poser.

"We don't need to get cleaned up," Marlo says. "We need some answers. And why the hell should we let this guy live?"

I slap my big sis on the back. "Seriously? Marlo's going Rambo on us."

"No. Your mother wouldn't want you to kill him. She

didn't send you here to avenge her."

"I don't think she's here to get a say-so," I tell him.

"We can't let him go. You know he's just going to come back for us." Peyton tries to move to get up, but Marlo kicks him down hard and he squeals in pain again followed by guttural sobs.

Blues Eyes nods. "He's been looking for your mother for years. We figured he might catch wind of your stay, which is why we beefed up security. Apparently the guards knew Mr. Santiago, so they let their guard down, as it were. He shot them both at point blank range. I've already called the authorities. They'll be the ones to take Mr. Santiago away."

"The authorities?" Amelia says. "They're the ones who raped our mother in the police van. Who says they're going to lock this guy up? Can't he just pay them off like he did the security guards at the prison?"

"No. The Santiagos are not what they once were. They have no power left. No money."

"Except an eighteen-million-dollar mansion and an asshole son with a gun." I wave my hands around in the air.

"It does not belong to Peyton. He's penniless. Even his own cartel kicked him out after he started using drugs again. He couldn't lead a horse to drink."

Three armed men with bulletproof jackets that read, *Policía*, rush through the front door. I see the body of one of the hulks lying on the front porch steps. I make the sign of the cross, without even thinking. They gave our lives for us. Unlucky bastards.

Blues Eyes sees me looking at the downed men. "Their families will be taken care of," he says coolly, and then begins talking to the police officer in Spanish. Whoever this guy is, he's smooth. I feel calmer in his presence, and Amelia can't stop staring at him.

Paul picks me up, spinning me around. His face is fierce, his body tense. I kiss him all over his face and neck.

"Thank God you're okay," he whispers in my ear, his voice cracking. He lets me down.

"Isn't that what I should be saying to you? You were the one with the gun to your head."

"I just kept thinking …" he starts, his eyes welling up.

I put my finger to his lips. "I know. Let's get out of here."

Paul and I make our statements to the police first, just as Rialdo and Karina come rushing in, screaming and babbling in Spanish. Karina hugs us, checking us over like a nurse herself. Our hands are bruised and cut and bleeding from beating Peyton.

He's her brother, yet when he looks at her, calling her name, pleading, she won't even look in his direction. She refuses to hear him, to acknowledge his existence.

In that moment, I think of my sisters and how lost I would be without them. I never allow myself to go there and want to take it back. I know I should stop thinking that not loving people will protect me. In the end, everyone has to go, whether I've loved them or not. Why not love them, unabashedly, crazily?

I leave Paul's side for just a moment to rush to my sisters and grab them for a quick hug. "If they're ever looking for three new Charlie's Angels, we'd have it in the bag."

Amelia doesn't want to let go of me. "Just don't say I'd

be Farrah Fawcett."

"Of course you'd be Farrah!"

Marlo laughs. "I don't know. I think my butt-kicking days are numbered. I'm a journalist for a reason. I prefer watching things from a distance."

"Come on," I goad her. "Tell me you didn't enjoy kicking that guy's ass after what he did to Elizabeth and Dimitri."

"Fine." Marlo makes an inch mark with her thumb and finger. "Just a little bit. But that was it. We go home now."

"Absolutely not!" Amelia says in the most big girl voice I'd ever heard from my lil sis.

"Get real, Amelia. Taryn nearly died of an infection and then we all nearly got killed this afternoon. I don't trust this place. Just like I said from the beginning. I don't trust any of this."

Tears rush down Amelia's face as the paramedics rush in. "Go then. Turn your backs. This has only made me want to meet her more. Leave me. I don't care!"

I'm not sure if it's because I nearly saw my beloved get his brains blown out that has turned me into a big softie, but as much as I'd like to go back to my old life with a renewed sense of it all, I can't leave my sister. I know our journey is not supposed to end here.

"I'll stay," I tell her.

"No!" Marlo argues before a paramedic blocks her view and starts tending to her wounds.

She may be used to us talking back to her, but in the end, she normally got her way. Not this time. I know how badly she wants to run. Who knows what could lie ahead. I don't believe in the bullshit about bad stuff happening in threes, but the wicked side of me kinda wants to hang out to see what the hell kind of doozy that number three would be to top what we've already been through so far.

Marlo may not realize it, but she needs to exorcise a few demons of her own. She'll come around.

As soon as the paramedics bandage us up and we give our statements to the police, Paul and I take Rialdo's car, no hulk driver by our side. Just us against the world.

Blue Eyes rushes out, just as we begin backing out of the long driveway. The brakes squeal. I never even got his name, or what he has to do with our journey or our mother. Too young to be her lover. And way too young to be a Keeper.

Paul rolls down the driver's window. "We'll be back," Paul says to him.

"We think it's not a good idea to stay here tonight."

You think? Geniuses, the whole lot of 'em. That "we" again. Is he doing mental telepathy with our mother or what?

"The guy who wanted us dead is going to jail," I tell him. Who else haven't they told us about?

"Word will hit the street. Who knows what could happen."

Paul shrugs and offers his handshake. "Exactly. We appreciate your concern man. We'll find a hotel and meet up with you tomorrow. If I can't talk her into going back to the states with me, that is."

I love that he wants me to return home, but I'm even happier that he'll be there when I'm good and ready. When my past is settled. When my heart is ready.

Blues Eyes takes a paper out of his jeans pocket and

scribbles an address on it then hands it to Paul.

"What is it?" I ask.

"*Chichén Itzá*. A nunnery."

17
AMELIA

"It's like a sorority of God girls," I say, as we enter the two-hundred-year-old nunnery the next morning, led by the head nun Sister Maria Cortez, who wears thin wire glasses and a traditional habit. Fine lines are etched in her soft face like notes in a prayer hymnal.

My sisters chuckle at my joke, but Rialdo and Blue Eyes ignore me. Sister Maria leads the pack, dropping the men off in the foyer, (no boys allowed) and taking us down the long hall of rooms. A holy dormitory of sorts.

"I hear you've had quite a time in Mexico," she says to us, unsmiling. "By God's grace you were able to join us."

Nothing like a near-death experience at the hands of a one-eyed lunatic to make you appreciate your life.

Karina is absent, heading back to the States on a red-eye flight, afraid that the police spread word that she's in Mexico. As unsafe as it was for us at the mansion, it is far worse for her; she is still a Santiago. So many people would love to punish her for the sins of her father. Paul has also left, and Taryn looks sad without him.

We have new guards, bigger than the hulks were, if that's humanly possible, but they remain outside the front gates, searching the great outdoors for intruders. I saw nothing for miles, except the occasional roadrunner and armadillo. No guns allowed in the hallowed chambers of the nunnery. The only reason Marlo stopped begging us to come home was because we were coming here. Any other place, and I swear she would've held on to our ankles until we gave in and went back home with her.

We're stored safely in the chambers of the Lord's heart, I think. What could possibly go wrong in this place?

Blue Eyes, whose real name is Lucas Kenney, hasn't taken his eyes off of us, and I mean that in the paternal sense. He's our protector, though he lacks the ammo and the muscle to do much about it. Still, I feel drawn to him, and want to bring him out of his quiet shell. He's barely said ten words to us since he came upon our beat-down of Peyton. I wonder what might have happened if he hadn't stopped us. If it was God's grace that brought him there in that moment – to save us from killing a man – to save a man from death.

Maria leads us down the path flanked by flower gardens kept up by the nuns who live in isolation there, sixty miles from the city. I have no idea why we're here, but it sure as hell beats the prison. The warm terracotta building looks inviting, if not comfortable.

We each carry an overnight bag, and I wonder why they would let someone as unholy as me in this place. Doesn't my body reek of sin, even after my absolution? Yet Maria doesn't look upon us with scorn or judgment. A relief.

The early morning sun rises over the expansive ten thousand square foot building, shards of light piercing through the windows. On the way, Rialdo had told us this is where seventy-five nuns, ranging in age from twenty-five to ninety-eight, call home.

The nuns are in silent morning prayer, so the place is quieter than quiet, with a stillness that causes you to catch your breath. I've never been very good at being alone. I fill my days and my nights with as much noise as possible.

Through the alcove, I see the cemetery plot full of more than two hundred grave markers. When these women die, they don't have far to go, unless you consider the trip to Heaven. Even then, wouldn't they get a one-way rocket shot? Skipping the whole purgatory bit?

Maria leads us in silence to the guest quarters, where visiting nuns usually stay, but I can't hold it in. "Are we the only sisters who aren't Sisters who have stayed here?" I ask.

Taryn and Marlo give me the dumb-question look, but I can't help it. I want to know why we might be the exception to the rule. I don't think I've ever been the exception before in my life. I've done whatever I could over the years to be accepted. I wore the right clothes, hung out with the right crowd, went to the right college, joined the right sorority. I've never known what it might be like to let all of that go – to not care what anyone thought of me. I didn't think even God could love me without a full face of makeup on.

"Father Castillo has arranged it. As it was, it is again," she says in a Mary Poppin-esque fashion.

Her eyes sparkle, but I can't for the life of me think how living here – without men of all things – could make anyone's eyes sparkle. Then I remember: they are brides of the Lord. I recall my penance: chastity. At least here the temptation has been removed. I don't let my mind think about the man in the corridor, the elusive, mysterious, impossibly handsome Lucas.

One sweep of the simple interior proves it's been stripped of material things, save the absolute necessities – a bed, linens, a dresser, a cross nailed to the wall- and I ache for the luxury of the mansion.

Three small twin beds line the walls of the room, the only light from a single lamp in the corner and a small window looking out on a desolate meadow. Only the tall sunflowers swaying in the wind provide a burst of color to the otherwise dull landscape.

"Lunch will be served at eleven," she says. "Praying makes us hungry early."

"What do you pray about?"

I see Marlo reach for her notebook and Taryn takes her camera out of its bag. Sister Maria folds her hands below her waist. "Everything under the sky," she answers. "Your guest will be waiting for you in the courtyard when you're ready."

With that, she closes the door and I fall back on the small bed. So much better than staying in a cell, surrounded by prisoners. Yes, I would take the nuns any day. I realize my discomfort has to do with not liking to be alone. Would that ever change?

"What in the world?" Taryn says with a sigh. She's not acting like herself, hardly said a mean thing all day. Still in some sort of love coma from spending the day with Paul the day before.

"Think our mother is here?" I ask, stretching my legs.

"A nun? I hardly think so," Marlo says, scratching notes.

"What if?"

Taryn lays back and closes her eyes. "Can we not play the what if game right now? I didn't get much sleep last night."

Marlo throws her notebook at Taryn. "Do tell."

"Talking about sex in a nunnery? This place is wired. Directly to the Big Guy in the Sky." Taryn laughs.

"Like you care," I add.

Taryn makes a zip motion with her hand to her lips, so we head out to the courtyard, a haven within a haven, to meet the special guest we were promised by Rialdo this morning.

To my disappointment, the woman in the habit is too old and too brown to be our mother. I smile through my sadness. I've grown tired of the wait, too impatient and so ready, so completely ready, to meet her. What more do I need to learn? Whatever it is I want to learn about it from my mom, in person.

What my mother had been missing all of these years only I could give her —a mother-daughter hug. As we step closer, the nun stands, and I know her, just as I knew Peyton.

She bows her head, no touching allowed, her big brown eyes fluttering beneath the headgear. "Girls, I am Sister Lucia Santiago. So very nice to finally meet you."

We stare at Lucia as if she's a mirage. My mouth drops, but one stern look from Marlo and I close it like a trap. I can see from the surprise on my sisters' faces that finding Lucia here seems somehow less likely than even our mother. A drug lord's wife? Absolution must pack a powerful punch.

"Please, sit," she says, softly. The way of the nuns. Speak softly, pray fervently, love fiercely.

We take a seat in the garden chairs, seated a few yards from the prayer labyrinth behind Lucia. "You must be in a bit of shock," she says in broken English. "First, let me begin by saying how sorry I am for what my son did to you yesterday. Lucas told me how very brave you girls were. Thank you for not killing him."

My face burns with shame. How do we respond? You're welcome? I mean, *awkward*. I clear my throat, feeling it thicken. I feel remorse for the pleasure I'd gotten in beating him. Marlo's face reddens, her words echoing in my head, *"why shouldn't we finish him off?"* In that instant I saw the Marlo I'd always known – the big sister who would go to any lengths to protect us.

"He's a troubled man," Lucia says. "Drugs change you."

Marlo leans forward, her elbows on her knees. "You would know that more than anyone, wouldn't you? Isn't that how you lived your grand lifestyle?" Perfect journalistic pitch.

Lucia nods. "I'll face the Lord on my judgment day. My past no longer defines me," she says coolly. "The only reason I revisit it now is to fulfill your mother's wishes. I want you to know that I loved your mother like a daughter. I saw her arrival as divine intervention. She gave Dimitri strength when he was weak. Rocco is a hard man to say no to."

"You say, 'is.' Is he still alive?"

"Rocco is in prison. He'll live out the rest of his life there unless he's murdered first." Her voice cracks.

"You still love him don't you?" I ask.

"He may have been a hard man, but there was a soft side that he showed only to a few. "

I flinch, knowing all too well how easy it is to love a

sinner.

Taryn pulls her knees up to her chest. "How did you get here?"

"Your mother convinced me to join her."

"Join her? Here?"

"Father Castillo did mass at the prison every Sunday evening and took penance. When she confessed what she'd done to Peyton, that she'd taken his eye and that she feared he would come back and kill her, he said he would pray on it and get back to her."

"He requested that she be transferred to the nunnery to live out the rest of her sentence there. A work-release program of sorts. Father Castillo is a powerful man and the prison needs him on their side."

"So in the end the Lord did help her more than Gonz," I say. I so wanted God to get the credit.

Lucia's gaze rests softly on me. "You look just like her. A spitting image. Each of you has something special of hers."

I fiddle with the rabbit charm, trying not to tear up.

"She took her vow of celibacy and committed to the convent. We don't hear much news from the outside, but Father Castillo told her of Rocco's arrest, that he feared for my life. She begged him to let me join her. It was an easy choice for me. I've always loved the Lord first. Not that it was easy to divorce Rocco or leave my home. I cried myself to sleep every night for months. Just as your mother had done in prison."

"Isn't this just the easy way out?" Taryn asks.

"Perhaps. But I would've been living in a prison of my own making if I'd stayed. I can't say I didn't enjoy the power and the prestige. I flew to Paris for fashion shows. Rocco and I spent every anniversary in a quaint Italian villa. I was delusional. I thought I had the perfect life, but it was all a lie. I felt like if I was a good Catholic, gave to the poor, went to mass every day, said my rosary, that I would not be held liable for our crimes. And when I lost Dimitri, I thought I lost everything. Karina was already gone to the States and Peyton was lost to the drugs."

"Why weren't you thrown to the lions along with your husband, then?" I ask.

"I didn't do anything with the business, and that's the truth."

Denial. It's a beautiful thing until it bites you in the ass.

"What's it like being a nun? Isn't it lonely?"

"Loneliness is only a state of mind," she answers. "Even those who are all alone can be filled with the Spirit, as I am. But I have the friendship of the Sisters to keep me grounded."

I begin thinking of all the things I'd have to give up to live a life of poverty, not to mention chastity. Except my lifestyle is all pretend. Living in an apartment my married lover pays for. The rest funded by bar tips and credit cards to keep me in fashionable clothes and gym memberships and spa appointments. Make that denial, party of *two*.

"Is that why you're selling the mansion?"

Lucia stands and hands each of us a small linen bag, tied with raffia.

"Give and it shall be given to you. When Rialdo sells it, we'll be able to help a lot of people. It's why I haven't taken the low offers we've received so far. Do you know how many loaves of bread you can buy with just twenty dollars?

Now multiply that by thousands. You can see why I need the best price possible."

"I'll leave you with your new charms. You'll find its meaning on the first page of the journal. I'll see you at lunch. The Sisters are all looking forward to meeting you." Lucia hands me a journal, bright pink, shocking against the black cloth of her robe. I take the journal and hug it to my chest.

As she leaves, we open the small bags. I shake mine, and smile. A tiny silver armadillo sits sturdily in the palm of my hand.

"He's an ugly little bastard, isn't he?" Taryn says. "That'll be interesting ink for sure."

"Don't even think about it!" Marlo says.

"Chill. Not until I get out of Mexico."

"I think he's cute." I hand the journal to Taryn for her to read while Marlo and I add the armadillo onto the charm bracelet next to the eagle and the rabbit.

May 15, 1998

I got a strange greeter when I arrived at the nunnery. He was short and stodgy, reminded me a bit of Rialdo and was the dirtiest brown color I've ever seen. He looked like the poor progeny of an anteater crossed with a tortoise and porcupine. I'd never seen one in person before.

During the whole drive to the nunnery with Father Castillo, I was plagued with worry. Sure, it paled in comparison with my daily worry of being knifed or raped again. As happy as I was to be out of the prison, and out from underneath Peyton, I was scared about life with these women who had given up everything for the Lord. I knew how to walk tough and talk tough, but inside my heart had hardened as solid as a rock. I worried they'd judge me — see that my faith had been shallow. The prison had changed me. My heart was beyond calloused. How could I live within the confines of this holy place without burning up in flames?

The armadillo seemed to be waiting for me. "Looks like you've made your first friend."

"He probably talks a lot less than Gonz," I'd said.

When Father left with a final, "Peace be with you," I tried to carry it with me like a locket and silently thanked the armadillo for his message.

See, during all those weekends sitting atop the Pyramid of the Sun, we often heard tour guides telling tales of Mayan legends, and the armadillo was known as one of the creatures of heaven.

The legends say the first armadillos were created to teach a lesson in humility to a couple of minor gods. The Maya Sun God Hachakyum sat the two egotistical deities down on a bench before all the other gods. Suddenly the bench transformed into a pair of armadillos, which jumped up in the air causing the two ungrateful gods to fall onto their butts in disgrace.

The armadillo wasn't there by chance. Nothing is, really. I can check my ego, and my past, at the door. I don't have to have all the answers. I don't have to be prisoner-tough. I must only be humble before the eyes of the Lord, and before these kind women with whom I'd live. I don't need to be tossed into the air any more than I already have to get that lesson. I suppose my new armor is supposed to be this place.

But I knew the first thing I would do in my new "freedom."

Write my girls without the shame of the prison return address on the outside of the envelope.

Taryn looks up from the pages, and we see three nuns

begin walking the labyrinth in the near distance, as they whisper prayers on their rosary beads. "What do you think Dad did with the letters?"

"Threw them away," Marlo says, standing and stretching. "No way he would've wanted us to stumble on them."

"Why not just read them to us?"

"You can't be serious. That would've made a nice tuck-in. My darlings, your mother has written us another letter from prison. Sweet dreams!"

I shake my head. "I don't think he would've thrown them out. He could've edited the information. Just to let us know that she was thinking of us. It would've changed everything."

"Would it? Or would it have made you want her all the more?" Marlo walks over to me, her hand resting on my shoulder.

I can't stop the tears, and I don't want to. "I don't think it's possible for me to have wanted her any more than I did. As much as I loved Cecelia, I knew the difference. When I saw her with her twin boys, I noticed that she looked at them differently than she'd ever looked at me. I knew she loved me in her own way. I still believe I'm her only girl, but when she left Daddy, she loosened the slack. She let me drift away from her and I didn't feel her trying to tug me back in. From then on, I wanted my mother. Our mother."

"We know you did, sweetie," Marlo says, her arms now wrapped around me. One of the nuns, a young one, about our age, has stopped and is watching us. I know she is curious. She must not have known our mother or our story.

Just three weeping sisters in the gardens. I hope she'll pray for us.

Taryn punches my thigh, her way of showing affection. "Look, sport. Daddy hated her for leaving us. He probably wanted to get back at her."

Marlo adds, "It's a father's job to protect his children. He thought he was doing what was in our best interest."

I jump out of the chair. "Like screwing around on his wife? How is that in our best interest, huh?"

"Shhh. Calm down."

"Don't shush me, Marlo. Do you know how sick and tired I am of you telling me to calm down? I don't want to be calm! And if that means shouting at the top of my lungs, then by God I'm going to do it."

The nuns have all stopped walking the labyrinth, their special messages to the heavens short-circuited by my scream. "I'm sorry, Sisters." Then I run, down the long halls, past the men waiting for us in the foyer, through the startled bodyguards and out into that meadow, headed for the sunflowers.

I sit among the stems for what seems like hours, closing my eyes and feeling the sun slide across my face and finally land on my back with the warmth of God's hand. I feel Him. I'm sure of it.

I'd missed lunch, but I don't care. My sisters know enough not to come and get me. They hate when I get this way, but it's like a switch is flipped and I can't flip it back off again.

If I know anything about the sun, it must be late afternoon by the time Lucas walks toward me. He's too preppy to be a guard, too handsome to be a private eye, too cool to be an accountant. Who is he to my mother? To us?

My stomach growls, but I have too much pride to go back in there and face anyone. I'll need to apologize. You'd think I'd be so good at it by now.

Lucas sits down next to me in the grass and removes his sunglasses. "I've been meaning to get out here sooner, but the women in there have been all over me."

"I can't believe you said that! That you said anything, really, but especially not that."

"Can you imagine the fights the Sisters have when it's Culligan man day?"

"Stop!"

"Sorry." He opens a small brown paper bag and hands me a turkey sandwich and an apple.

"I'm starving."

"I suspected. Your sisters told me you were upset and that you required a long cooling off period. But I was curious how one cools off when it's ninety degrees outside in direct sunlight."

"Good point. I guess it's your job to come out here and make sure I haven't gotten sunburned to death or attacked by a herd of rabid armadillo?"

He shrugs his round shoulders. I want to lie in the grass and count the constellations of freckles on his fair skin. I remove the straw cowboy hat from his head and stick it on mine. "That's better."

He looks at me, shrugs and searches my face, opening his mouth and then closing it again. I can tell he wants to say something.

"What is it?"

"Nothing."

"No. What? Am I as a red as a crab or something? Tell me."

"It's nothing, really. I'll let you get back to it. In closing, it is air conditioned in there. And an ice-cold pitcher of tea is waiting for you in the dining hall. Not that you'd be interested in either."

"I don't succumb easily to bribes."

He gets up, dusting off his beige shorts. His legs are long and muscular. Big thighs, round calves. "You must be a runner," I say to him.

"Five miles a day," he says. "Just to unwind."

"Me, too. Will you run with me in the morning?"

He looks at me in that way again, a twinge of … something, then looks away, down the row of sunflowers and beyond. "I don't think that's a good idea."

"Because you're the shepherd and I'm the sheep?"

"Something like that."

"What better way to protect me than to be right by my side?"

"It's not that easy." He gets up, but I grab his hand. It's warm and strong, and I yank on his middle finger.

"Who are you, Lucas Kenney? Stay awhile longer." I hate the pleading whine in my voice. I recognize it from all the times I begged Alex to stay a little longer when I knew I should let him go. How painful to watch him get dressed so he could return to his wife and to kiss his baby girl.

The memory helps me to release Lucas. "Fine. Go."

He jogs away, as if he can't get away from me fast enough.

18
MARLO

A nun's day begins at the break of dawn. Morning prayers. A simple breakfast. Mass. Hymns. Chores. Lunch. Prayers. More chores. A light dinner. Evening worship and an hour to recreate before bed. Board games, spiritual reading. It may not be prison, but it certainly is regimented. And nothing like the fantasy life I had created for my mother. I'd envisioned her on big adventures, and though she'd lived in Paradise and resided in a heavenly mansion, her life so far seemed far worse than the deaths I had imagined for her.

The one thread of consistency between my bad thoughts growing up and the life revealed to us through her Keepers and her diaries is this: she has played the hero as much as the victim.

I try to swallow the belief that I had somehow caused all those bad things to happen to her. I didn't curse her to Hell. I was just a kid. But I didn't pray for her, either. I damned her in the way only a child's mind is able. I told her, repeatedly, how much I hated her. I shouted it to anyone who would listen. My teddy bear. The same tree in the backyard I'd lain under with her. The clouds in the day and the stars at night. Wherever she was, I thought she should know how I felt. Of course, I told my father. He told me I shouldn't, but that glint I saw in his eye was the hatred he had for her, too. He couldn't defend her completely.

No. I didn't cause this. She chose this life, and one

thing led to another. Isn't that the way it is? I'm not saying she got what she deserved, because, well, I'm not that evil. I'm glad she was strong. A survivor. She was as brave as I imagined she might be. And less selfish than I'd thought. I still couldn't like her, and found my heart still filled with too much rage even after we'd seen everything that had led us to this place.

I understand her heart-as-a-rock problem. How had it softened? Are prayers some sort of tenderizer to a tough heart? Does isolation work wonders for worry instead of multiply them?

I want to go on a nun diet. A spiritual fast. Whatever this place is, I need to eat and drink and breathe it.

The nuns are nothing like I'd imagined, either. I expected a quiet succession of graying women with reverent expressions walking in line to Communion wearing their black uniforms like penguins heading out to the sea. Instead the women are just regular girls from the block. Mother Sister Maria is the most serene, and probably stern if this place calls for such a thing. How hard can it be to keep a bunch of nuns in line?

"They're unruly," Sister Maria tells us at dinner, and the sisters howl around her. It's men's poker night without the men or the poker. There is booze, though. Wine, but not the watered down kind they serve at mass. This is the good stuff. They don't indulge, *much*. But tonight is special. Former Sister Elizabeth's children have joined them, and so we get the best wine they have to offer. A vintage Shiraz from Sonoma, 1998, the year our mother came to live in the nunnery.

The round table seats ten, with eight total tables in the large, open dining hall. A single sunflower adorns the vases in the middle of the table, thanks to Amelia's thoughtfulness. She had counted the tables during our tour and didn't want to return empty-handed from her meltdown.

It seems Sister Maria and Sister Lucia have taken special care to invite the right grouping of women to the hostess table. Sisters Phoebe, Therese, Ruth, Naomi, and Eve.

Lucia is by far the most glamorous, like the rich woman dressing up like a nun for a charity Halloween party. Years of great skincare and designer hats to protect her skin, I imagine. Sisters Phoebe and Therese are sisters, dropped off at the nunnery when they were eighteen and twenty, respectively, by their father. Therese's husband had left her for another woman, and unable to have children, she decided not to try to marry again. Their mother had died in childbirth and Phoebe couldn't stand the thought of being separated from her sister, and so she gave up a future life of poverty with husband and children to pursue a life of poverty without them. The women were now in their '40s and quick with jokes and compliments.

Ruth is a published writer with a regular column in the Catholic News & Opinion, heavy on the opinion. Naomi is the painter. "I make it a point never to put a cross or a rosary bead in any of my work," she says with pointed finger. Her artwork lines the halls, full of bright colors inspired by nature and her dreams. She promises to give us a tour after dinner.

Rounding out the group is Eve, the teacher, who didn't join the convent until her husband passed away, her children were grown and she retired from teaching.

The commonalities bind us together, and I imagine we could talk about anything. Docile couldn't be further from the truth.

Ruth is the chatter bug. "One of the high school volunteers set up an e-newsletter for me so people can subscribe to my column through the site. Before, the magazine distribution was only 10,000 in the United States. I passed 10,000 subscribers within the first month." Ruth's chest puffs up as if she'd just told a scandalous secret.

"Why do you think we call her Superstar? She has 100,000 subscribers all over the world."

"They rolled out a red carpet for me down the hall and up to my door," Ruth says. "I think my face was redder than that carpet."

Amelia laughs. "You gals are a riot. I just never expected nuns to have this much fun."

"What's not fun about living with a bunch of friends and doing the Lord's work?" Phoebe asks.

"It's nice to have my message reach people in their own homes, through their inboxes, but our primary purpose here is to pray for you to the great inbox in the sky."

"The 'you' meaning all people, right?" Taryn asks.

Sister Maria raises her fork. "We did a lot of praying for you three in particular when your mother was here."

I take another sip of wine, trying not to choke on it. "You prayed for us?"

Ruth refills her wine glass. "We know it was very healing for Elizabeth to put your names in the prayer log. I remember we prayed for your first day of school every year. We prayed for you to be filled with the Christmas spirit on the first day of Advent and to get what you wanted for Christmas."

"Well, it didn't work," Amelia adds, her hands beginning to shake, her mouth to quiver. "All I wanted every year was her. I don't think you ever grow out of that wish. And to not know whether or not she was dead or alive? It was torture."

"I'm so sorry," Sister Maria says. "I'm sure this doesn't ease your pain, but we just wanted you to know how much she thought of you."

Naomi smiles. "Remember how nervous Elizabeth was when Marlo turned sixteen? She didn't like the idea of you being on the road with all those crazy drivers. And boys, oh my, she was up many a late night worrying about boys."

"And I taught her to knit one winter," Therese muses. "First thing she says is, I want to knit scarves for my girls. We must get three of them done before Christmas! She was terrible at it at first, but she used every social hour getting them done to get them to you before Christmas. Did you like them?"

Amelia sucks in her cheek, her eyes welling again.

"We didn't get them," Taryn says curtly. "Apparently she sent us letters and drawings and scarves, but we didn't get anything. Okay?"

"Oh, you poor dears," Ruth says.

Taryn throws her napkin on her plate. "Just for grins, let's say our mother had come back to us instead of joining the convent or wherever she went next, then she could've made us those scarves while sitting in our warm living room next to the fireplace, and after Daddy died, Amelia wouldn't have had to go live with Aunt Darla."

Lucia raised both hands towards Taryn. "It's not like that," she says. "Before the crash, she was hopeful. She tried to be tough on the outside, but we knew how much pain she was in. She was afraid she had nothing to offer you. That her time, her one chance to be a mother, had passed."

With my eyes, I plead Taryn to sit back down, and she does. I try to soften my voice; afraid we'll hurt their feelings. "All we mean is that if she'd had seventy-five nuns praying for our father, maybe he would've lived. But I guess Karina had stopped spying on us by then. If you'll excuse me."

I scoot out my chair, knocking over my water glass in the process. I've already grown tired of seeing pity in their eyes, and I'm sure we're bound to wind up in their prayer log again.

"Are you okay?" Lucia asks, coming around the table to console me.

I feel faint just looking at them. All those nights I'd lain in bed wondering where she was, and she was here, *praying* for God's sake. "I haven't been sleeping very well. If you'll excuse me I think I'll retire to my room. Eve, I'd love to see your paintings tomorrow." I look to my sisters, who are about to dig in to their homemade apple pie. "Are you coming?"

Amelia picks up her fork, her earlier tears dried, her shakes gone. Well, that was quick. "I want to hear some more about Mom."

Taryn shrugs her tiny shoulders. "I better stay with Amelia."

"Of course."

I head back to the room, praying, actual honest-to-God praying that I could lay my head down and sleep. Could God not grant me that one tiny request? To sleep and rest my weary mind? I won't even ask for the big stuff yet, like how to fix my marriage or stop obsessing about Peyton's attack or Taryn's near death experience or that Shane is doing just fine and dandy without me.

As I remove my shoes and lay down on the bed, my cell phone vibrates. A text message from Shane. "Going out with the gang."

I'd been hoping for the greatest proclamation of love via text ever. "I MISS U & CAN'T WAIT 2 MAKE MAD LOVE 2U WHEN U RETURN".

I need that damn armadillo bench to kick my ass up into the air and shake the ego out of me.

I groan. I don't even want to know where they're going or what he'll be wearing or what *they'll* be wearing or how great he'll smell or how close he'll sit next to the girls or how many times he'll smile at them or if I'll come up in the conversation at all.

And, finally, I drift off.

Two hours later, a light rap at my door wakes me. I wipe the drool from my mouth, amazed that I've slept at all and lift my head, marveling that it feels like a bowling ball. But I slept! Two whole hours. Who knows how long I could have gone had I not been interrupted? I want to stake the person at the door with the cross on the wall.

I open it, the heavy wood creaking, revealing the small, young woman who stared at us in the garden earlier. A teenager, no more than sixteen or so.

"I'm so sorry to wake you. I had no idea you'd be sleeping."

I rub my eyes. I must look like death warmed over, and I did retire at a toddler's bedtime. "How can I help you?"

"Where are my manners? I'm Rebekkah Gonzales. I go to an all-girls school in Mexico City and volunteer here on the weekends." She pauses. "My mother was Maria Gonzales."

I stare at her blankly, slowly waking up. Gonzales? My eyes widen. *Gonz.*

"You were Gonz's daughter?"

"I was a prison baby," she says to me. "Elizabeth was like a mother to me."

I can't help it. My brain still isn't talking to my hand. I close the door in her face and crawl back in bed, cocooning myself under the quilt and shutting out the world again.

I am certain I've gained some Heaven demerits for that one, but I don't care.

"Where's your next Mexico piece?" Ken asks the next morning on the phone. Amelia has gone for a run, stirring up a fight with the bodyguards who demanded that one of them go with her.

She said they would only run behind her and stare at her ass the whole time, so Lucas agreed to run with her. Taryn went to the craft room to paint with Eve, and I took my laptop to the foyer, the only place where I could get an Internet connection.

"It's coming along slower than expected," I told him. "But did you like the papantla flyers and the Spanish cuisine with the drink recipe?"

"They were beautiful, but that was this week's column. I've got a big white space with your name on it. I need something by noon."

My silence speaks volumes.

"Is there a problem?" Ken asks, as compassionately as he can muster, but then again he's an old school journalist, not a nun.

"No, sir. It's just..." I consider telling him about the attack and the dead bodyguards and being stuck in the nunnery, but there's time for that later, after deadline. Ken's not a sentimental sort, which is why I like him.

I think about the resemblances between the prison and the nunnery and the one person who has first-hand experience with both. I don't want to talk to anyone who says the woman who *unmothered* me was like a mother to her, but I have no choice. I have to do an interview and write the article in three hours.

"I've got an in-depth story for you," I tell him with a sigh.

"That's my girl."

I wonder how many heavenly demerits Rebekkah will get for pulling out of Morning Prayer to talk to a journalist.

"I took my first breath behind the walls of a prison and I hope to breathe my last behind the walls of All Soul's." Rebekkah sits with her hands folded on her knees, fingers worn from gardening and nightly knitting for Mexican orphans. Her voice is small, a perfect match for her slight physique. Impossible to think a tough-as-nails inmate gave birth to her.

I lean forward to hear her without asking her to speak up. It seems her whole life she has been told to be quiet, until it became second nature, her only nature. Prison, foster homes, an all-girls Catholic school and a nunnery.

Her mother: a legendary inmate. Her father, a guard, had raped Gonz and was killed by her mother's hands just days before her birth, ensuring her mother would live out the rest of her days in prison. She still corresponds with her by mail. I bet she even prays for her, too.

"Prison was just another word for home," Rebekkah says softly. "You may have grown up with three bedrooms and a kitchen and a back yard. I grew up in a house with five hundred cells, a dining hall and a rec yard. I learned only recently that moms decorate nurseries for their babies. I slept in a box beside my mother's bed. I have no baby pictures. The only photo I have from my childhood other than the prison-issued birth photo was taken on the day of my mother's cell mate's release."

Rebekkah pauses and pulls a photo out from the Bible she is holding and hands it to me. I catch my breath and hold it. My mother, beautiful and serene, though far from happy, hugs the preschooler, and looks into the camera. I can clearly see the bond between them and hate how jealous I feel. I try not to think that I would've been twelve at the time, when our health teacher had assigned us a report to interview our mother for our birth experience. After class

Mrs. Simpson had come to my desk, leaned over and said, "you can ask your father, dear."

I feel small suddenly, much smaller than Rebekkah or her Bible or her photo or the speck of dust on the stained concrete floor. "So by the grace of God she goes," I think. Created by two monsters. One who pledged to protect and serve, but ravaged inmates. Another who turned to drugs to self-medicate and profit and led the most dangerous prison gang in the history of the prison. A mother who told her cellmate to scratch out the eyes of her attacker and her commandments were followed.

How had such troubled souls created such goodness? *Surely* the grace of God.

"Why are you crying?" Rebekkah says, her brows wrinkling in puzzlement.

"I'm sorry." I wipe my tears with the back of my hand. "I've been so angry with you. All night long, really. She mentioned you in her diary. Often. And I was so jealous that she was the one that had held you and spent the first four years of your life with you. But then she left you, just like she left me."

Rebekkah reaches out her hand, and I take it. "But we're here, aren't we?"

19
MARLO

"Remember when I fell off the trampoline when I was eight?" Amelia asks, kicking the stones as she walks.

Taryn, Amelia and I walk arm in arm along the singular dirt road outside of the nunnery at dusk.

"I remember," Taryn says. "Daddy let you eat ice cream for dinner, you little drama queen. I figured you were just faking for extra attention." Taryn knocks her hip against Amelia's, sending me tumbling on the other side.

"I was bawling my eyes out, screaming in pain, and Daddy was just sure I'd broken my arm. But I didn't. Not even a sprain. *And* it got me to thinking that we had many falls and whatnot growing up but we never had any broken bones whatsoever. If you think about it, it's like some great umbrella hung over us, shielding us from things. I think our good health all those years was because our mother and the nuns were praying for us."

Taryn scoffs. "Umbrella? More like a dark cloud. Marlo, come on, talk some sense into our little sis here."

I stop and look at them earnestly. "I don't know. Amelia may have a point."

Amelia raises her hands in victory. Taryn shakes her head. "Unbelievable."

"Well, what do you have to lose to believe in the power of prayer? What if it really works? At the very least you believe in the energy of all living things. That the universe if full of matter, right? So prayer is directed thought, whether or not it's delivered to an omniscient being."

We turn around, eying the bodyguards waiting for us in the distance, and our Keeper duo, Rialdo and Lucas, talking just outside the gates. Before we reach them, Taryn sighs. "There's something I never told you guys. It's weird and I just thought I was dreaming it anyway. Besides, I was three sheets to the wind."

"What?" Amelia and I say together, stopping in our tracks.

"When I was seventeen, I snuck out of the house to see a biker dude you didn't know about. Ray. Total dickwad. Anyway, we were doing tequila shots at this shit hole bar and Ray gets so wasted he passes out cold, so I thought I could drive myself back home, thinking I'll take the lake road so there won't be as much traffic, or cops. The road was blurry, but I blasted the AC and blared the radio to keep myself awake. Sylvania Road has so many curves I struggled to stay in the lines, especially when I saw a few oncoming cars. The next thing I know I hear, "Taryn Elizabeth" and feel a hand shaking my shoulder. I slam on the brakes. I'd fallen asleep and gone off the road. My wheels were two feet from the drop off into the lake."

The hairs on my arm stand on end. "Who said your name?"

"I don't know. My heart was racing. I looked in the backseat. Empty. Outside? No one. Just the shimmery reflection of the moon on the water." She bites her bottom lip. "As crazy as it sounds, I thought it was our mother or a guardian angel. By the time I got home and snuck back into bed, I had convinced myself I'd dreamed it. It was just too hard for me to believe in either one."

Tomorrow, we'll leave for our next destination, but they won't tell us if it's our final stop, or if we finally get to meet the enigmatic woman who birthed us, left us, and enlisted the gift of prayer by the faithful for years thereafter.

Before bed, I ask for help of my own. For Rebekkah to teach me how to pray the rosary, something my mother had done, day in and day out for seven years at All Soul's. The sanctuary is quiet, and Rebekkah is breaking curfew to stay up to help me. We patter barefoot and genuflect, me awkwardly bending and making the sign of the cross before we slip into the pew, let down the kneeler and face the large painted cross of the Risen Jesus before us. I can't believe she'd rather spend her weekends here than back at the dormitory with her friends, but I know how it feels to not have a place to "go back home" like all your friends do.

The wooden beads of the rosary feel foreign in my hands, yet I follow Rebekkah's lead as she quietly explains the rosary's purpose to remember key events and mysteries and thank and praise God.

After each decade of beads, we say the prayer by the Blessed Virgin Mary at Fatima: "O my Jesus, forgive us our sins, save us from the fires of hell, lead all souls to Heaven, especially those who have most need of your mercy."

Especially those who have most need of your mercy.

Like the Santiagos.

Like Gonz.

My mother.

And even me.

Rialdo is crying like a baby when my sisters and I stand

outside the nunnery the next morning, the black Escalade waiting to take my sisters and I and Lucas to the airport.

"Please don't," Taryn says. "Crying makes me incredibly uncomfortable." This makes Rialdo smile and Taryn wipes his tears and wraps him in a big bear hug. "I have a feeling I'll smell your Old Spice in my dreams."

"Ah, you," he pats her back. "It is Armani, not Old Spice."

"Whatever it is," Taryn says. "Take it from one American girl and go easy on the stuff, 'kay?"

"For you, I shall consider this." He hugs Amelia, and Amelia can't hide the fact she's happy Lucas is going with us for the rest of our journey.

Rialdo sighs. "The Lord has blessed me. To spend the last week with such beautiful girls." He hugs me, his head coming just above my breasts, and I kiss him on the forehead. What a nice little round man.

"Good luck with the house," I say. "And thank you. For everything."

Lucia kisses our cheeks, all six of them, then holds my shoulders and looks me squarely in the eyes while my sisters are gabbing with Rialdo. "I meant what I said about your mother. We understood her, and accepted her, as is. There were times she couldn't leave her room. She'd be bedridden for days at a time, though the doctor could find nothing physically wrong with her. Eventually we knew it was just her way. We only expected of her what she was willing to give."

I swallow the lump in my throat, thankful my sisters didn't hear Lucia's confession. She still had days like I remembered. Our mother didn't belong in a prison or a nunnery. Surely she belonged in a mental ward. Where could she possibly go from here?

"Send a postcard," Rialdo shouts as we pack in to the SUV, Lucas holding the door open for us and one Mexican guard sitting in the passenger's seat.

Lucas grins, putting on his aviator shades, ready to get in to the driver's seat. "Rialdo, my friend, where we're going there are no postcards."

DESTINATION 3: KENYA, AFRICA
"THE ULTIMATE SAFARI EXPERIENCE"

"Western Kenya is an area of great geographic, cultural and natural diversity, offering tourists just as much, if not more, than many of Kenya's better-known tourist areas. Most travelers dream of finding a new and unknown destination, somewhere far from the beaten tourist path, where the thrill of real discovery and exploration reward the visitor with new and unexpected experiences, sights and sounds. Kenya's western region offers this and more."

—Magicalkenya.com

20
AMELIA

"We need those cool safari hats," I tell my sisters as we step out of the Jeep onto the flat, dry terrain near a village in Kenya. Somehow a baseball cap just feels *wrong*.

"Sure. Let's swing by the mall and get one for you," Taryn says in a Valley girl accent. "Oh, wait a minute! We're in the middle of nowhere. No malls!" She slaps her forehead. "Silly me!"

Lucas opens a brown leather bag and produces three khaki hats, to match the one he's wearing. He tosses them like Frisbees to us.

"What the princess wants, the princess gets," Taryn says as she pulls the hat onto her head.

"Now we're twinkies," I say, satisfied. "Remember how Cecelia used to dress us in matching dresses for Easter?"

"Don't remind me," Taryn grunts. "I've burned all photographic evidence. Damn, it's hot out here."

"It's the humidity." Lucas grabs a few more items out of the back of the jeep. Sunscreen, sunglasses, bug spray, our backpacks. Taryn snaps more pictures, though Lucas tells her to respect the privacy of the Maasai tribe. She must only photograph them with permission and must agree to list their names in the magazine, to not treat them like nameless wild animals.

"I think you're more like our genie than our Keeper,"

Marlo says, accepting the large, trendy sunglasses he passes out.

No label. Drugstore quality, but I want to pretend our mother picked them out for us. My sisters look nothing like Jackie O in the glasses and Taryn resembles a fly.

"I'm not your Keeper," Lucas says matter-of-factly. "But you're about to meet her."

My eyes sweep the landscape after pausing long and hard on Lucas. He's still a mystery and he wouldn't take the bait on the flight, answering my questions with short, sometimes evasive answers. He's extremely frustrating. I have a feeling he doesn't want me to get to know him, though I don't know why.

Sitting next to him, I tried to touch him as often as possible, our arms brushing up against each other, my elbow jostling his. My flirting techniques usually work like a charm, yet they don't seem to have an effect on him. My abstinence pledge is working, despite my best efforts otherwise.

The landscape stretches out for miles, golden dirt and distant hills dotted with ancient trees. Kenya is worlds apart from lush Hawaii and exotic Mexico City, yet breathtaking in its own right. Raw. Natural. I hear a stream in the distance, which must be why the villagers settled here.

On the long Jeep ride to the remote Maasai village of *Maji Moto*, meaning 'Hot Water' in reference to thermal springs close by, Lucas explained the dry climate, the diverse topography, and most importantly, that we would see the big five – elephants, giraffes, rhinos, zebras and lions.

We would spend an entire week here to experience the

cultural riches Kenya provides, along with learning the history of our mother in Africa. Unfortunately, though, we would be roughing it. My stomach churns at the thought. The last time I'd slept in a tent was with Alex, making love over a long weekend that was supposed to be a corporate fishing expedition with some vendors. My code name was "business."

We'd spent the weekend mating like wild beasts, next to the campfire, on the picnic table under the stars, on a blanket next to a rustling stream, and in the safety of the tent, over and over again as he whispered sweet lies about our future. He said I made him feel young, but I see now I could've been any hot, young big-boobed blonde chick. In fact, he was probably already banging some girl in my absence, setting up extra credit cards and cozy apartments for his next affair.

As we turned down the long, winding road to the village, I watched a leopard carry a baby orynx up a tree. The circle of life, indeed. It's so much cuter when Disney does it.

I take it as a sign and stop thinking about Alex. He was the leopard. I was the orynx.

Lucas takes a moment to explain the Maasai, Africa's most primal, independent tribe. They shun the modern world to keep their traditional rites and customs. Lord Almighty, I'd stepped into a *National Geographic* magazine. At least the journalist and the photographer would get a kick out of this. I can't imagine my mother living in a place that smells like dirt and sweat 24/7. Sure, the prison wasn't her choice, but at least it smelled like bleach. Lucas assures us we'll get used to the smell, but do we really want to?

We follow a small trail on foot. "I can't believe we're in freakin' Africa!" I grab my small backpack and follow Lucas's lead to the village a hundred meters away.

"So you've said. A hundred times since we landed," Taryn says, clearly annoyed.

"Remind me why you were never a cheerleader in high school," Marlo says to me, stepping in line behind us.

Taryn scoffs. "Too busy sleeping with the athletes."

Lucas doesn't even turn around to acknowledge he heard it, but I give Taryn a good push off the trail. "Is there some natural law I don't know about that says you have to be a mean bitch to me?"

Marlo must be tired of getting on to us by now, as she doesn't say anything, either, and Lucas doesn't stop for our spat.

I decide to ignore Taryn and hope the mosquitoes eat her for dinner.

A mild wind cools our sweat-beaded brows, but I'm overcome with the stench of a cattle farm back home in Kansas.

"Is that cow manure?" I ask, holding my nose.

"Among other things," Lucas answers, as if the smell doesn't bother him.

"Well, I remember reading in geography class that these homes are made with dung and sticks," I tell them.

"Nothing says 'home sweet home like a house made of shit," Taryn says.

I want to defend our childhood, but know it's futile. Taryn always has the best comebacks.

"We'll be in tents," Lucas says as we get closer to the

huts.

We hear the villagers before we see them. Loud music rolls through the village, catching on like a wildfire, beginning at one end and growing like a snowball until it reaches us. They sing in English, "We celebrate, we celebrate this day. Because I woke up and I'm alive."

"Is this some sort of holiday?" Marlo asks.

Lucas shakes his head. "It's like this every day."

"Every day? What do they have to be so happy about?" Taryn adds.

"The day starts and end with song. They're grateful." Lucas waves to a woman who is singing and clapping at the entrance of her hut, very happy to see us.

"The Maasai villages are called *Manyattas*," Lucas tells us as we view the low, round houses, twelve in all.

"Maasai mythology believes in a time when the earth and sky were joined together, until they were torn apart, leaving only the wild fig trees as bridges between them. God, called *Enkai*, sent herds of cattle down through the trees to earth."

A pair of goats stands on either side of the trail like stone lions at the entrance of a grand mansion. An elderly woman wearing a long red garment with yellow stripes walks toward us. Her hair is cropped short, her skin bluish black in the afternoon light. Her ears, ankles and wrists are strapped with colorful beads and a disc necklace hangs down her chest. Simple beige sandals adorn her feet.

She calls out to the other villagers, mostly women and children, who race from their afternoon activities to greet their western visitors. I feel like I've stepped into a documentary as I watch the colorful tribe with big smiles swarm us. They are not hungry or anxious like the children we met on the streets of Mexico City, but seem happy simply to see us. The singing continues, even louder, and I smile back, the universal peace sign.

The elderly woman, whom Lucas calls Asha, hugs him and kisses both cheeks. He has been here before. How many times?

Asha greets each of us with a hug, and repeats our names in English.

"Come. We have a-much to talk about," Asha says to us, surprising me with her dialect. Had Lucas taught her English?

None of the other women or children speak to us, though they stare at our clothes. We follow Asha to an open field behind the huts, where two trees provide afternoon shade. Four lounge chairs sit in a circle and several bowls and plates are covered with cloth. "Sit, please. You must be hungry from your long journey." Asha's eyes are bright and big, and a younger woman with a baby tied around her chest takes the cloths off the dishes revealing goat cheese, a loaf of bread, nuts and mangos.

I stare at the food, my stomach churning this time in hunger, but worry about refrigeration, germs, dirt, flies and all the reasons I hate roughing it. I'm a city girl, spoiled to the hilt by modern amenities. This place makes Kansas look like the Taj Mahal. Lucas nods and digs right in, filling his small bowl with the food, and my sisters do the same.

I'm suddenly very thirsty and I'm thankful we've packed lots of bottled water. I can't imagine not going to the fridge to refill my water glass whenever I want. What in the world was my mother doing in a place like this, with indigenous people? This place made the nunnery seem like a cakewalk, and the prison? Well, at least it had commodes.

I blink back tears, ashamed I can't appreciate this experience or feel as joyous just to be alive as these people do. Not many people get to see the Maasai culture. I fill my bowl, and think at least I'll lose the few pounds I gained in Mexico.

The younger woman, Kya, leaves us and Asha claps her hands together. "So you have a journeyed far in the search for your mother. I have a looked forward to this day for many years."

"Did our mother talk of having us visit Africa?" Marlo asks.

"Many a time. By the time she lived here, she was a mostly cut off from western civilization. She had a come here three summers in a row, as a part of a mission trip from the nunnery. Finally on a the third visit, she said she was being called to stay in Africa."

"Called?" Taryn asks.

"By God." Asha crosses her legs, something she says our mother taught her on her first visit. I shoo the envy. She'd left too soon to teach me the basic animal instincts a cub gets from her mother. I had to learn it all from someone else, and mostly from my sisters. I still hear the echoes of the "we celebrate" song in the distance. I try it on for size, but only in my head. *We celebrate, these sisters by my side. We celebrate, new friends around the world.* I'm trying.

"I can't imagine Elizabeth here," Taryn says, taking a bite of the mango.

Asha tilts her head. "Your mother was a hard worker. She liked simple living. She had a much to teach and we were a willing to learn."

My heart pounds in my chest. My mother, a teacher. Just like me. But how could she stand the heat? The mosquitoes? How had she so easily answered God's calling to help them, but hadn't been called to return to us? I'm not sure I could stand a week in this place, but I suppose I'd find out.

"How long did she live here?" I ask.

Asha claps her hands and stands. "Not here. Come. I'll show you. Your mother was our orphanage director for two years."

I see Taryn's jaw tighten. So this was where the nuns at All Soul's sent their knitted blankets. Marlo brushes off her bottom and Lucas helps me stand. I can't help feel the electricity from his touch. I meet his eyes, but he looks away.

It takes half an hour to reach the orphanage by foot. Well, everything is by foot. A long cement building stands in the distance, and a dozen children greet us in the yard, save one, who continues to swing on the lone tire swing on the tree. I'll bet the little tyke had to wait all morning to get her turn on the swing. I wouldn't give it up, either.

Since Asha's children are grown, she took over some of our mother's duties at the orphanage, accompanied by Kya, a young woman with energy to burn. Kya wears a bright blue garment with a red head wrap.

The orphanage is simple, two large bedrooms with ten beds each, three old wooden cribs and two wicker bassinets, each with sleeping babies. Asha makes the walk each day and sleeps over every third night to relieve Kya of night duties with the babies. They also rely on western volunteers—missionaries like Lucas, who comes at least twice a year to help out with the orphanage and bring supplies.

I recall Alex saying he'd done mission trips in Africa, but I know a man can do good work and do bad things, too. A good person can break a heart. Alex did. So did my parents.

The children are excited to see Lucas, who seems much more animated with them than he is with us. He relaxes and lets down his guard. I have no idea why he has to be guarded with us, except that whatever relationship he has with our mother, she has asked him to watch over us.

While my sisters play Red Rover with the children and Lucas, I follow Asha into the building and the small kitchen, which doesn't really resemble a modern kitchen as it lacks appliances. An open shelf houses pots and pans and tin coffee cups, and a pantry full of dried goods with white labels from all over the world—mostly Europe and the U.S.

A tiny fridge is plugged in to a generator for the goat's milk and medicine that must be kept cold, such as the HIV medicine for the AIDS babies.

Asha hums a song, grabs an old rickety step stool and climbs it to retrieve a notebook inside a plastic bag from the top shelf and hands it to me. My mother's journal.

My brow wrinkles. "She left it here?"

"Yes. Your mother saw no reason to take her journals with her. When it's out of her mind, and onto paper, she let them be."

I wonder if, when she wrote them, she had in mind that she'd share them with us someday, or if it was just therapy to put them on paper.

I hug the journal to my chest and instinctively respond to the baby's cry in the other room. I don't think. I just act, briskly walking to the bassinet and scoop up the tiny baby, bones mostly, a jaunt face with deep-set eyes the color of dark chocolate and a round Pooh tummy. Not an ounce of fat on him.

As I cradle the baby and hold the bottle to his mouth, I wonder if I'd cried before my mother left, if she'd known that the last time she'd kissed my baby-soft mouth, it would be the last. If I'd seen a tear fall down her cheek after I'd said, "Mama," and if it had made any difference at all if I had learned to walk by my first birthday so I could toddle after her and grab her pants' leg and not let go.

After her feeding, I take the baby with me into the sunshine to watch my sisters and the children play Duck, Duck, Goose. I still can't take my eyes off of Lucas. He is primitive and simple and gentle, much like this place. Yet he is strong, much like the lion guardians that make up this tribe.

As the sun sets, we've made the campfire and three tents. Kya invites us to stay in the orphanage, but I'm not sure with the sounds of all those children that I'll be able to sleep much, so we opt for the tents instead.

Marlo, the snorer, shall get her own, while I'll bunk with Taryn, and Lucas makes his own. We are just beyond the village, but not far enough out to be in any danger of wild animals. By nightfall, the stars are as brilliant as an LCD screen.

Lucas says he'll leave us to read in peace, but we insist he stay.

Taryn reads first.

August 22, 2001

Asha has taught me to do bead work, which I do by candlelight after the children have gone to bed. Like much about the Maassai culture, the beading is highly symbolic. With more than forty varieties, both women and men wear them. Red is the color of the Maasai, and you see it everywhere you turn. Blue beads are considered Godly, reflecting the color of the sky, and green is the color of God's greatest blessing, fresh grass after rainfall.

When Asha told me this, I recalled a memory from when Marlo was three. I'd had a particularly hard day. Taryn was crying non-stop from tummy aches and Richard had yelled at me before he left for work for not getting his laundry done. "What are you good for," he'd yelled. "Let me know when you figure it out." He dug a pair of britches out of the dirty laundry he'd worn the day before and wore them again. Shame seeped through my bones like poison.

He was right. I couldn't seem to keep up with the laundry or the dishes or the cooking or the babies. Everything was a mess. To make matters worse, I was feeling nauseous myself. Whatever Taryn had, she'd given it to me. But when Richard's sister Darla came over to help out after I told her how Richard had yelled at me, she said I looked faint and put me to bed.

"Could you be knocked up?"

"Don't even say those words, devil woman!" I'd laughed, but terror struck my heart. Richard often drank at night after work, just a six-pack or so, and demanded sex even if I didn't feel like it. He said I couldn't fulfill the most basic wifely duties. Sometimes he wore a condom, but often not. I couldn't even believe he wanted to have sex with me since he repeatedly told me how ugly I'd become. How I'd let my body go after having babies. Then he'd smile that handsome smile and I felt lucky he wanted to be with me at all.

He was stressed at work and he often brought his work home with him. His team kept missing their sales numbers, but he was the sales rock star. He could charm anyone into anything. His number one priority was climbing the corporate ladder. His dreams were so much different than mine. He painted a big landscape full of a big house in the suburbs and a BMW and a VP title. He told me he would win sales trips and take me away somewhere, someplace exotic like Hawaii or Mexico, to give me a break from the babies, but I just sighed. I knew not to get my hopes up.

I couldn't bear to look at the pregnancy test when it was ready and made Darla do it.

One worried look. "You're going to be okay."

She hadn't said it with a sigh of relief, but like a warning. I screamed, waking the baby again. Marlo was still in the front room watching the Flintstones, but ran to the bedroom to see what was the matter. How often I seemed to frighten the girl!

I don't think mothers should let their children see them cry too much, but I couldn't stop myself. Darla whispered in my ear that she would help me "take care of it." She knew I couldn't handle another baby. Not now. Maybe not ever.

"Don't cry," Marlo said, taking my hand by my middle finger.

She led me to the backyard where the spring sunshine was on full blast. Honestly I hadn't even noticed the sun was up that day, or that the days were growing warmer. In her other hand she carried a baby blanket from her bed and spread it out in the middle of our lawn.

"Come on," she said excitedly. She lay on the blanket, her full body fitting in the tiny space, whereas only my back fit on the blanket and the rest of me hung off onto the grass.

"That color is blue," she said pointing to the sky.

"Who taught you that?" I asked, astonished that she knew.

"Daddy," she said proudly. "Daddy teaches me everything." She

flopped over on her belly and ran her pudgy fingers through the blades of grass, freshly cut by Richard the night before. "And this is green. And do you know where the colors come from?"

My tears had dried from the wind. "Tell me."

"God has the biggest crayon box you've ever seen. He uses it to color the world."

The black cloud over my heart lifted for the moment. She was three and she got it. God colors the world, and gives us the gift of children. I didn't need Darla to help me take care of anything. I would take care of it by having the baby and somehow, someway learn how to be a better mother.

I shudder and look over to see Marlo crying. She quickly wipes her tears away with the back of her hand. "I don't remember it," she says. "I wish I did. It would be a nice memory to have."

Did Marlo know she saved my life before I was even born?

September 11, 2001

Planes have hit the Twin Towers in New York, the Pentagon in D.C., and another plane crashed, killing all the passengers aboard. Terrorists, they say. Orubi brought the news from a neighboring village. We have no outside communication here. I've been paralyzed with fear ever since that my girls could be there. Had they moved to New York for college?

No. Father insisted I leave all worries to Christ. Why is this so hard to do? My girls were probably not on any of the planes, but I am plagued by the future. After all this, I know have to add terrorist attacks on American soil to my long list of Could Be's. I must write to the Sisters at All Soul's and ask them to please put my girls back on their prayer list. This calms my fears.

I feel safer out here with nothing— no running water or electricity or phone service— than I ever did at home. It hits me. Home was not my home. This is my home, yet I doubt it will be my last. I will fast and pray. I don't know where I'm going but I know I'm not quite there yet. I feel like my future will visit me soon and show me the Way.

I pass it to Lucas, but he passes it on to Marlo. He doesn't look uncomfortable hearing these things. I wonder if he's heard them before. If he has been my mother's confidante.

June 8, 2003

I awoke this morning with such an aching in my soul I was sure I'd been speared. The black night just before dawn keeps my nightmares prisoner, yet I return to them, time and again, like a fool to love.

I dreamt of Dimitri, and he was alive. I'd always felt he had survived the crash because I hadn't seen his body. I could feel his presence and I whispered into the dark.

"Is that you my love?"

I stumbled around for the flashlight I kept by my bed. My fingers clumsily clawed the wood floor, when a voice said, "Si. It is I, rayito de luz."

My shoulders shook, and I demanded that I wake. How could my dream go on? But then he was there, on my cot, holding my head in his hands, kissing away my tears and I gave in because ghost or hallucination or nightmare, I wanted this so much.

He made love to me on the cot and it was just as I'd remembered. His skin was hot, and my body trembled beneath him. Every cell within me lit up by his touch. Yet it wasn't like I remembered entirely.

He was thinner in this dream, with a short beard and longer hair. We lay there after and to my surprise, he did not disappear. I kept poking and prodding him, but he only laughed.

"Dimitri, is it really you?"

And by the faint light of the sunrise through the window, I could see he was no mirage.

"I told you nothing could keep us apart," he said to me, holding my hand in his.

And so before the children clamored from their sleep, Dimitri told me of his head injuries from the flight, the amnesia that went away after six months, and his ten years in prison for the crimes he had committed. His mother and father believed he was dead because Peyton had planted a burnt dead body at the scene, unidentifiable. The government kept Dimitri's imprisonment a secret, hoping to get Dimitri's help in building a case against his father, yet he refused. He'd been told I'd died, and he knew his father's guards were more dangerous than the government's. Really, he was dead either way.

Dimitri didn't know if my captors were from Peyton's gang, but he suspects they had stolen an ambulance to torture me before dumping me at the hospital where the police were waiting for me. Unfortunately, Tamira had died in the crash just as we'd been told.

When he was released and went back to the priest for his first confession outside of prison, Father Castillo told him that I was alive and in Africa at the orphanage.

He had no money and worked construction jobs to save for the plane ticket to Africa without ever telling his loved ones that he was alive. He still feared his brother would kill him.

Dimitri has shown me that there is nothing you won't do to get back to the people you love.

In the middle of the night, with Taryn curled up like a

sleeping jungle cat beside me, I unzip the tent and walk the five paces to Lucas's tent. No lions in sight. I unzip it as quietly as I can, and step inside, hunching over, careful not to trip over his sleeping body. The cover on the top of the screen is open, keeping out the mosquitoes but letting the light in. The moon shines softly on his face.

My tank top sticks to my flesh, my men's boxer shorts a breezy relief in the heat. I miss air conditioning. I miss my nightly bath. I miss the smell of the beach in Hawaii and the taste of fresh lime margaritas in Mexico, but right now what I miss most of all is this.

I sit on my heels, my hands on my knees, afraid to even breathe, and Lucas's eyes shoot open, his body jerking awake, lying on his back, shirtless, looking up at me in surprise and, I sense, fear.

Like an animal, I crawl on top of him, but he doesn't move. His body stiffens as I lay my body out over his, thighs on thighs, hips on hips. I run my fingers over his chest, his nipples hardening under my touch. His breath shortens.

I lift up, straddling him, aching to have nothing between us. I remove my tank top, revealing my bare breasts. He gasps and I feel him harden underneath me. This is the response I wanted from him in the sunflower field and on the plane and every moment in between.

Gently, I slide my body back down the length of his body. He's wearing khaki shorts, and I unbutton them, but he grabs my hand before I can remove them. He starts to speak my name but I cover his mouth with mine. His tongue is hot and explores my mouth with urgency. I press my breasts on his chest and my whole body comes alive.

Lucas pushes me up and away from him. "We can't." His eyes say even more: danger, confusion, lust.

"Don't you want me?" I whisper, hurt.

I sit back, crossing my arms over my breasts. He rests on his arms, nearly panting, staring up at me.

"I can't," he says, firmly. "Even if I wanted to."

"Everything is working fine," I tell him. I'm breathless and can't believe this may not happen.

"It's not *that*."

"What is it? Is it because you work for my mother?"

He exhales. "I'm a Buddhist monk. I've taken a vow of celibacy."

I laugh, and then remember my sisters can probably hear me, and I cover my mouth. "You're shitting me."

"Amelia."

"But you were so …"

"Into you?"

"Well, you were almost *into* me."

"You know what I meant."

"So that's why you've been so quiet?"

"We don't believe in senseless chatter."

"And why you've been avoiding me?"

"To avoid this."

"But what if this was inevitable?"

"You mean fated?"

I nod.

He shakes his head. "I want enlightenment." His voice is strong, assured. His eyes are intense but the lust has passed.

I put on my tank top and wipe away a tear. "Well, I guess it's for the best anyway. The priest said the penance for my sins was abstinence."

Lucas smiles. "I see you take your penance very seriously."

I flip him off, monk or not. "I'm not Catholic. I can't believe I just tried to seduce a monk! How do I go from sleeping with a married man to sinning with a monk? Why do I always fall for the wrong guy?" I throw my hands up to the air.

"May I share an observation?"

"Since that seems to be the main thing you do, sure."

"You don't just fall for the wrong guy – you fall for any guy. As if each conquest proves that you deserve to live. But then you feel worse about yourself than before. You like the thrill of the chase, which could be why you thought you loved the married man and you think you want me. But it isn't a game to win."

"I'm disappointed. I expected more from you than a slut-shaming sermon. And just so you know, in my humble opinion, climax is the closest one ever gets to enlightenment."

Lucas takes my hand. "I wish you could see that it's because I have feelings for you that I can't be with you. I want you to know you are worthy just because you are."

"Well, I'm sure you're heart's in the right place and all, but a self-help talk in the middle of the jungle wasn't what I had in mind." I bite my bottom lip. "Marlo and Taryn think I'm addicted to love. So being a professional in the abstinence department, what do you suggest?"

"Start with loving yourself and see where that goes." Lucas lets go of my hand.

He made it sound so easy. The bigger picture of love.

"Please don't tell my sisters," I say as I unzip the tent.

"Don't tell us what?" Taryn says from the tent over. "Stop your jabberin' and leave the monk alone for Christ's sake."

No secrets between sisters.

21
TARYN

Asha hands us the charms the next morning. I half expected it would be a charm of a cow or a goat, but thankfully it's the lion. In a prophetic voice, Asha says, "Africa is where your mother's strength returned to her."

She goes on to tell us Dimitri didn't like the indigenous life. The secular nature of this lifestyle reminded him too much of prison, being shut out from the civilization he had missed out on for ten years. He had so much he wanted to catch up on, yet he couldn't show his face again in Mexico. He wanted to visit his mother at the nunnery, but it was still too dangerous. Instead, he decided he must go to the United States to visit his sister Karina, who lived in New York. Naturally, he wanted Elizabeth to go with him. "We can visit your girls finally," he told her.

He wanted to get back to helping others and promised Elizabeth they would spend part of the year in Africa. It was her main stipulation before leaving. She had grown to love the orphans, and felt the familiar pang of abandonment as she said goodbye to them. Yet as she had done with her own girls, she left her orphans in good, capable hands.

With every breath in Dimitri's body, he would live life to the fullest and not let a second go by.

As Asha is talking, I can tell Amelia thinks all this is romantic, but it makes me want to puke. I'm not used to guys going to any length to get the girl back. I didn't think it really existed. Until Paul. He came for me. It blows my mind.

Gotta admit, I'm sucked in to the story, but I still feel more like a detective than a daughter. *Where In The World is Elizabeth?*

Life is short. Let's fly to Paris!

Life is short. Let's sail the world!

Life is short. Make amends.

Let go.

Forgive.

Move on.

Something about nearly dying had changed Dimitri. Something about losing what was most precious to my mother over and over again had made her strong. So what do you do? Where do you go? And why didn't she visit us five years ago?

And how does a handsome Buddhist monk who doesn't shave his head bald or wear a weird toga sheet fit into it?

Lucas throws our bags into the back of our Jeep. Monk Lucas. *Brother* Lucas. Poor Amelia. One look at my baby sister and I see she's a spurned, lovesick puppy. How does she fall in love so easily while I find it so incredibly hard? She's so humiliated this morning she can't even look Lucas in the eye. Fortunately he wasn't much of a talker to begin with, so at least that hasn't changed.

Amelia fakes it, putting on a smile and singing as if she hadn't thrown herself on him the night before. She teaches the young villagers a new song, clapping "Can't you hear the rumble, rumble, deep inside the jungle, jungle. Let's all go on safari and see how the animals live!"

Marlo, in chipper spirits because she'd actually slept through the night, begins singing it with her. Finally a lion guardian emerges from his house and Lucas agrees to translate so Marlo can get her interview for the magazine.

Since I can't get a tattoo for the time being, I ask Asha if she'll pierce me. Just two. But I don't want an ear piercing in the traditional place, the lobe, which is even forbade in the Maasai culture for girls until they are women.

Asha places the holes high on my ear. She puts the lion and armadillo charms on two earrings in less than a minute, both charms secured on my upper right ear, the armadillo on the bottom and the lion just above it. The charms tickle my ear as I turn my head, but I'll get used to it. Besides, it's only temporary until I can ink their images onto my permanent ankle bracelet.

I pack up a small bag full of beads in my backpack to bring home and sell in my tattoo shop. This news, which I didn't think was a big deal, causes the tribal women to cheer and dance around me. I look forward to helping the orphanage in a small way and help these people get more goats. Besides, it won't kill me to give back. In fact, it's been the one thing that's made me less angry over the years. It dulls the edges. Volunteering at soup kitchens, wrapping gifts to give to disadvantaged kids during toy drives at Christmas, teaching art workshops at the Boys & Girls Clubs every summer. I have so much; I never knew it before, but yeah, I do.

"Did you know it was love when you heard him speak Maa?" I ask Amelia as we stand by the Jeep waiting for Marlo and Lucas to join us.

Amelia curls her lips in and blinks back tears. "How could I be so stupid? Why don't guys just come right out and say it, you know? I just thought he was playing hard to get."

"And you like what you can't have."

Amelia sighs. "Do you think I have a problem?"

"Love junkie? Sexaholic? Maybe. I'm the last one to ask shit about love. But I have spent my time on the couch."

"I guess I should see another therapist. One that I don't end up sleeping with this time."

"Splendid idea. Get a fat, hairy female."

She waves away my idea in disgust. "You think Shane and Marlo will make it?"

"I don't know. I guess if you want something bad enough, you can make it happen. 'Thoughts are destiny' sort of thing."

"Like you and Paul? Didn't you feel closer to him after … you know?"

I swallow the insta-lump in my throat. Still can't talk about it. I nod.

"You think Dimitri and Mom lasted? After this I can't see her in a place like New York. Too … I don't know, busy and loud."

"Tough times can bring you together or tear you apart."

"Kind of like what it's done for us."

"Us?"

"You, me and Marlo. Brought us together."

I shrug, but know she's right. I hop into the passenger seat so Amelia won't be stuck riding next to the sexy monk as we wait for he and Marlo. I turn around and slip my glasses down my nose. "Look, since we're being all open and shit, I want to say I'm sorry I was so wrapped up with my band and my boyfriends after Dad died. I was looking for escape, but I should've paid more attention to you. I feel bad now that I wasn't there for you more. I shouldn't have missed your junior and senior proms."

"Just a stupid ball gown and gussied up hair," Amelia says, tears in her eyes.

"I know you and it was more important than that. That kind of stuff meant a lot to you, as it should've. I should've been there to snap your pictures and make sure your corsage didn't look too cornball."

"Marlo was there with the 'don't drink and drive' speech, so I think it was covered."

"Still. I should've been around more. I see that now. And I want to tell you how proud I am that you're letting Alex go. You deserve someone who can give himself to you completely. I'm tired of guys using you."

"Maybe I was using them."

"But no more, right? You're not half bad, kid. Don't ever think otherwise, you hear me?"

She smiles, her blue eyes shining underneath her blonde bangs. "I love you, too, Taryn."

Lucas and Marlo head our way. My sister raises her hand high in the air. "Who's ready for a safari?"

22
MARLO

I dreamt that Shane had been eaten by a giant crocodile that left nothing behind but Shane's favorite orange Nike shoes he liked to wear on rounds. I grabbed the shoe, hugging it to my bosom like a baby and chased the crocodile, begging him to come back. The him being Shane, not the man-eating croc.

I'd awoken in the tent the following morning relieved it had just been a dream, yet disappointed I couldn't turn to Shane in bed and tell him. Like some sort of Freud, he would dissect it, but I'm not sure I wanted him to.

Meaning: I'm leaving you.

Meaning: Another life is swallowing me whole.

Meaning: You don't hate my orange Nike shoes as much as you claim you do.

Alas, no cell phone service. I couldn't even text him my dream. Or tell him how much I loved him, despite the bumpy road or how different I felt in the two weeks without him – a little *less,* whatever that means. He might say my feelings don't change "the facts." Perhaps. But certain things are no longer gray for me. And the facts have changed.

Fact: I don't like sleeping in a mansion, a nunnery or a tent in Africa without him by my side.

Fact: After sharing a bucket with my sisters, I swear I'll never complain about sharing the sink with him ever again, or how he leaves the glop of toothpaste behind. As for the toilet seat lid? Leave it up! I really don't care. At least we have a toilet.

Fact: Our so-called "scheduled" lives seem pretty great after watching inmates get ordered around and nuns shooed into prayer time. Yes, he works long hours, but he comes home to me, doesn't he? As tired as he is at the end of the day (or morning, as it may be), he still manages to hug and kiss me, even when I don't feel very huggable or kissable, or even likeable for that matter. Why don't I let him know that I couldn't sleep until he's fallen into sleep beside me? I never told him I used to do that with my dad, first because he worked so late or he stayed out late with women or drank too much, then after when he got cancer and I listened to his raspy breaths, wondering if each would be his last.

Fact: My little "rituals" he makes fun of, like how I line up the food in the pantry in alphabetical order and put his shoes neatly in the closet after he's removed them seem kind of silly now. I suppose the world won't crumble if he puts the Raisin Bran where the Corn Flakes belong. I watched a ritual involving cow blood. Enough said.

Fact: I'll never again complain when he calls me from work to ask me to go out and get his soymilk and wheat bread, even after I've already gotten home. The grocery store is a five-minute drive. All my life I've kept things on a strict schedule. So much to get done. I like things in order, but I see that the only perfectionist I'm trying to please now is me. He doesn't need the house or our schedules to be as regimented as the one I grew up in. I like order in chaos, but I suppose a spontaneous schedule wouldn't be bad every now and then. Besides, a trip to the store is not exactly an hour-long walk to the well or a half-hour spent milking a cow, now is it?

Fact: My bad thoughts have nothing to do with him. He is the lead actor in them, sure, but he didn't cause them. I've had them all of my life, since I was a little girl. I know if I don't control them, they will swallow me whole. Just like that damn crocodile.

See, babe, I'm coming around. I may still get eaten by a lion on this trip, but dammit, I love you! If you haven't given up on me yet then by God I haven't given up on you.

I would tell him all of this, but we're two days from a good Internet connection, which gives me an extra day to get my next story written, but two days late – no scratch that – about *two years* late in telling Shane that I was a fool for letting fear get in the way of what could be a perfectly good marriage, with no perfection necessary.

When I look over at my sisters, Amelia by my side, bruised ego but otherwise in good spirits on our way to a safari, and Taryn in the front seat like a snake uncoiled, I see peace. There is something about "getting away from it all" that makes those pesky people issues melt away.

Asha told me people visit Africa because all walks of life are drawn to it, though they have no idea why. "It's one of the original homes of mankind," she had said, her voice wispy and light. "In Africa you are able to a free your soul."

And learn about ancient giant crocodiles that once roamed the land in the Mesozoic Era, over 200 million years ago. *She's* the real reason I dreamed of a crocodile, no Freud needed.

The ancient tribal lore fascinates me, but not as much as the vista from our unique viewpoint an hour later – from atop the hump of a camel.

The safari is led by Helena Hargatay, the owner of Wild Side Safaris, and her troupe of Samburu men, dressed in their ancestral garb, cardinal red sarongs which make the men look even more beautiful. They are handsome – high cheek-boned, pouty-mouthed, gorgeous skinned Africans.

On a rest, I pulled out my notebook to write a short sidebar piece while it was fresh on my mind:

Things to Bring to a Camel Safari
By Marlo Thompson

"It's not all tank tops and khakis. Leave your flip-flops at home. Cool clothes, a set of warm clothes, a light raincoat, two pairs of comfortable walking shoes or boots, hat, suncreen, sunglasses, insect repellent and a water bottle. You will be walking. A lot. Depending on the terrain, you can't always ride the camel. Don't forget to tip. The porter, not the camel.

You are now a nomad. If it's been awhile since you were last in college, this may remind you of how much you walked on campus from class to class and what great calves you had. (And how little you walk now and where your calves have gone.) You will travel in the morning and evening and rest in the afternoon. You may or may not be blessed by moonlight. If you are claustrophobic, you will relish the space. If, on the other hand, you fear being marched out into the middle of a faraway place and then left there, this may not be the trip for you.

This irrational fear is why I will tip better than my sisters or the elderly couple with us, The Professor and Mary Ann. Not their real names, of course, but they resemble the Gilligan's Island stars, just thirty years older. Besides, I'm terrible at remembering names.

Six camels accompany us – one for each member, minus our porters. Called "ships of the desert," the camels carry our supplies, lightening our load. I also can't remember their names because they are African, so Amelia names them after the Seven Dwarfs, minus Happy because, well, have you ever met a camel?"

*

"You need a breath mint there, big guy," Taryn tells Sneezy, her camel for the day as I put away my notebook. Camels suffer from halitosis, and you don't have to be within kissing distance to smell it, either.

Amelia can't get over how much the Samburu men's sarongs look like her junior prom dress. We have to hide our giggles every time the Professor and Mary Ann "ooh" and "aah" and "oh, honey." Amelia says it sounds like they're having simultaneous orgasms every time they shout. I've come to believe everything reminds Amelia of sex. Yes, I said 'come.' God, she's got my mind in the gutter now, too.

I like the old couple. For me they represent the ideal I thought I could never have – looking into the future and finding that by some strange force of nature you were able to stay married to one person for forty years and raise kids and spoil the grandkids and Jiminy Christmas, have enough money saved up for retirement that you can go on a freaking safari in Africa! I used to never believe that was possible for Shane and I, but the last couple of days, I've been reconsidering. What if? What. If.

Let me just get through my twenties first.

Grand, sweeping storyteller Helena regales us with another story of an African god. Amelia, who cannot for the life of her keep her mouth shut, has told Helena that we are on a journey to meet with our estranged mother, but of course she already knows this. Everything about this trip is pre-planned if not pre-destined. Helena took Dimitri and Elizabeth on this very same route five years earlier. I wonder if she is in possession of a journal, but she tells us that much like the ancestors here, the stories will be passed down orally. But first, she insists we know about Elegua. "The trickster God of Crossroads, Beginnings and Opportunity," she hisses with a smile.

Taryn and I look at each other and raise our brows. Amelia eats it up. She still loves story time.

"He is the Guardian of the Crossroads of Life. When there are decisions to be made, he provides opportunities and second chances."

"Then what's the trick?" Taryn asks.

"Elegua is child-like and can turn something that seems simple into something very complicated."

"Like the fork in the road," I ask.

"Exactly. Which way do you go? You become confused and then miss the opportunity you've been given."

I wonder what the Buddhist thinks of this talk of an African god, but don't ask. I'm still not convinced I want to meet Elizabeth when it's time. Now I blame Elegua. I'm confused.

Helena rarely stops talking, only long enough to take another question, and the Professor is full of them. He's done his research and wants to know about every bug, plant and animal along the way. It may be awhile before we hear those oral stories of our mother.

Mary Ann is more fascinated by Taryn's tattoos more than the life cycle of the spider monkey.

"I always wanted a tattoo, but didn't think it would be proper to get one," Mary Ann says, smoothing back her silver, shellacked hair. "I was always trying to please my parents. I was the do-no-wrong child who became the do-no-wrong wife. But I want a tattoo for me. Just me."

"Women your age get tattoos all the time," Taryn says. "In fact, seniors are a growing market for us."

"Is that so? In your professional opinion, what do you think I should get?"

I don't want to picture sweet old Mary Ann with a tramp stamp, the nickname given to the tattoos above the butt crack, so I slow down and walk with Lucas and Amelia instead. She's gotten over her awkwardness, and he's still not talking much, but Amelia doesn't care. She needs a listener. I resist the temptation to reach over and yank up her tank top, which is showing two inches of cleavage.

She's going on about her decision to teach and her new fascination with world traveling. My gut shrivels into a tiny knot. I inhale and try not to think about my baby sister on expeditions like this one, without me. She's asking Lucas about his travels, and he speaks. Actual words.

"I was a spoiled rich kid from the suburbs," he says. "So for my college graduation gift, my parents gave me a trip to Europe. And I haven't been back home since."

My shriveled gut turns to dust. How could the monk be such a bad influence? I can now see visions of Europe dancing in my little sister's head. I imagine all the European lovers she'll take. She'll drink too much wine and even take up smoking. She'll eat too much cheese and not eat her broccoli.

"I was walking by the Louvre at dawn. I hadn't been to bed yet. And in the distance I saw a row of monks walking towards me. Full robes, baldheads and all. They stopped about twenty feet in front of me, not even looking at me. They were looking at something behind me. So I turn to see what it was."

Amelia and I shake our heads, waiting for his answer.

"The rising sun. The monks stood there for a full ten minutes, not saying a word, not taking their eyes off of the sun. Now I'd never meditated before. I'd never stared at anything for ten minutes before, so I start doing it, too. I'd been in France for a month, and yet it was the first time I'd ever really looked at the sun. Where would we be without it? We curse it when it's too hot and we moan when it's missing, but we never really just appreciate it. The longer I sat there, the more at peace I felt. My restlessness disappeared. So when the monks finally walked away, I followed them. I took it as a sign. I converted to Buddhism, after being a lapsed Catholic since high school, and began studying the Tao. Now I try to never miss a sunrise, or if possible, a sunset. Every one is unique. But I'm particularly partial to the ones in Africa."

The sun, huh? I decide to try it on for size. Has to be a

much healthier way to start and end the day than my bad thoughts.

We eat by candlelight that evening, while darkness erases the magnificent pink, orange and blue watercolors in the sky. A lion roars in the distance, reminding us again of our place. A lion's roar can be heard from five miles away, which reassures me. A little.

The Professor and Mary Ann retire to their tent early, the only effect of age I'd seen on them all day. I wonder if they still make love after all these years together. I wonder, yet I don't want to picture it.

A simple meal of fruit, nuts, beef jerky and wine re-energize the rest of us. The buzz of the wine eases my aches and pains as I splay out on a blanket, watching the flickering of the candlelight on the faces around me.

Helena grabs her knee and pulls it in to her, resting her chin on it. "I met your mother just after Dimitri arrived in Africa. Elizabeth made arrangements with Asha to cover the orphanage until they could find a new director," Helena began. "She didn't talk much, nor did Dimitri, but I'd never seen a happier couple in all of my years doing these tours. So many people come to Africa because something is broken. Their marriage, their spirit, unsure of where life should take them. But these two behaved as if they had already drank from the wine of everlasting life and wanted nothing more than to just be. I only knew your mother for three days. I had no idea she'd been a prisoner or a nun until she called to book this trip for you. When she told me her brief story, I got it. I'd wondered all those years what she and Dimitri had to be so happy about, and now I knew."

"What was it?" Amelia asks.

"They possessed the Gift of Now. They didn't carry the energy of the past with them or the anxiety about the future. The reason they seemed so happy is that they were only focused on the very step we were taking as we took it. Their minds were uncluttered, their hearts broken open. For someone like me, who lives in my head all of the time, so full of stories that I sometimes forget their purpose, it was a teaching moment. I never take a single safari for granted anymore. I never yearn for the start of a new one or look forward to the end when I'll go back to my home. This is my home, wherever I am. The nomads know this. But it took me much longer to get it. Your mother reminds me of that."

"And you?" Taryn asks Lucas, who sits across the fire, next to Amelia. "How did you meet our mother?"

Lucas turns onto his belly on the blanket, staring into the fire, remembering. "Your mother knocked me out cold after I'd been sent by the monks to work in the orphanage. The Buddhist faith is based on compassion, something I'll admit I'd fallen short of all of my life. Before that, I'd never especially liked children. I'd seen them as nuisances growing up, and I'd been a spoiled brat myself. But my teacher told me to look at children not as little people but as spirits. See through their size and just acknowledge the energy they possess."

"Back up," I say, shaking my wine glass in the air. "Knocked out cold?"

"Ah, yes. I arrived a day earlier than your mother expected so I caught her off guard. I'd gone to the outhouse first. She thought I was hiding, I suppose, and when I came out, she knocked me over the head with a pan. When I came to I had a goose egg on my forehead. Kids started calling me unicorn. That's how I met your mother. She was protecting her children." He catches what he's said, and inhales, but we let it slide. I like this story. It's much closer to the ones I'd imagined all those years, curled into my bed at night. Only in my dreams, she would've ended up dying while saving the orphans.

"When I came to, and actually remembered my name, she profusely apologized. She told me that a few months prior, a missionary had tried to molest a young boy. Your mother beat the man with her bare hands. With the help of some of the older children, she tied him to a tree to wait until authorities could take him away."

"How did she know to trust you then?" I ask.

"She didn't. But Elizabeth knew that one man's sin couldn't taint the good of the whole. Of course she told me this story while my head was still zinging from the blow. I didn't blame her. I'd surprised her. I think any mother would've reacted the same way."

I have to swallow hard. I still don't feel comfortable with her being called a mother. Anybody's mother. "What did the children call her?"

"Sister Elizabeth, though she broke ties with the Church after Dimitri returned."

My mother, the drifter. Moving on. Is there nothing she held on to?

Lucas goes on. "I've learned a lot from your mother. One of my favorites is her idea that the soul is like silly putty. The more I thought about it, the more I knew it to be true. The soul sits within you like a lump of Silly Putty. You have the ability to shape it, to mold it into something beyond yourself. Others may try to hurt it, to use it as a punching bag. But even if someone smashes it, you have the ability, the gift, to reshape it, to fill yourself up with it to make yourself whole."

Amelia smiles. "I like that."

Lucas nods. "And the part I like best? The soul is stretchy. Its purpose is not just to live within you, but also to reach out to others. All spirits are connected, but we are so busy judging others that we can't see that we are all the same inside. But when we reach out to help others, it stretches our soul, and we feel more fulfilled."

I stare up at the Milky Way, wishing again that Shane could be here to see it with me. He was the first person that got me out into nature. Science is everywhere, he'd told me. He fell in love with medicine because he first fell in love with nature. I'd been waiting for Shane to shape my soul without any responsibility to do it for myself.

Taryn leans forward. "What I really want to know is how you know our mother now, five years after she hit you over the head."

Lucas nods. "Where your mother is, so am I."

And with that, he gets up and heads to his tent, but not before Taryn yells after him. "Then tell us why you gave up being a monk."

Lucas looks over to Amelia, nearly apologizing. "I suppose a part of me will always be a monk, just as a part of your mother will always be a nun."

At this, Amelia gets up, brushes off her shorts and leads the poor ex-monk to his tent.

Helena blows out the candles, with a tiny smile on her

face.

"This should be interesting," Taryn says looking back at me. "Ten bucks says she talks her way into his tent."

"Lucas isn't like her," I say in his defense, shaking her hand and taking the bet.

Taryn scoffs. "Did you not hear his whole sinner/saint speech? Tonight, he's bringing out the sinner to play."

I retreat to my tent, hoping I'm wrong, but as I open the tent flap to stare at the starry sky, I suddenly don't want to think at all. What if I could lie in bed, or anywhere for that matter, and just *be*?

23
AMELIA

"You shouldn't be here," Lucas says, kicking off his sandals and avoiding eye contact with me outside of his tent.

"Why did you lie and tell me you're a Buddhist monk when you're not?" My heart is beating out of my chest, but I don't care. I have to know. If he doesn't like me, fine, but I deserve the truth.

"I still practice much of what I've learned. Like I said, it's a part of who I am now."

"So you're celibate by choice?" Seriously, no *comprende*.

"I am. Eight years."

"But for god sake, *why*?" I try not to see him as a ridiculously handsome guy, a conquest, someone to ease my pain, like all good lovers do. I just want to see him as a person, even just as a spirit if that's at all possible.

He shakes his head and smiles in the moonlight. "I don't expect you to understand, Amelia."

"Please don't treat me like a child. My sisters have done that to me all of my life. Just try me."

"The story I told you about France. See before I met those monks, I'd been with women all over Europe. And before that, as many women as I could in college."

My heart drops. I can't see that guy in him. "So you were a male slut."

"To put it mildly. And it was, well, a distraction. It felt good in the moment, especially the moment before the moment, like with you last night. But after, I felt empty. I used to believe to get that feeling again, that I just needed to do it again. And I told myself I just hadn't found the right woman yet. But the women didn't feel the same way. Some of them did. If they knew I was just passing through town, then yes, it was just one night for them. You tell a woman you don't want a relationship and she says okay to get in bed with you, but then she wants more. So my trying to be truthful upfront just sounded like a line to them. They all thought they could change me. But going to different continents didn't help, either. I was still the same. Still empty. Filling up that hole inside of me with booze and women and new adventures. Until the monks found me."

I no longer see Lucas, but the reflection of myself in his eyes. His story is mine. I'd filled up with men and had caused all the drama he spoke of. Even Alex, who I blamed for seducing me, told me time and again we couldn't have a relationship, until I'd broken him down and then he tried to live dual lives. Lucas was right to keep as far away from me as possible. I shifted the weight of my legs, my chest full of heartache from all the dumb mistakes I've made. "I think I understand. So tell me what I can do to feel as free as you do right now. You know, Zen, or enlightenment, or whatever."

"It's not that easy. Besides, I'm far, far away from being enlightened."

"Then just talk to me. I don't see why we can't be friends."

His shoulders relax, and we look out at the brilliant sky

above us. "Have you ever been just friends with a guy before?"

"No. You ever been just friends with a girl?"

"Probably not until I met your mother."

I raise a brow. "You weren't even friends with girls in elementary school?"

"Nope. Had crushes on all of them."

I turn to staring at Lucas's profile. I resist reaching out to touch his jaw line, one of my favorite parts of the male body. Nope. No thinking about male body parts.

"Do you think we could be friends?" I ask.

"Stranger things have happened."

My heart skips. "So what if we just take each day as it comes? Just live in the here and now, not worrying about what could happen or thinking about our screwed up pasts?"

Finally, he turns to face me, and really looks at me. If my mom's right about the whole Silly Putty soul thing, then that look just melted it from my head all the way down to my toes. I can't help but feel connected to Lucas, and I'm pretty sure it's more than simple attraction or feeding my addiction. But how would I know the difference?

"I'm willing to try," he says finally and reaches out to touch my chin, rubbing his thumb across the dimple there. Putty. Pure putty.

"You better go back now," he says. "Why don't you join Taryn and me for yoga at sunrise?"

"It's a date," I say, and force myself away from him, dragging my intoxicated soul with me.

The Half Moon. The Pyramid. Even the Eagle pose. So

many of the yoga poses have something to do with our journey, and I'm terrible at nearly all of them. Even for a runner with great leg strength, I don't have decent balance. And Marlo? As wobbly as a spoonful of Jell-O. She just hates to be left out, and I'm glad she joined us so I don't look quite so bad.

I've been a runner all of my life, but I've never once tried yoga. Too still, I'd thought, which is the whole point of yoga. Learning to breathe, balance and feel the flow of energy throughout your body.

Taryn tells us she's been doing yoga since she graduated high school. I had no idea my sister, who chugs energy drinks like you should drink water, was into this peaceful practice.

Lucas tells us that you should face the east, the sunrise, to draw energy from the sun as you do yoga. The great big ball of fire over the horizon feeds me a spiritual breakfast, but doesn't seem to keep Marlo and me from tumbling into each other, especially on the "intermediate" Eagle pose.

I'm fairly sure I've done this pose before, horizontal, with a man. But standing up? Marlo and I are like downed trees, falling into each other. Taryn and Lucas ignore us, reminding us to keep breathing, which is kind of hard when you're laughing your ass off.

To our surprise, after our sweaty sunrise yoga and quick outdoor showers (regrettably, one at a time), Helena tells us this is where we must part.

"I thought it was a three-day safari?" Taryn asks.

"Normally it is. But your mother wanted you to see things from another viewpoint today." Helena points up.

Lucas, freshly showered and delicious enough to *eat* for

breakfast, claps his hands together. "Get ready to take to the skies."

A Jeep driven by a Samburu man rumbles down the road to take us away. I'm so thankful we won't spend the morning walking that I nearly cry.

After cheerful goodbyes with our safari team and final pictures with my favorite camel, the bright-eyed Dopey with her long eyelashes, we are off on our next great adventure.

Instinctively, I grab Lucas's hand on our way to the Jeep, and he squeezes it before letting go.

24
TARYN

The hot air balloon hisses as we step inside the basket. I've already shot nearly a thousand pictures in two and a half weeks. Photography comes as easily to me as breathing, yet each shot is a challenge, like piecing together a puzzle: the right light, the right angle, the right elements. When it all works, you can see God. The energy within the object.

My father shipped us off to Sunday school each week until we were old enough to decide for ourselves how we wanted to spend our Sundays. He was by no means a religious man, and obviously couldn't keep the Ten Commandments to save his life. He ate too much, drank too much, yelled too much, cheated on his wives, and cursed like a sailor. But when he told me he saw the divine in all things, I knew I wanted to see that, too, and every so often, in a tattoo or in a painting or in a photo, I thought I saw glimpses of it.

Marlo makes notes in her small voice recorder as our basket joins the sky, unhitched by the group of men on the ground. Amelia stands on her tiptoes, waving at the people below who grow smaller by the minute.

I snap pictures, first inside the basket, looking straight up into the balloon, followed by the champagne-colored hills in the distance, profiles of my basket brethren, mouths agape and the rich land below. From this view, we can see the differences in the elevation of the terrain and the majestic kiss of sky and earth. We soar across the painted landscape, to the rain-ripened green grass and see our first wildlife, the unusual wildebeest. Not just a few of them, a thousand. No, tens of thousands. I have to pull the camera away from my face to take it all in.

"The annual migration of the wildebeest is one of the great wonders of the world," Lucas tells us. "A natural cycle that replenishes and renews the grasslands of East Africa. More than a million wildebeest gather in the Serengeti to mate each June."

The cycle of life. You are born. You eat. You mate. You die.

Among the masculine animals, we see herds of zebra and gazelle, flocking to the grassland for their share of the majesty. I can't take pictures fast enough: the sturdiness of the wildebeest, the elegance of the gazelle, the royalty of the zebra.

The wind whips my sisters' hair and I switch the camera setting to take black and white photos. I take one of Amelia nestled against Lucas's shoulder, their eyes cast down to the spectacle below, and their body language telling more than their mouths could.

And my big sis, her notebook back in her pocket, her voice recorder on pause, her eyes dancing with delight at the movie playing out before us. Her mind is free, for once. I bet Shane would like this one. I'll send it to him as a surprise.

We float above a herd of elephants next to a winding river, and a half hour later, the biggie I've been waiting for:

a pride of lions. This particular pride has about twenty-five lions, with several lionesses and about a dozen young cubs. I shudder at the thought that these lions may be hunting the very same wildebeest and zebras and gazelles we saw earlier.

"They really are family animals," the pilot, an older African gentleman, tells us. "They ferociously protect each other and rely on teamwork. The females are the primary hunters, but usually hunt together because a lot of their prey is faster than they are. They stalk and then surround their prey, usually after dark."

"The family that kills together, stays together," I say dryly as I snap on my wide-angle lens.

"All the females are related," the pilot continues. "Mothers, grandmothers, sisters, all working together. They even nurse each other's cubs. The females usually stay with the pride for life, while the males leave within two to four years, to take over a pride of their own."

This much I'm sure of: what my mother did goes against nature.

We finally land for a late country breakfast, which is waiting for us at a small lodge on a reserve, and Lucas fills our glasses with chilled sparkling wine.

"To Mother Earth," Marlo says, holding her champagne glass high for a toast.

After what I've seen, that's something I can toast, perhaps the only kind of mother I can toast. We drink down the wine, bubbly and cold.

Lucas turns to me. "A little birdie told me your favorite animal is the giraffe."

My sisters shake their heads, as if it didn't come from them. I nearly choke on my biscuit. The little birdie being my mother? I faintly recall visiting the zoo with her before she left. Since she was the one who took all the photos, she was rarely in any of them. With my father, yes. I always lingered by the fence staring up at the giraffes with their spotted brown bodies and long necks high into the trees where they could pluck their lunch of leaves. They seemed so ... *content.*

"Remember your giraffe?" Marlo asks. Elizabeth had given me a stuffed animal giraffe for my third birthday. My only memory of that day is opening that particular gift.

From then on, I'd slept with Gertie every night, watched cartoons with her, and even begged to take her on car rides with me. Then one day, when I was in second grade and thought it was time to be done with childish things, I decided I was through falsely hoping that our mother would return and didn't want anything she'd ever given me, including my precious Gertie.

If our mother could throw us away so easily, how hard could it be to throw out a stuffed animal?

I'd cried myself to sleep for weeks after the trash truck took Gertie away, but with each night I lay and thought about her at the bottom of a garbage pile, the more my young mind believed that's where I belonged, too. I was piled under mounds of grief, though no one could see it. It suffocated me. Changed me.

My therapist says I have attachment issues, but unlike Amelia, who seems to thrive on unhealthy attachments, I don't bond to begin with. I'd tried with my father, but what good did that do me? The fact that I had stayed with Paul as long as I had was short of a miracle.

When my father asked what happened to Gertie, I lied

and said I lost it. I'd probably even blamed Amelia. I was forever blaming the baby. I'd even blamed Amelia for our mother leaving. Amelia cried all the time. I was a big girl. At three, I rarely cried, especially since it upset our mother so.

"Well, this next leg of our trip is in your honor," Lucas says.

"I think she likes you," Amelia says three hours later, as I feed the giraffe from the second story window of the Giraffe Manor.

I can't help it. I feel like a kid again, as warm and filled up as I'd always felt with Gertie in my arms. This giraffe, and the six like it on the property, are gorgeous beasts, even more beautiful than the ones in the zoo. The giraffes, like Lakota, stick their necks literally into the house to be fed by the visitors. Lakota lets me pet her long neck and I'm in love. I don't care if it's impractical. I want a giraffe. I'd asked Santa every year for one for Christmas—well, that and my mother. I figured since she'd given me Gertie in the first place, maybe they'd come together as a package. She'd be riding my real giraffe on Christmas Day. I gave up on Santa and God that same second grade year.

"Thank God we're not sleeping in a tent again," Amelia says, stretching her back. "I need a nice soft mattress."

"Not me," Marlo says. "Sleeping in the tent the past few nights has been the best sleep I've had in months."

"So maybe you and Shane should start going camping again."

"I might just do that." Marlo takes her laptop and her ice tea up to her room with her to finish her final story on Africa to send to her editor, and to call Shane. Maybe I shouldn't care either way, but I want them to work things out. I want us to believe in the natural order of things — sticking together throughout life.

I've tried Paul all morning, but he's in some boring banker's meeting. Seriously, I can't imagine my Paul, who rides his Harley every weekend, going to stuffy after-hours networking events. But he does. And then he comes home and rips open a beer and we go to a hard rock club. He's a mystery to me, but a good one.

Finally, I get the call I've been waiting for.

"Damn I miss you," he says.

"Are you still in your meeting?"

"Just stepped out, like a millisecond ago."

"Tie?"

"Coming off as we speak."

"Hot?"

"Me or the weather?"

"Funny."

"Blazing. I might have to ride the Harley naked."

"Not without me, you won't."

"In that case, I don't think the Harley is what I'd be riding."

"You sure don't sound like a banker."

"I don't make love like one, either."

"How would you know?"

"Oh, word gets around, believe me. God, Taryn. I need you back here."

"You just saw me a week ago. Or have you blocked it out?"

"You kidding? Shit. I could piss my pants thinking about it right now. But you wouldn't believe how famous I am around here. Everyone wants me to tell the story. I'm a rock star. But I told them it was the *Charlie's Angels* who were badass."

"I won't go down without a fight."

"That's why I love you so damn much. You're a lover and a fighter. Speaking of the former, how long would it take for me to get to Africa?"

"You're not coming to Africa. Besides, we're about to leave here anyway. I think our next stop is the big one."

"Oh, shit."

"Yeah. You can say that again."

"You ready to meet her?"

"Yes. No. I mean, I don't know. Maybe. Probably. It would be for the best, right? Just get it over with?"

"Of course. Damn. I can't imagine not knowing my mother."

"Yeah, but you're mom is like Betty Crocker incarnate."

"She does make a bad-ass chocolate cake."

"If I'm lucky, she won't sound like a lunatic."

"You really think that?"

"I don't know what to think. She's been a recluse most of her life. If you think about it, she was all alone with us, too. Her prison was with three little babies she couldn't take care of."

"You know it wasn't you. Tell me you know that."

I can't help but feel the cry pulsing behind my eyes. I do know that, don't I? And yet some small part of me, the little girl that will never die, still blames herself, and her sisters.

"Babe, come on. She was messed up, but her prison

was in her own mind."

"I guess." I don't want to cry, but I'm not even sure the tears would be for Elizabeth. The trip has brought up all the old feelings, feeling like an outsider, turning me into a rebel that pretends she doesn't care, when inside maybe I do. I may miss Paul as much as he misses me. For him, my soul is stretchy, but I can't quite make it the distance. Yet. "Hey, guess what I'm doing right now?"

"Is it dirty? If so, let me call you back when I get to my house."

"No. I'm feeding a giraffe, eye to eye. We're at the Giraffe Manor."

"Oh, babe. You must be in hog heaven."

"Giraffe heaven. Even better."

"Kinda takes the surprise out of your birthday party then. I swear I was going to give you a giraffe birthday party at the zoo."

"Get out. That's ridiculous."

"I know! But the zoo banks with us and we just sponsored a big new exhibit, so they said they'd let a few of us in there for an hour."

"No way. That's the sweetest thing ever. Like sickly sweet."

"Too mushy?"

Of course it's too mushy, but by now I should expect no less from the man. "No. Perfect. I mean it. I don't know what I did to deserve you."

"You didn't have to do anything, T. Just being you. Like the time you made us pull the bike over this spring so we could run through the sunflower field. And last winter when you insisted we get in on the snowball fight with the neighborhood kids. You don't let a moment slip by. Something about you brings out the best in me."

I do? God, two words I never thought I'd be saying when it comes to a man. Maybe I'm just fun, fun, fun. Some might call it reckless and stupid. Doesn't mean I'd make a great life partner.

On second thought, I could do a whole helluva lot worse than let this man love me.

That night on my bed, my sisters crash, bringing their Orange Crush cans, pretzel sticks and reading materials with them. Amelia thumbs through *People* magazine. Marlo reads *Out of Africa*. As together as we've been the last few weeks, separating again is harder to do than we realize.

When we were little, Marlo had slept in the middle of us in the queen-sized bed. She'd squeeze my hand when I was sure I'd seen a ghost in the closet. "It's just your imagination," she'd tell me before braving the dark to climb into the scary closet and jump up and down and wave her arms around wildly to prove that a ghost didn't exist. At least it never took her hostage in front of me.

I know now that a ghost did exist, always has, and maybe always will. She haunted us since she left and I've never been as brave as Marlo about waving it away. But I wonder if Marlo's stoicism is just an act, if she's internalized her fears and simply balled ours up along with hers.

"Can you believe we leave tomorrow?" Amelia tosses the magazine onto the floor and crams a pillow behind her head. "I'll miss this place. Think we'll ever come back?"

I shrug. "Why would you want to? You said you hate the wilderness."

"After I gave it a chance, it wasn't so bad. I guess the creature comforts back home were some sort of padding keeping me from feeling what I needed to feel."

"Like Alex is an asshole who doesn't deserve you?"

"Yeah, but I can't place all the blame on him. It's the other stuff, too. I keep thinking about those kids at the orphanage. And there's more where that came from."

Marlo props the open novel onto her chest and taps her bare feet together. "So, you're going to leave your flatiron and hairdryer and massive makeup collection behind to become a missionary?"

Amelia crosses her hands over her belly. "I don't know. I think I'd be making a bigger difference here than being a teacher back home."

I raise a brow. "So it was the *monk* that led to this revelation?" I put my head on her arm, but she shoves it off.

"I don't need a guy to influence my life. Not anymore. I *do* want to make a difference. Even if it's just me. By my lonesome."

Marlo picks up her book, but then sets it down again. If she really wanted to read in private, she wouldn't have joined us. "Did something happen with you and Lucas?"

"Why?"

I grunt. "We have a bet."

"For the record, I didn't think anything would happen," Marlo says.

Amelia huffs. "You two should be ashamed of yourselves. He's a man of … Buddha."

"With a not-broken penis," I add.

Amelia can't help but smile at me, and neither can

Marlo. "We're just friends. Besides, I need to get my life together before I get mixed up with a guy again. A non-married, available guy who hasn't made an abstinence pledge."

"Shit," I say. "I lose."

"Told you!" Marlo sticks her pink tongue out at me. "Good for you. There's so much to love about you, Ames. I wish you would see that."

"I guess," Amelia says, her eyes tearing up. "Actually talking to Lucas made me see what I've been doing. After Dad died, you both were gone and I was at Aunt Darla's feeling like an orphan, feeling sorry for myself. I figured if I found a man to love me, then I wouldn't be so lonely. I didn't think it would take quite so many men. Now I see I was looking outside when I should've been looking within."

"You got all that from one pillow talk?"

"No, but it all makes sense now. I see my pattern and it sucks and I don't want to hop from man to man or marriage to marriage. Besides, right now I just want to focus on meeting Mom."

Marlo crosses her arms. "What do you think will happen when you meet her?"

"I just want to hug her."

I shake my head. "That's it?"

"Yeah. When I've dreamed about her, it's the first thing I think of. Isn't that what a mom and child do when they see each other again? A big, long hug."

I jump off the bed and pace. "I don't know. That's something you do when you know someone. I'd still be more inclined to punch her. Especially after nearly getting Paul and us killed."

"No, you won't," Marlo says.

"I *dare* you to dare me. What about you? You want to *hug*, too?" I snicker.

Marlo sighs. "I still don't know what to think. It'll just be so *awkward*. Maybe even more so after knowing all these private things about her."

"You're the queen of awkward avoidance. Same reason you feel uncomfortable in therapy. You'd rather hide than fess up that something is broken and try to fix it. The great pretender."

Amelia pipes up. "Like you should talk. You're avoiding a commitment with Paul. If that's not hiding, I don't know what is."

"It's okay," Marlo says. "I know I need to work on some things. And there's another part of me that thinks after all Elizabeth has gone through, the parts of her that needed changing have changed. And what remains … what remains might be our mother."

We lock eyes. I'd never considered that it all might actually not suck in the end.

A soft knock at the door startles us. "Come in."

Lucas's head appears followed by his sculpted body, wearing a fitted athletic shirt and running shorts. "Sorry to interrupt. I'm going out for a run, but wanted to let you know that we leave right after breakfast tomorrow."

"Where are we going, pray tell?" Marlo asks.

"Your final destination." He pauses, seemingly enjoying the anticipation on our faces. "Have you ever been to Grand Canyon?"

DESTINATION 4: GRAND CANYON

A powerful and inspiring landscape, the Grand Canyon overwhelms our senses through its immense size; 277 river miles long, up to 18 miles wide, and a mile deep. The oldest rocks at the canyon bottom are close to 2000 million years old. The Canyon itself—an erosional feature—has formed only in the past five or six million years. Geologically speaking, Grand Canyon is very young.

—National Park Service (nps.gov)

25
MARLO

I am in no mood to meet my mother.

We flew first class from Africa to Arizona, changing planes twice, and eventually crawled into a car twenty hours later to drive the final way to Grand Canyon. I hadn't slept in nearly two days. The refreshment I'd felt in Africa had gone with the miles. While my sisters managed to sleep any time of day in any mode of transportation, I seemed to need a tent or at the very least a hard bed. I couldn't wait to tell Shane that I may have cured one problem in our marriage: our marital bed. Our mattress was too soft. We'd need one of those sleep number beds to save our marriage. His side soft, my side hard, like our dispositions. It was, at least, a start.

Even the B-12 vitamin drops Amelia pushed on us don't help. Taryn sucks down an energy drink, but my stomach is sour. I'm not sure if it's the travel (I hope), or the impending meeting, to blame.

"I. Can't. Wait!" Amelia slaps her bronzed legs with her palms. She sits by Lucas in the back of the limo, across from Taryn and me. The limo is tricked out. I took one eerily similar to my senior prom. Neon lights. Cheesy maroon carpeting. Only this bar is filled with nothing but healthy drinks, no alcohol. Good thing. I might down something I shouldn't.

Taryn rests her head against the window, staring out at the Arizona afternoon. "I can't wait for the truth," she says flatly. "I want to get it over with and get back to real life."

Amelia shrugs. "Hello! That's what we've been getting this whole time. Bits and pieces of her truth as she lived them."

I place my hand on my stomach, willing the butterflies to settle. "In my book, our own truth is the only one that matters."

We look at Lucas. He knows the woman. If he has something to say about her, this would be a real swell time to spill it. We all watch him. And wait.

He clears his throat. "A young widower, who had a five-year-old son he loved very much, was away on business when thieves came and burned down the whole village and took his son away. When the man returned, he saw the ruins and panicked. He took the burnt corpse of an infant to be his son and cried uncontrollably. He organized a cremation ceremony, collected the ashes and put them in a beautiful little bag, which he always kept with him. Soon afterwards, his real son escaped from the thieves and found his way home. He arrived at his father's new cottage at midnight and knocked at the door. The father, still grieving asked: 'Who is it?' The child answered, it is me Papa, open the door!' But in his agitated state of mind, convinced his son was dead, the father thought that some young boy was making fun of him. He shouted: 'Go away' and continued to cry. After some time, the child left. Father and son never saw each other again.' After this story, the Buddha said: 'Sometime, somewhere, you take something to be the truth. If you cling to it so much, even when the truth comes in person and knocks on your door, you will not open it.'"

Amelia shakes her head. "I don't get it."

Taryn shoves her sunglasses on top of her head. "It means if we are clinging to our beliefs about her about our judgment of her, then we really can't be open to the truth. Isn't that it?"

I look at Lucas. "She knew that story, didn't she? She knew we wouldn't be ready to meet her unless we went to all of those places. To see where and how she'd lived."

"She knew that the last thing you knew was that she was there and then she left. If, as she figured, you had not received any of her letters or gifts she had sent to you over the years, then you would believe this was some sort of magical act. One day here, the next day gone. You would have skipped over twenty years, because the space in the middle meant nothing to you."

"I beg to differ." Taryn's voice echoes in the car. "That space meant everything."

"Precisely. But you might have taken her years for granted. A flesh and blood person who hurt and ached and yearned and aged as you did."

"Whatever," Taryn says, looking out the window again. I know she cares more than she lets on. She's wearing the charms as earrings, isn't she? I bet she'll find the nearest tattoo shop, if there is one near a canyon, and get them etched for life onto her bracelet tattoo. This is why I've always hugged her even though we both found it difficult. We both needed it and were ashamed to admit it.

Amelia is crying again, though I doubt it's Taryn's outburst. We're all tired and hungry. This is all too much.

"Elizabeth would like you to rest tonight and she'll see

you tomorrow."

We all breathe a collective sigh of relief. We wouldn't have to break down without adequate sleep and nourishment at least. Our bodies needn't be weary like our hearts.

The mountains rise up like earthen gods in the distance, guarding the passage to our mother. I try to stay present, but my mind keeps slipping both backwards thinking of Iolana and Rialdo and Karina and Asha and forward to five days from now when I will decide if I'm returning to Shane for good.

I still don't get the Gift of Now. My mind tumbles back and barrels forward with little respect for the present. I don't know what this says about me, but I am certain it can't be good.

"We're here," Lucas says with a smile, just as happy as we are to be done with traveling for a bit.

It is no paradise. No mansion. No slum. No wildlife. Just an unassuming road leading to a large Santa-Fe style home sitting by itself, nestled by mountains on two sides. When I'd e-mailed Ken about our final destination, he requested three stories while I'm here: The Canyon. Santa Fe style homes for a residential story, and an off-the-beaten path feature. I figure with this place, I might be able to tackle the final two stories in one stop. Yes, it felt better thinking about work than my mother.

He'd attached architectural information about Santa Fe-style and this home, this very, very large home, fit the profile. The right way to build in the Southwest is to make the homes appear to be one with nature, creating harmony. Perhaps this is why the home didn't appear obnoxious like the large homes in Kansas.

But, it turns out this is not a home at all.

A small sign at the end of the road reads *Zen & Now*. The limo pulls around to a side parking lot where a dozen or so cars are parked. "What is this place?" Amelia asks, barely waiting for the car to park before opening her door and escaping.

"It's a retreat," Lucas says, climbing out and stretching, showing us the bottom third of his abs.

"I note you didn't say a resort." Taryn stands and stretches.

"People come here not just to unwind, but to learn how to live healthier lives. Inside and out."

"I've heard of places like this." We follow him up the stone path. "A place to get the body, mind, spirit in alignment sort of thing?"

"Precisely," Lucas says.

Elizabeth. Is she a guest here? The place, though different in style and location, shares some of the characteristics of the other places she has lived. Remote. Quiet. Sanctuary. She is a loner in isolation whether by her own doing or that of others. I allow my mind to think all the things I'd pushed away these weeks before. Will she be meek? Strong? Brash? Sorry? Graceful? Beautiful?

Then with a breeze, they are gone. I concentrate on the retreat. It imbues both hominess and sophistication.

The earth-colored stucco and flat roof has three elevations and a large, curved entrance that reminds me of the mansion in Mexico City, though I don't see a cross anywhere. Rounded corners and window ledges give the place a comforting feel.

"It's lovely," Amelia gushes.

The building has more patios than a regular home, extending the home out into the yard to enjoy the natural vistas during the warm season. I see one near the front and the side of the home, and I can't wait to see the back of the home where it faces the mountains. Perhaps with a hard cot to sleep on.

We arrive at the front desk, where a naturally pretty blonde woman smiles broadly at our arrival. "Welcome to Zen & Now. I'm Carmen Shirkey," she says. She pushes a button on the sleek Mac computer. "You're all checked in. I'll show you to your suite."

Taryn rolls her eyes. "Great. Looks like we'll be roomies again."

Carmen hands us three room keys. "I think you'll find the accommodations to your liking. Summer is a very busy time of the year for us. Lots of corporate suits and couples and girlfriend get-aways."

Great. A spiritual detox for the elite. If I have to sing Kumbaya with them, I'm so outta here. From the looks of things, no more Keepers. Only Carmen wheeling our bags up to our room for us.

Heavy wood beams above us provide the only dark colors in the whole place. A few older women sit in the sunlight reading novels in the great room near a curved corner fireplace.

The halls and walls are full of nichos, small carved-out spaces to display Santos (Carvings of Saints) and pieces of art. I swear I've seen them before. Some remind me of the nun's paintings and Mexican artwork from the mansion. In one *nicho,* a grouping of three painted wooden giraffes stands tall in three different heights. I watch Taryn pause and look at them and move on. Coincidence?

Carmen leads us down a corridor with private rooms that face an interior courtyard full of flowering plants and a fountain. A mother and daughter sun themselves on the lounge chairs. My gut churns at the sight.

"It's free hour," Carmen tells us. "The workshops start back up in a bit."

I wonder if we'll be expected to participate. Lucas says his goodbyes at the elevator, inviting us to join him for hot Vishnu yoga before a light dinner.

My eyes, weary, widen all the same. "I have no idea what you just said, but I don't think I like it."

"I got the dinner part," Amelia says. "Though I'm not too fond of the word 'light' in front of it."

Taryn raises a pierced brow. "Ooh. We don't have Vishnu classes back home. I'll definitely take you up on that."

"Very well, then. Carmen will explain everything."

By explain 'everything', he meant this place, whatever it was, and our orders, er, *choices* for the day. I'd go with Sleep, Slumber or Conk Out. Any of those on the workshop list?

Our suite lives up to the retreat title. Bright and airy, the space is a roomful of sunshine, with pale yellow walls, a curved white couch and an ash brown coffee table topped by fresh flowers and a card.

Amelia plucks the card from the bouquet and reads it aloud. "You've made it. Truly a dream come true for me. Please make yourselves at home. I can't wait to see you tomorrow. Love – your mother." She tries to pass it to me, but I shake my head. I don't need to see it. She has some kind of nerve signing it that way.

Taryn plops on the couch. "I don't know about making it home, but it ain't too shabby."

A fresh pitcher of lemonade sits on the table and I pour us a glass while Carmen points to the brochures on the table. "We offer classes in health & nutrition, spirituality, cooking and relationships. We also provide exercises programs throughout the day, starting at five a.m. We lead both a morning and an afternoon hike as well as moonlight yoga on the portal. We also offer daily silence retreats at Grand Canyon. Dinner is served at 5:30. You can join us in the banquet room, or if you're too tired, call up room service."

Now she's talking. Room service. I see the bed and march towards it. I don't care what my sisters do, but I need a nap way more than I need a workshop, even if "Letting Go of the Past" might prove helpful. That's what tomorrow is for.

Amelia is already busy checking things in the brochure, my impulsive little doer, sponging up change with fervor. Taryn is more skeptical, laying on the couch and contemplating the choices, the energy drink aiding her ability to stay awake. I'm certain she'll try the most unusual workshops and activities.

Carmen shows me the controls on the bed. "You can change the softness or firmness by changing the dial," she instructs. "It's important for you to get a good sleep while you're here."

Sleep Number. She may as well have said a troupe of Sleep Fairies would sprinkle me with the Dust of Nod.

When I awake, my sisters are gone. The sun is about to set and I realize I'm too late for dinner in the banquet room. I nearly call Taryn's cell, but opt against it. We don't have to experience everything together.

Instead, I pluck my phone from my bag and dial Aunt Darla's number. She picks up on the second ring. I explain to her what I need and ask her to call me back as soon as she knows anything. She agrees and I call room service, only to find there is nothing remotely greasy or delicious on the menu. Everything is low fat, organic and "good for you." Shane would love this place. I married a health nut, though I try not to hold it against him.

I groan and order a chicken breast and salad (no cheese, no ranch, not even upon request.) Shane eats this crap and he's been begging me to try new foods and learn to cook this kind of stuff. Swears it will help with my energy level and depression. The only thing I'm sure cures depression is M&Ms. By the bagful.

I circle a cooking class for the following morning, but wonder if I'll be weeping in the arms of my mother instead. No, I can't see myself weeping. I would stare at her like a statue of the Virgin Mary. I would scream or I would say nothing at all. I want to meet her; I don't want to meet her.

Just as my chicken arrives, my phone rings. I had made a pact with myself. If Aunt Darla indeed found evidence that our mother had tried to contact us over the years but my father had kept it from us, I'd be more willing to meet her.

If she found no evidence, I'd see how I feel tomorrow.

Lucas said to be open to the truth, but I'm a journalist, and I like evidence. Aunt Darla is my source. She'd cleaned out our house after Daddy had died and moved things into storage in her attic and a shed out back. She recalled there being a heavy trunk her husband had moved up to the attic. She'd assumed it had our things in it, things from our childhood, but our father had never once mentioned Elizabeth sending us anything. If she had, he'd kept it to himself.

"I'm not sure if this is good news or bad news," Darla says.

My face whitens. My blood feels cold. I'm not even sure if my heart is beating any longer. "What did you find?"

"It's all here, Marlo. At least two-dozen letters, birthday cards, a few paintings and the scarves you mentioned. Looks like some years there were several things and other years nothing at all. My favorite is some drawings she did of you girls dressed up for Halloween."

I feel my heart beat again, but it pounds in my chest like a sledgehammer. I want it to slow down. I'd almost wanted her to find nothing. To find that my mother was delusional. That she'd never sent anything. That her journals were just made up stories of a sick or creative mind. I wanted the journey we'd just seen with our eyes to not have been real. The pain of what we'd experienced the last few weeks implodes within me. My God. My poor mother.

"I don't know what to say." It would've been nice to have them before we meet her, but now it's too late. We only have what she's given us on this trip. Which is so much I still can't swallow it all.

I hear the faint sounds of weeping through the phone line. Aunt Darla had been best friends with Elizabeth before she left. Had she not told my mother she'd "take care of it" when she got pregnant with Amelia?

"This is the Elizabeth I knew," she sobs. "I knew she couldn't just walk out and never look back. This proves she looked back. And back, and back, and back."

"You knew about her problems, didn't you?"

"I knew how awful Richard treated her. I knew she was depressed, yes. I'd convinced her to stay, time and again. I told him if things didn't change, if she didn't get some help, she would leave, but he never believed she would go. He said, 'where would she go? What would she do?'"

"I guess we know now."

"He underestimated her."

"Well, most fathers wouldn't like to believe that a mother could abandon her children."

Darla sucks in her breath. "She was sick, honey. It's tough to grasp. Lord knows I couldn't have left my children, but she wasn't in her right mind."

I close my eyes and remember seeing my mother lying in her bed, raccoon eyes from no sleep, the uneaten bowl of Fruit Loops I'd brought her that morning still untouched and soggy on her nightstand. I hushed my sisters. "Let's play the quiet game." I'd thought if she had a good sleep she'd wake up happy. She'd act like home was where she wanted to be.

"What if she still isn't?"

"Well, you're all grown now."

"I don't feel very grown right now."

"Honey, there's something else you need to know. Something I'm not proud of, that's been weighing on me for twenty years. I drove your mama to the airport the day she left."

I have to lie back on the bed. My voice is small, a whisper of a whisper. "You what?"

"She told me she needed to get away for a bit, and I agreed. Just to get rested up, you know? She said she was going to think things through and then she'd be back. I figured she meant whether or not she'd divorce Richard. She wouldn't even tell me where she was going. Had me drop her off at the front gates, and that's the last I saw of her. The authorities tracked her down in Hawaii, but Richard refused to go get her."

I toss the now-cold chicken into the trash. I want to be angry with Aunt Darla for driving the get-away car, but she had no idea the getaway would last twenty years. For a second, I'm angrier for my father for not going to get her. Would Shane come after me, fight for me, or would he just let me go?

"What did she say? When she left?"

"She said, 'take care of my girls.' I'm so sorry, Marlo."

I want, no, I *need*, to believe that my mother *couldn't* return to us. But she had the chance, every day on the beach before she decided to step off Hoary Head. And then again when she recuperated and left with a new man and a new life. Time after time. Better, worse, broken, healed, beaten, begin again.

I try to push away the anger at my father, but it takes over my whole being. All the hours I'd sat with him during chemo, so he'd have company, and we'd talked about frivolous things: like what happened on *Friends* the night before, or who would win the World Series. I'd kept my sisters from the dirty work, watching our father disappear before my eyes. I'd fed him, chauffeured him, changed his wet sheets when he was too weak to make it to the bathroom before he gave up his pride and agreed to let me start buying him Depends. I hate that I could be so angry with a man who was so sick, but he should've used those hours and hours we spent together to confess. Even just one minute, to utter the sentence that could've rewritten my history.

Your mother did care, Marlo. There's a trunk I've been keeping, to show you when you're old enough. You need to know while there's still time. I'll be gone and what you do now is up to you.

He knew the day he was going to die. But, before he'd breathed his last, he just told me to take care of my sisters and to never let anyone stand in the way of my success. No grand speech about not making the dumb mistakes he made in life: living selfishly, placing money above people or treating women liked used playing cards to be traded when a better one comes along. He should've apologized for how he treated Cecelia, as well as Elizabeth. He'd let pride get in the way of truth, even at the end.

How had I not seen it before?

I clear my throat. I don't want to find blame, but I would like to know how to step off the merry-go-round my ancestors put us on. "And what about Grandfather? How did he treat you growing up? Treat Grandmama?" Even when my dad was alive, we only saw my paternal grandparents on an irregular basis. They weren't wealthy, though they lived as if they were, preferring to spend holidays in ski resorts or on cruises instead of in Kansas, with their only son and daughter. They'd retired to Florida as soon as Darla left the house.

"I wish I really knew him. He was hard on us growing

up. If you didn't bring home straight A's on your report card you better not come home at all."

He'd turned my father into a perfectionist and passed it on to me. So much better to try to be perfect than to risk disappointing him.

Darla went on. "When Richard died, my father wept in my arms. First time I ever saw him cry. 'Course that didn't really change his behavior. Calls a little more often, but still mostly talks about himself. Sometimes forgets to ask about me, or my kids or you girls at all."

As kids, we'd gotten birthday cards and holiday cards with three checks, one made out to each of us. At least they were always on time, but I would've preferred a phone call, a visit. The cards were so impersonal, despite the jovial messages from the Hallmark copywriter. "Why didn't he and Grandmama offer to move back and take care of us and be with their son when he had cancer?"

"Well, he assumed I would step up and do that, and besides you were nearly grown. Richard tried to sound so upbeat to our parents, like he'd lick cancer. I think he was in denial, even at the end."

"As for how he treated your grandma, I think she lived through a lot of hanky panky I don't care to think about."

I pause to let the news sink in. "Did you and my father know about the affairs?"

"Well, we certainly weren't deaf. We could hear the fights. My mom threatened to leave, of course, but she was a housewife and it was the '60s. What would she have done? Mostly she just appealed to his ego. It would look bad on him at his company if his wife left. She did what she knew how to do, which was smoke and drink the pain away."

I close my eyes and picture my grandfather from the year before, crying over my grandmama's shiny, lavender casket. I wonder if he ever confessed his sins while she struggled with each breath, homebound and strapped to an oxygen machine? Did he regret not being faithful, or was he simply grateful she never left?

Darla sighs. "I'd like to believe it's never too early to turn the train around. Especially if you know where you're going."

I press my lips into a hard smile. I like the idea of shaping my future, of willing a happy life for myself and Shane and my sisters.

But where does this leave the reunion? Could I appear cloaked in the objectivity of a journalist? A third-party witness? However hard I try, Little Girl Marlo will be there, screaming, begging to be heard. My past and future require me to be present now.

I have no right to make that little girl wait or wonder any longer.

26
MARLO

How does one top paradise and camel rides and hot air balloons and ancient pyramids?

She'd played her cards well. Buttered us up with great food and wine and adventure. I remind myself not to get too caught up in the hoopla. She is just a woman who gave birth to us. But not so fast. If I had been adopted at birth, this scene would be easier. Instead, she birthed us, loved us, earned our trust and then crushed us. I wanted to hate her as rampantly as Taryn seems to. Yet I also want to love her as fully as Amelia does, sight unseen.

Taryn had stolen away into a nearby town and gotten her charms tattooed onto her leg the evening before. Her ankle bracelet of ink now looks identical to the ones of silver dangling from our wrists. She has removed the charms from her ears and tossed them onto the Bible in the nightstand, next to the book on Enlightenment by the Dalai Lama. And a book on relationships by Rabbi Shmuley. Either this place believes in everything, or nothing at all.

We eat breakfast in the dining hall group eating, just like we witnessed in the prison and the nunnery and the orphanage. As I look around at the retreat's decor, and it's as if we brought our adventures around the world right back here with us, like a tornado swooping up bits and pieces of our travels and tossing them here in one collective heap. Odd.

"I hope to see you in some workshops later," Lucas says after breakfast, dropping us off at a guest door at the corner of the second floor near the back of the retreat.

"That hot Vishnu yoga kicked my ass," Taryn says after him. So that's what it takes to impress my sister. I'm hopeless, then.

"There's more where that came from," he says. "Peace."

Peace. *Right.* My insides are churning like an ice cream maker. I can barely hear myself think. Taryn, Amelia and I stand outside of the door, holding hands. I'm not sure who grabbed whose hand first, but Taryn's is cold and Amelia's is clammy. Or am I feeling my own? Cold *and* clammy.

I nod and exhale. Nothing can really prepare you, can it?

Taryn reaches up and raps hard three times on the door. I would've rapped softly, but that's our Taryn.

We hear the shuffling of footsteps. Two voices. One male. One female.

I try to swallow but find it impossible.

The door swings open and the woman who once was my mother is standing just twelve inches away from me. I don't hear anything.

I see her eyes. They are just like Amelia's and mine, as blue as that Pacific Ocean she jumped into in Hawaii. Her eyes are smiling, every crow's foot turned skyward.

Her cheekbones mirror Taryn's, high and pointy. A model's cheeks, rouged like the color of pink Hibiscus.

Her smile is wide and genuine, with nearly straight white teeth. Amelia inherited that dimple in her chin and I got that crooked bicuspid I had fixed with braces in the eighth grade.

Her body is toned and sculpted, like an actor in a Pilates commercial. She is lithe and strong, at least on the outside.

She definitely *looks* like our mother. God has sprinkled bits of her among the three of us.

Her arms open like an eagle in flight, the whoosh of her floral perfume filling the space between us, and just like that, we fall into her grand wingspan like birds coming home to nest. The Hug.

My sisters take each side, their chins nestled inside the crook of Elizabeth's neck, so I step back, staring eye to eye. I'm afraid to touch her again, after all this time. Are those her tears or are they just reflections of my own? I can hear my heartbeat or is it the collective heartbeats of four women, a symphony of years gone by rising to a crescendo? My heart once grew within her body, and I can't pretend a piece of me doesn't belong with her.

We will never truly be separate. We never were.

I stand there, my shoulders shaking, overcome with such emotion that I can no longer think.

"My girls," Elizabeth says, her hands touching our hair, her mouth kissing our heads, our cheeks. "It's so good to see you. My God, you're all so beautiful."

"So are you," Amelia says, wiping her eyes.

Elizabeth is pretty. Fragile and petite like Taryn, but naturally pretty like Amelia. I'd expected she might be slumped over, or look sickly like I remembered her from those days when she'd taken to her bed.

This woman is the one who had lain out on the blanket with me in the backyard, full of hope. The stress she once wore like a second skin is gone, revealing a glowing beauty underneath: *peace,* both the tranquility and the truce. My emotions call for a cease-fire.

Over her shoulder, I see Dimitri, nearly as striking as his portrait back in the mansion. He looks even more distinguished with age, with a muscular build and salt-and-pepper hair. He's crying, his arms crossed in front of him. I can tell how much he wanted this for the woman he loved. How he'd wanted it from the first time she'd told him about us back on the beaches of Hawaii. How close he'd gotten to bringing her to us before his plane went down in Mexico.

I step aside, hugging Amelia's back and mouth, "Thank you," and Dimitri responds by blowing me a kiss and touching his hand to his heart.

The whole journey was worth it just for the look on Amelia's face. I'd do it all over again for my baby sister. When she sobs, "Mommy," I lose it. I'd so often hoped Cecelia would be a replacement for our mother, at least for Amelia. Cecelia hadn't really wanted three girls, she'd wanted our father and thought the only way to keep him was to move in and take care of his children. She wasn't unloving, but it's not the future she saw for herself. Despite her best efforts, he cheated on her, anyway.

Amelia not only wants this, she needs this, to know the woman who gave birth to her, who didn't strike her from her womb when she had the chance.

I'm not sure if it's the little Marlo who is crying or the mature Marlo who knows she would make it in the world without ever seeing her mother again, but here I am, crying my eyes out because however crazy this feels, I'm in the Now and I'm not going anywhere.

The haunting questions I'd been asked all my life, the ones that hung around like stubborn ghosts, slowly drift away. We've moved out to the patio, like any mother and daughters might be prone to do on a gorgeous Arizona afternoon, to hear how Elizabeth got from Africa, to here, as owner of Zen & Now. My mother, a builder of Zen. Go figure.

Dimitri checks on us like a doting father might. He doesn't even try to hide his excitement.

"We're fine, darling," Elizabeth says each time. I love the way he holds Elizabeth's gaze before walking back in the house, how they communicate with that one long look that everything is okay.

"He just wants to be a fly on the wall," she says after he leaves earshot.

I don't blame him. I'd want to know, too. Until then, I'd only thought about how my sisters and I would handle meeting our mother. I hadn't considered Elizabeth's feelings—the bulldozer of emotions she had to plow through to be okay with facing us again. If I hadn't walked in her shoes on our journey, I would never have known how she was able to get here, physically or psychologically.

The children's voices echoing in my head through the years finally got answered, as well. My classmates couldn't have known how much it hurt me to hear them. How I'd felt dirty and ashamed that I couldn't answer them.

Where is your mother?
Why did she give you up?
Don't you miss her?
Why doesn't she visit you?

And the ones who passed on the opinions of their own mothers. *My mom says your mom should be shot. My mom thinks your mom ran away with another man and didn't want the responsibility. My mom, my mom, my mom.*

I had to hit ERASE and wipe those judgments from my mind. The tape recorder in my head needed a reboot, a clean tape. One that only I could record. I had walked in her shoes and they'd walked us here. Why not give her, give us, a chance?

We travel in the limo to Grand Canyon, twenty minutes from Zen & Now. Taryn and I let Amelia do most of the talking, as if we could get a word in edgewise. We drive to Yavapai Point, already packed with visitors from around the world.

As much beauty as we'd seen on our journey, Grand Canyon, by far, leaves me speechless. If anywhere could make us feel like tiny specks in the grand scheme of things, this is it. The miles of canyon, the tiny stream below, which isn't a stream at all, but the roaring Colorado River. The stripes of wild color across the canyon proudly flaunt its age. *I've been eroded, washed away, pummeled and beaten, but here I stand, more majestic than ever.*

Elizabeth leads us to a clearing where no tourists roam, just the four of us, and the canyon. Party of five. We near the edge, and for an instant, I wonder if she has ever thought of jumping. She sits on the ground, and we do the same, like ducklings following her lead.

We face the bowing sun, watching its finale, saving the best for last. Blue, purple, orange and yellow ribbons frame the star. I've never seen it this large, or close, as if I could reach out and touch it with my fingertips.

"Each time Dimitri and I come out here, we watch the sunset from a different vantage point. Each one is uniquely exquisite. But I knew when I saw it from here that this is where we needed to begin."

Not end. *Begin.* She unzips her shoulder bag and pulls out three tiny turquoise bags and hands one to each of us.

Our final charm? "A cactus," I say, holding it up to the skyline.

"Not an animal this time," Amelia says, hooking it on to her bracelet. I hold mine in my palm. Nothing prickly about this charm, though I still feel tiny pricks in my heart every time I look over at my mother. I feel tangled and don't know how to break free.

"That ought to look cute on my ankle," Taryn says. "Better find a good inker for that one." She presses it against her anklebone.

"Like you're afraid of the prick of a needle," Amelia says. She's so tickled; it wouldn't have mattered if the gift had been a mound of dirt, or the grains of sand from Hawaii. Anything from our mother.

I watch Elizabeth watch us. "I know it must mean something," I say.

She nods. "When I was a little girl, I used to beg my father to let me water the flowers outside. He said watering the flowers was harder than it looked. You couldn't overwater them or they'd die. You couldn't underwater them or they would die. Then one day he brought home a cactus in a tiny hot pink pot. He said we'd start with the cactus and if I did a good job taking care of it, I could have my own area of the garden to take care of."

Elizabeth wipes her eyes. I never knew my maternal grandparents. Her mother committed suicide when Elizabeth was just eight years old, so her father raised her.

Her mother left. Her father stayed.

Then her father died in a motorcycle accident when I was just three years old. A year before our mother left. My only memory of him is a big gap-toothed smile and the faint smell of cigar.

I bite my lip. I think of Lucas's words, looking within the person, where the spirit dwells. I try to see the eight-year-old girl who lost her mother. I try to see the Daddy's Little Girl who hadn't fully grown up when she started having babies of her own. Just when she reaches a breaking point with postpartum depression again her father dies tragically. He left without saying goodbye.

And so she runs because it's too hard to stay.

I think of what Iolana and Rebekkah both told me. "We are all the same."

I feel paralyzed, my heart thick in my throat.

"I told Dimitri about my childhood cactus when we moved to Arizona. He told me the cactus is a symbol for protection, endurance and maternal love. I'm sure my father didn't know what it meant, but I knew right then I had to find the charms to give to you girls."

I place the charm on my bracelet and watch it clink against the lion. Endurance. *Endurecer.* Yes, I could more than toughen up and endure. I could let myself feel something good again - even love.

I look at my mother's small wrist and see her charm bracelet, the one my father had given her with a new charm the days we were born. Perhaps he'd tried to love her, but came up short. Just like the bracelet, only half full, unfinished.

Had she used it as a reminder all these years? A physical thing to tether her to the past? Or a rope of hope to hold on to until the time was right?

When I'd first received the letter, I couldn't believe she'd survived all the imaginary deaths I'd put her through. Now I couldn't believe she'd survived her own brushes with near-death to come full circle.

"It's perfect," Amelia picks up a pebble and tosses down into the canyon. I wonder what it might be like to fly through it.

"But ..." Amelia pauses.

We look away from the sunset. Its reflection blazes in her eyes. "But I don't like feeling that you chose Dimitri over us."

"It's hard to explain, but he chose me. I'd only chosen death. He showed me compassion when I felt like no one else did. Everyone was trying to tell me that everything would be all right. Your father told me I needed to change my attitude. Quoted a bunch of business leaders, as if that would do it. Your aunt told me to be grateful for what I had. Did they not know I had been trying that for years? I felt like a big failure for not being able to fix myself. I was a terrible mother. Couldn't do the simplest tasks. Changing a diaper was as hard as lifting a two-ton boulder some days. Marlo remembers this, I'm sure. And I'd depended on my father to tell me what to do all my life. I wanted to join him in Heaven. Having children of my own made me miss my mother desperately and I wasn't sure how to do it right.

After my daddy died, I'd gone to pack up his things and sell his house. I wanted to get some picture of my parents for you girls, and pictures of me growing up so you could have them someday. But what I found instead ..."

She pauses, looking off into the distance, her eyes watering. She shudders and pulls herself back. "I found some medical documents, about my mother. My father had told me she'd had a heart condition. Funny, I'd been worried about my heart ever since. Always afraid if it was beating too fast or beating too slow or how it might explode with love when I held you all in my arms." She rubs her arms, as if feeling our tiny bodies lying there.

"Her heart was fine, well the physical part of it, anyway. She'd hung herself."

"And your father never told you?"

Elizabeth's shoulders shook. "No. He told me the most wonderful stories of my mother. Some of them I remember. She was known as the eccentric in the neighborhood. I just thought she was so full of life. If we woke up and it had snowed in the night, we'd run through the snow barefoot in our pajamas. We'd make a snowman as the rest of the neighborhood kids were bundled off to walk to the bus stop but she'd let me stay home. Life is too short not to relish the first snow day, she'd say to me. So then we'd be half-frozen and we'd sit inside and drink hot cocoa and she'd read me *Little Women* by the fire."

"Sounds wonderful," Amelia says.

"She was crazy," Taryn responds.

Elizabeth rests her chin on her knee. "Sometimes I'm not sure what to think. She'd disappear for days at a time. Once she was even gone for two whole weeks of the summer. Said she was visiting sick relatives. I had no idea she was the sick one."

"When you found out about her suicide, you were already depressed, weren't you?"

"Certainly! I just thought of it as a fog at the time, a fog that lifted so rarely I could barely squint to see through it. But I know why he kept the truth about her death from me. He wanted me to remember her before her last act. I'm sure your father was only trying to do the same thing."

"Knowing that your mother did that. You had to feel full of ... shame," Taryn adds.

"Of course. Since my father wasn't around to talk me out of it, I felt perhaps I'd been too much for her. She wanted a way out. I guess in a way it gave me permission, too. I felt a connection with my mother I'd never felt before. Almost euphoric. She'd found a way out of the pain. She'd opened a door I hadn't considered before. I became obsessed by it."

"You left us so you could die."

Amelia is shaking her head, but she needs to hear the truth. Elizabeth looks at me directly. "I couldn't do it in front of you. I had tried once ..."

I nod, but don't say anything.

"With the help of my Keepers, I began to hold on to hope of a better life. And that I could return to you someday when I was better. I'd go back and get on the right medication and deal with my past and fix my marriage and join the PTA and not me the neighborhood kook, but just a normal, fun-loving mom. I'd wear sexy lingerie and work out to Suzanne Somer's videos so your father wouldn't want to cheat. And then I decided to see Mexico. I'd never been out of the United States before and Dimitri already loved me very differently than your father ever had. But I didn't think he'd give you over to me. He had your futures all lined out, right from the time you were in my belly. He'd talk to my tummy and say things like, 'I bet there's an Olympic athlete in there. Or the next Miss America. The first female President of the United States.' His dreams were much bigger for you. I hadn't even graduated from college."

"I was determined to see you again. And then the plane crash. I, I began to wonder if it was the universe telling me to stay away from you, that I was no good for you. And yet, I dreamed."

"Your Keepers," I say, almost in a whisper. "Why do you call them that?"

"It started when I laid on that cot in Hawaii after my jump. I hadn't spoken in days, was barely eating, when Iolana looks into my eyes and says to me, 'You're a keeper.' In those few words, she said to me that my life had value. I couldn't throw it away. Yet, just like back home, I wasn't sure what to do. I was still trying to fix myself and didn't know the way. So on my long journey, I found other Keepers – people who showed me compassion – they were like keepers of my soul. They believed in me when I no longer believed in myself."

"Why not come visit us instead of having Karina spy on us?" Taryn asks.

"I just wanted to see how you were before I arrived out of the blue. I wanted someone to wave a magic wand over me and turn me into a wonderful mother. Any progress I'd made was destroyed when I went to prison. I almost didn't feel human when I joined the nunnery, but with prayer and faith, I began to come alive again. I could never repair the damage I'd done to you. That's why I tried to stay in contact with you through the letters and gifts. I wanted you to know that I loved you even if I couldn't care for you."

"I'm sorry for what Daddy did to you," Amelia says. "As much as I loved him, I hate that he made things worse for you. I wish he'd given us the things you sent."

"Your father was your Keeper. I suppose he was right to protect you from me. I can't blame my leaving solely on his cheating. It was just another thing that pushed me over the edge. Bad choice of words."

"What did you do when Dimitri came for you?" I ask.

"Truthfully, I was in shock for a while. I'm not sure what I believe about reincarnation, but I looked at Dimitri's rising from the dead as an awakening. I started to believe I could live a different life, maybe even a normal one, with a small table in a kitchen instead of rows of tables in a mess hall. I always pictured a table with five chairs. That's what I wanted. But a table with a leaf and extra folding chairs in the garage so when your families grew we would make room for more. We'd add high chairs for babies and move into the bigger dining room. Both Dimitri and Lucas told me it wasn't an impossible dream.

"Lucas told me the story of an old monk who could see fate in people's faces. One day the monk looked at a young novice's and saw there that he would die within the next few months. Saddened by this, he told the boy to take a long holiday and go and visit his parents.

"'Take your time,' he said. 'Don't hurry back.' He felt the boy should be with his family when he died. Three months later, to his surprise, the monk saw the boy walking back up the mountain. When he arrived he looked intently at his face and saw that the boy would now live to a ripe old age.

"'Tell me everything that happened while you were away.' So the boy started to tell of his journey down from the mountain. He told of villages and towns he passed through, of rivers forded and mountains climbed. Then he told how one day he came upon a stream in flood. As he tried to get across the flowing stream, he saw that a colony of ants had become trapped on a small island formed by the flooding stream. Moved by compassion for these poor creatures, he took a branch of a tree and laid it across one flow of the stream until it touched the little island. The boy held the branch steady as the ants made their way across, until he was sure all the ants had escaped to dry land. Then he went on his way.

"'So,' thought the old monk, 'that is why the gods have lengthened his days.' Compassionate acts can alter your fate. I wept after Lucas told me this. He told me to consider the possibility that I had given myself a leash on life with acts of kindness."

"But you broke the law," Taryn reminds her.

"We did. Even Dimitri agrees we were rash and young and foolish then. I'd already risked death, and he thought he was indestructible. We tried to do the right thing by doing wrong things. But would I do it again, if the choice were the same? To run away to die but live a sometimes uncomfortable, simple life over a certain death if I'd stayed? Looking back, I have to believe I made the better choice."

Even with the heat, goosebumps cover my flesh. I can't imagine how that would've changed me. To come home from my first day of school to find my father weeping, not because she'd run away, but because he'd found her body.

"And now you're what, ready?" Taryn asks.

"A mother's heart lives outside of her. Wherever you go, I go. But I wanted to be well. Just like the song we sang every day in Africa, I was thankful to be alive, but I wanted more than that. When Dimitri and I came back to America, I was still attached to the past as much as I tried to live in the present. As long as I kept hold of the label of the Mother Who Abandoned Her Children, I could never return to you. The self-loathing and shame were tattoos on my soul. I wasn't sure how to remove them. I'd fooled myself that I could go on without you forever."

Taryn's tiny shoulders rise and she exhales. "Guess that answers the 'what do you have to say for yourself' question."

"I was afraid nothing I could ever say would be good enough."

Taryn nods. "So we get an apology-by-way-of-whirlwind-trip, huh?"

Elizabeth's hand reaches out, but stops in mid-air as if she doesn't have the right to touch Taryn. "I *am* sorry. If I could, I'd fill this canyon with apologies. I'd fill the Colorado River and carry them to the ocean and fill it, too."

Amelia leans her head on Elizabeth's shoulder and takes her hand, lacing her fingers through hers. "I'd rather have this."

Taryn looks at me, and I see that the anger is gone, but she is still unsure. So am I. How can we trust this woman? Is she good for us? Do we need her in our life, or is this meeting all there is, or all there will ever be?

"Where do we go from here?" I ask.

Elizabeth smiles as we watch the sun dip behind the canyon, casting an amber glow over us. She looks at me, and then my sisters, deeply, as one might study works of art. It's up to us, isn't it? We're grown. We don't need our mother to figure this out.

Taryn clears her throat. "Forward. I think we should go forward. And it should involve food."

"Something with cheese," Amelia adds. "And preferably fried."

Elizabeth laughs. "Well, I do have a key to the kitchen. I suppose we can make anything we want. The cooks back in Mexico were good teachers. I make a mean quesadilla."

We get up and bid a silent farewell to the sunset. *Forward.* My new favorite direction. As soon as we turn away from the drop-off.

I link arms with Taryn and watch my mother walk, still as graceful as a nun, and Amelia, glowing from within. I recall what Amelia had asked as a little girl, every time we gathered the ingredients and set them on the counter. *"Do you think Mommy ever bakes cookies where she lives?"*

I lean over and meet my mother's gaze. "Got any sugar hidden in your cupboards?"

27
AMELIA

"You've got some chocolate goo," Mom says, reaching over with her napkin and wiping it from my chin. It's late. Past midnight. Early to bed, early to rise is my mother's way of life, as well as the guests who come here for rejuvenation. But she's staying up late for us. I purposely outlasted my sisters, both in cookie consumption and bedtime.

We laugh and I reach for another cookie. My third. Yeah, I get it. I'm not a child anymore and my mom's not a cookie-baking type of mom. She was the Mom Who Couldn't/Didn't/Shouldn't Stay. She doesn't eat sugar and she didn't raise us, but I won't let that take away this moment.

My sisters have turned in, so it's just the two of us in the kitchen, both of us perched on the countertops. Thanks to the sugar, I'm wide-awake, but I know it's more than that. I finally got my Christmas wish, smack dab in the middle of the summer, in the middle of the desert, and *before* the middle of my lifetime.

I know we have years to get to know each other, and I'm certain, beyond certain, that I want this. We both may be damaged goods, but I don't care that she's part of the reason I'm damaged. I still think I can learn from her and if things get weird, I know how to run. There's a place for misfits, and I say why can't misfits make up a family and create who we want to be from here on out? *Forward.*

"Do you ever leave here?"

"Not often. I know my limits."

"You mean people? Crowds?"

"Yes. Noise. Stress. Unfortunately, it's a very long list."

"Is it okay if I come visit you then?"

Mom's eyes tear up. "There's nothing I'd like more. I was so afraid you girls would just look at me and run."

"No. I want to stay. I mean, could I? Just through the summer? Before school starts in the fall? Maybe I could even apply out here somewhere. In Arizona."

"Oh, baby. I'd love that. I mean it. Nothing would make me happier." She wraps her arms around me and it doesn't feel as foreign as it did that day in her doorway.

"You said happy. Are you happy now? With your life?"

"Absolutely. I can't say I don't have my moments, but it's the ups and downs a regular person has. Not the drastic roller coaster ride I used to be on. I also can't say I'm normal, Amelia, but I've found no one is, entirely. We are all works in progress. But I may not be who you need me to be, Amelia. I don't want to give you false expectations."

"I understand. But I feel like I need this. I think it will help sort things out. Not just because Lucas is here, either."

"I'm happy to have you here. And Lucas is a gentle soul with natural charm. If it's meant to be, I'm sure it will work out."

"I need to give us both space and if this trip has taught me anything, it's that I could use some therapy. I hadn't stopped to realize why I'd done all the things I'd done until I started listing them all out in the confessional. I don't want to like Lucas or anyone else for the wrong reasons."

Mom nods. "Things are slower out here, but slow is good for therapy. You get to see things more clearly, and make decisions from a better place."

"I might feel stir-crazy at first, but I'm willing to try. I don't want to become obsessed with the wrong things, you know? And as for my future, I don't know if I should be a teacher, or go do mission work, or travel first."

Mom puts her hand on her chest and gives me a small smile. "Oh, dear. That sounds awfully close to you asking me for motherly advice."

I blush, and goosebumps cover my arm. "I guess so."

Mom wraps her arm around me and squeezes. "You are like a fresh butterfly from a cocoon, darling. Where you fly is entirely up to you."

28
TARYN

On the third morning, after sunrise yoga, the guests disperse, leaving Elizabeth and I standing on our mats as the Arizona morning comes to life around us. It's the first time I've been alone with her, and my heart still feels uneasy about her, but thanks to the yoga, my head and body feel clear.

"Would you like a juice?" She asks as she dabs her chest and neck with a towel.

"Sure."

We sit on the patio, where a few other early risers enjoy oatmeal and fresh fruit around us. Elizabeth pours me a glass of OJ and smiles. I know the difference between a fake smile, which I get most of the time from onlookers, and a real one. Hers is genuine. She seems comfortable around me, which few people are. This alone puts me at ease.

"Your tattoos are beautiful. I'd love to hear the stories behind them."

My body feels prickly and hot. Revealing the meaning of my tattoos means sharing the geography of being me. I don't want her to "get me." I don't want a "bonding moment." I know she put a lot of thought into those charms, as I do with my art. Yet I do feel compelled to share, as if a tiny door to my heart as been opened and everything comes rushing out. *She wants to know me.*

"That could take awhile," I tell her. I'm so used to them, they may as well be dated wallpaper in a vintage kitchen. To her, my body is a foreign land.

"I don't mind," she says, as if she could just sit here all day and listen to me.

I clear my throat and point to my left upper arm, to the Buddhist golden fish tattoo, depicted by a pair of fish. "I'm sure you've heard a lot of Buddhist stories from Lucas. It's not like I was all deep and existential when I was sixteen. Basically, this was my teen rebellion tattoo. Dad said I couldn't get one, so I ran away from home—just a weekend, and I let my boyfriend pick it out. Dad had just found out his cancer had returned and I just couldn't deal, you know? My boyfriend chose the fish because he said it stood for freedom and emancipation. Of course, back then I thought it was freedom from Dad's strict rules and kind of a 'fuck you' to cancer, not to let it take over our lives, not some symbol of spiritual life, because, basically, until recently, I didn't have one."

"What did your father do when you came home?"

"Cried. And hugged me. He said he was afraid I wouldn't come back."

Elizabeth doesn't flinch.

"And this," I say as I lower my tank top to reveal the ten-inch wide lotus tattoo on my chest, "I got for my eighteenth birthday. The book said it was God's favorite flower, so I figured that was good enough for me. I named my new rock band Lotus and moved out before graduation. Dad said I couldn't be in a band until I graduated so my bags were all packed and I was out the door on my birthday. Played my first gig that night, actually. I still managed to graduate, though I have no idea how. We'd play college frat parties during the week and I'd crawl into bed at like four a.m. and have to get up at seven to get ready for school. That's why I moved out. Besides, I was never as strong as Marlo. I hated watching him waste away."

"I'm proud of you for graduating."

It seems stupid to care now, after all this time, that she'd say she's proud of anything, but my heart softens a little. I can tell she means it. "Well, Dad would've killed me, otherwise. I promised him my band wouldn't get in the way of school, so I kinda had to prove it to him, you know? Didn't want him to know he was right."

Elizabeth laughs easily.

"So for graduation, I got the bluebird." I flex my right arm, showing the bluebird holding a ribbon with the words, "Carpe diem."

"Seize the day."

"And I sure as hell did! The bluebird has no dark side. It's a popular nautical symbol for sailors, for happiness, so I was feeling rather optimistic that I'd made it to graduation in one piece. Gloating is more like it." Next, I stand and remove my shirt, revealing my sports bra, and turn around, showing her my back. Angel wings start at my spine and cover the width and length of my back. Inside the wings, my pride and joy: my snake tattoo. Three snakes, intertwined, each one biting the tail of another.

"It's gorgeous," Elizabeth says.

"I call it my eternity tattoo. I got it right after Dad's funeral. He said when he was sick that he'd be our angel looking out for us. And when I went in to get it and saw the three snake tattoo in the book, I immediately thought of me and my sisters."

"What do the snakes mean?"

"It's an ancient Egyptian myth, like 1600 BC or something. An enormous serpent devoured its own tail, surviving by devouring itself, symbolizing an unending, eternal cycle of renewal. The concept of infinity. I figured we were in this together. Forever."

"Do your sisters know that? That you got the tattoo because of them?"

I pull my tank back down. "No. I didn't think they'd care one way or another. And unfortunately I haven't put that idea into action enough."

"And do you still feel that your sisters don't care?"

"I'm sure they *do* care. I was just afraid they'd find the snake tattoo creepy. Which it sort of is, I suppose."

"And what about Paul?"

"How do you know about him?"

"Well, Mexico for one thing. I'm very sorry that I put you all in harm's way. I told Lucas I was on my way, next flight out, but he insisted it was too dangerous and he would handle it. Karina called me and said you were safe and she was on her way out, too. I had the shakes for two days after."

I don't like to imagine her so fragile, worrying about us. Isn't that what pushed her to the edge the first time? "Do you see Karina?"

"She comes a couple of times a year. She's the sister I never had, and of course she and Dimitri are close."

"I like her. She was cool."

"And so … Paul."

I point to my chest and show her the half-heart tattoo with its jagged center.

"Like a friendship charm," Elizabeth says. "And Paul has the other half, I take it?"

"Yeah. Dumb, huh?"

"Not dumb at all. I think that shows real commitment. Anyone can slip a ring on and off, but a tattoo…"

"You're right. He's the first guy I've really loved. And I think he's the first guy that doesn't want me to be anything other than what I am."

"What you are is pretty great, Taryn. I'm only sorry I didn't have anything to do with what a bright, beautiful woman you became."

I choke down some OJ, willing myself not to break down. "But you did. Your absence shaped me more than your presence ever would have."

After a long silent moment, Elizabeth speaks softly.

"So it's not all bad then."

"I suppose the fact that I'm tattooing the charm bracelet instead of just slipping it on and off says something, too."

"It does. I only wish the charms could've been different. You know, the things we'd have experienced together: dance recitals and soccer and choir and vacations we'd gone on together." Elizabeth shrugs and has to look away. I like that it pains her that things couldn't have been different.

"I believe in fate. This existence, the way things have gone in my life, yeah, some of it's really been shitty. But the rest, and what's to come, I think I'll be luckier than most."

Elizabeth puts her head down, her hand over her face, and I know that for once I haven't said the wrong thing, but maybe, just maybe, I've gotten it right. It's as close to saying I forgive her as I'll get.

Perhaps an hour has passed when Lucas comes out, followed by his puppy dog, my little sis.

"We're ready when you are," Lucas says with a smile, clasping his hands together.

"Ready for what?" I look to Amelia, but she only looks up to the sky and smiles coyly.

"A surprise!" She says, unable to contain herself.

"Great. You know how I feel about surprises," I tell her dryly.

Lucas leads us to Elizabeth's suite door, just as we'd done two days prior. I know she couldn't fit a giraffe in there.

Marlo has joined us and looks oblivious. Neither of us

have a clue what could make Amelia this excited, jumping up and down on her toes, while Dimitri and Elizabeth stand behind us, watching and waiting.

We open the door and inside, basked in the sunlight-filled room, are our guys, Paul and Shane.

Paul lunges forward, his big chest wide, his arms out, his face beaming. "Hey, babe," he says and I jump up into his embrace, wrapping my legs around his waist.

I forget there are other people in the room. I know what I want now and the confusion I'd felt for so long is wiped away. Forward, I think. I know *this*, Paul, feels right.

He kisses me, a long soulful kiss, then hoops and hollers to the crowd. "Who's ready to hike the canyon?"

29
MARLO

The next morning I wake early, my muscles stiff from the ten-mile descent on Bright Angel trail into the canyon. We'd hiked all afternoon in the 120-degree heat, four couples, a mish mash of people trying to become a family after years of not knowing how. It's dark still, and the crickets and the bats still dominate the night. I feel safe inside the tent, cocooned with my better half still sleeping soundly on the air mattress beside me.

By dusk we had made it to Phantom Ranch and pitched our tents. The men got along well, and Lucas talked more than usual. Everyone loves Dimitri, the life of the party, gregarious and charming. I can see why my mother fell in love with him. While no child wants to see their parent with someone else, I can see how doting Dimitri is, and feel the love between them. I never felt that between my parents, but then I only remember the fights.

We'd dined on a steak dinner at the bottom of the canyon, save for Elizabeth and Taryn, our vegetarians, who ate baked potatoes and salad. I'd hung up my reporter's hat for the night, no notes, no observations. I could be one of them, a daughter, a sister, a wife.

My favorite part of the morning is just before dawn, when bad thoughts have yet to catch up with me, and I can watch Shane sleep, amazed that he's mine. He's always slept like a baby, quick to sleep and all through the night. Even if he's had a traumatic day at work, like losing a patient, he still manages to shut down his brain and get his slumber on. Only an insomniac like me marvels at the wonders of easy sleep.

I only woke once, but instead of a nightmare, it was a rare, good dream. I was flying in Hawaii, soaring down Hoary Head, only there were no ropes, no harness. My arms were spread eagle, soaring through the valley. I felt connected to all things, the animals and flowers and water an extension of myself. I felt another presence, too, so I looked back and saw Shane flying with me, wearing his orange Nikes.

Within minutes, nature's light switch has gone from moonlight to sunlight, and I don't want to miss it. I sigh heavily, and Shane's eyes open and a smile creeps across his face. "Mornin', or is it still night?"

"Morning almost. I don't need to ask how you slept. Sawed logs all night."

He turns and puts his hand on my hip. "Last night was amazing."

I smile. Nothing better than make up sex *plus* reunion sex. "Do you want to watch the sunrise?"

Shane lifts his brows. "Is my wife a morning person now?"

My body lightens at the word "wife." I want to tell him I'm so many things now, things undiscovered and unplanned and unexpected. I am more. And I am even more with him.

We gather up our blankets and I'm pleased to see everyone else is still in their tents. From our position in the canyon, the sun appears to be breaking through the earth, its rays splitting open the dirt.

We pick a large rock, surrounded by prickly pear cactus, and perch on top of it. The charm bracelet is still on my arm, and I think of the cactus charm and its meaning. Maternal protection. I wonder if I'll ever have that. Wonder, but not worry. I'm happy my mother is safe, and that finally, I'll stop worrying about her. Now I *know*. My Forward involves trying not to worry at all.

Shane wraps the blanket around me as we stare up at the blazing ball in the horizon.

"Thank you for coming," I say, not even looking at him. Now I know what Shane would do. He wouldn't let me run away. He would come for me. He would fight for me.

Shane nuzzles my cheek with his nose and pulls me closer. "I know I can be insensitive sometimes and work too damn much, but this much I know, Marlo. We belong together. No ifs, ands or buts."

I feel hot tears fill my eyes. I know this, too. This sureness that we are meant to be. I'm just sorry I buried it under so many boulders.

Shane inhales then exhales the crisp morning air. "I get the feeling this is one of those memories we'll look back and reflect on when we're rocking in our chairs at the old folks' home."

I feel the familiar swell of shame in my throat. "You can see that far into the future?"

Shane nods. "I've always imagined us together forever. You telling me it's time to trim my nose hairs and me rubbing you down with arthritis cream."

"How romantic!" I playfully hit him, but I mean it. Arthritis cream is the most romantic thing he could ever say to me. He wants to take care of me for the long haul, and I, him.

I think of my suitcase packed at home, the one I thought would be enough to start a new life without Shane.

"I want to come back home," I say softly, watching Shane's face light up from the sun's glow and something else, a happiness the sun didn't put there.

"Are you sure?"

"No matter where I was in the world, my first thought was how much I wanted you there with me. I've been so afraid of giving myself to you completely, afraid you would leave me, or someone would steal you from me. I thought marrying you would make my insecurity go away, but I'm not ready to give up."

"I was afraid you'd tell me you'd decided to stay gone for good."

My chest warms, and I take his left hand in mine and squeeze. "Are your favorite hospitals still Boston, Chicago and Newport Beach?"

"Yeah. But you said you could never live any of those places."

I tap my foot on the rock. "After what I've been through, I'm pretty sure I could live anywhere. As long as you're there with me. And there's running water."

"What about your sisters?"

"I think it's time I let them grow up. Look how they've turned out? Not so bad. Pretty great, really. I think I can stop worrying and start living now."

His hand drops to my lower back and he leans in, our

faces just inches apart. "You up for more traveling?"

"I'm up for a lot of things. Though an airlift out of this canyon would be a nice start."

He laughs. "I say we start with a trip back into the tent." He raises one brow.

I don't want to think. For once, I want to feel and not be afraid of it.

I kiss him my answer.

ABOUT THE AUTHOR

Malena Lott is a married mother of three in the Midwest. A den mom, dance mom and brand strategist, she enjoys zumba, yoga, wine and strong coffee. She writes about creativity, mojo and zen on her author blog at www.MalenaLott.com and is the founder of www.BookEndBabes.com, a book blogging site, and Buzz Books USA, an imprint of her creative firm, Athena Institute.

Novels:

Something New

Fixer Upper

The Stork Reality

Dating da Vinci

Novellas:

Life's a Beach

The Last Resort

Non-fiction:

Dance Mom Survival Guide

ACKNOWLEDGMENTS

Most importantly, to my sisters, Tina and Amanda, you have taught me so much about life and all of our trials have made us stronger. Though I won't be getting a serpent infinity tattoo, I'll love you forever.

To my editor Mari Farthing and all the supportive writers in the Hive, I love being a part of the publishing community with you. We are indeed celebrating stories and I can't think of anyone I'd rather celebrate with.

While it sounds obvious to say a book isn't possible without your parents, in this case it's even truer. My parents did the right thing in letting my grandparents raise us, and I had a wonderful upbringing. I can never, ever express enough gratitude to my grandparents, may they rest in peace, for giving us such a loving home. They encouraged my reading and writing, college and dreaming big.

To my larger sisterhood – my sorority sisters at Alpha Chi Omega, my Girlfriend Book Club authors, girlfriends and readers – you have given me a safe place to be myself and know just how to lift me up. Thank you.

To Jason and Tisha King, owners of Atomic Lotus Tattoo in Oklahoma City, for being so gracious to answer my questions all those years ago about tattoos and the business. Now we find ourselves block neighbors and I feel lucky to know you.